the Forgotten King

LEGACY OF DRAGONS

The Forgotten King

LEGACY OF DRAGONS

MARK STALLINGS

Eldros Legacy Press
P.O. Box 292
Englewood, Colorado 80151

Cover Art by:
Jake Caleb

Cover Design by:
Rashed AlAkroka, Sean Olsen, Melissa Gay & Quincy J. Allen

Map Design by:
Sean Stallings

Ordering Information:

Quantity sales. Special discounts are available on quantity purchases by corporations, associations, and others. For details, contact us at the address above or via our website.

The Forgotten King / Mark Stallings — 1st ed.

ISBN: 978-1-959994-18-3

DEDICATION

To Becky, without whom this would never have happened.

In Memory of David Farland

WHAT IS ELDROS LEGACY?

The Eldros Legacy is a multi-author, shared-world, mega-epic fantasy project managed by four Founders who share the vision of a new, expansive, epic fantasy world. In the coming years the Founders committed themselves to creating multiple storylines where they and many others will explore and write about a world once ruled by tyrannical giants.

The Founders are working on four different primary storylines on four different continents. Over the coming years, those four storylines will merge into a single meta story where fates of all races on Eldros will be decided.

In addition, a growing list of guest authors, short story writers, and other contributors will delve into virtually every corner of each continent. It's a grand design, and the Founders have high hopes that readers will delight in exploring every nook and cranny of the Eldros Legacy.

So, please join us and explore the world of Eldros and the epic tales that will be told by great story tellers, for Here There Be Giants!

We encourage you to follow us at www.eldroslegacy.com to keep up with everything going on. If you sign up there, you'll get our newsletter and announcements of new book releases. You can also follow up on FaceBook at

facebook.com/groups/eldroslegacy.

Sincerely,

Todd, Marie, Mark, and Quincy
(The Founders)

ACKNOWLEDGEMENTS

I would like to thank my partners at Eldros Legacy—Rob, Todd, Quincy and Marie. It has been a hard road to travel, but a really fun journey.

Next, I would like to thank my beta readers—Nick, Dan and Zach. Those three had excellent feedback and found the issues as I pushed out the chapters.

Also, I would like to thank the crazy people of the Peacemaker Cantina. They have been my cheerleaders every Saturday providing a mental and emotional outlet during these turbulent times.

Finally, I would like to acknowledge my brother, Sean. He did all of the maps that we put in the books for Eldros Legacy. His map drawing began in 1981 when he discovered D&D.

THE CHRONICLER

The man in the stocks had been there for longer than anyone could guess.

He stood on a rise before a valley that contained broken buildings, collapsed walls, and a single metal tower. The ancient city behind him had been abandoned in another age, but the man remained, bent over, gnarled hands and gray-haired head stuffed through the holes of his forever prison.

Since he'd first begun telling his tales, only one man had stayed. The young, blond man still sat there, cowl pulled low. The old man never tired, but neither did the young man. He stayed. He ate. He drank. He listened:

"Do you know the story of the Second War of the Giants...?" the old man asked again. "I have told you about Khyven the Unkillable and the Guardian Rellen...

"But I have not told you about Ora Lightbringer, immortal king and slayer of Giants. Though Khyven and Rellen braced the Giants at Drastone Rock, it was Ora who saw the whole field.

"How do I know? Oh, I know, young man. I know because I was there.

"I was there the day the dragons fought openly in the skies over Drakanon. I was there when Kishar rose as the goddess of the Delvers. And I was there the day Ora Lightbringer wedded the Heart of the Dragon.

"A thousand years before the Second War of the Giants, Ora killed the Giant known as Wrok, blowing a crater in the center of Drakanon. The magical blast also turned him immortal, and he stewarded Drakanon through a thousand years of peace. But when Houshkulu the Deceiver tried to invade Ora's lands, the Lightbringer rose to do battle once more. And when Nhevalos the Betrayer orchestrated his final web, it was Ora Lightbringer who saw it for what it was. And because he did, Drakanon endured.

"I'm going to tell you his story, the true story of Ora Lightbringer, the first Human to make an alliance with Dragons...."

MAPS

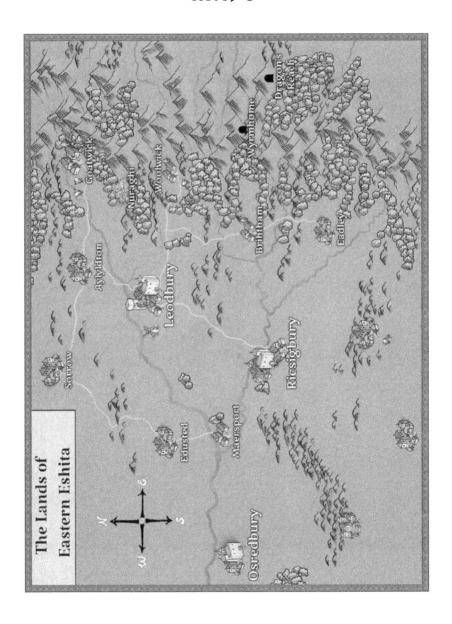

CHAPTER ONE

ORA EARL

R emind me again why we took this contract?" Ora grunted as he blocked a cleaver with the short sword in his left hand and thrust his long sword through the Goblin's chest. The razor-sharp blade easily parted bone and armor. "I hate Goblins."

Black blood gushed out of the creature's mouth. It gurgled as it slid backward off Ora's blade. The rank smell of Goblin blood mixed with the musty smell of mold.

"Because they kidnapped a little girl," Sera replied, sweeping the head off another Goblin.

The body just stood there, spurting dark ichor from the stump of its neck. Sera front kicked it in the chest, sending it back into the next Goblin rushing at them. "They're filthy creatures."

"That they are." Ora swatted an arrow out of the air. He yelled toward another member of the party, "Gverth, archer."

"On it." Gverth, student of the elements, pointed a finger at the Goblin archer. *"Pir,"* he uttered the Old Akkermenian word for fire, and an incandescent bolt shot from his hand. For a brief moment, the two beings were connected.

The Goblin screamed as the flame bored a hole into its chest. The smell of burnt flesh flooded the room.

"Well done." Hohan, a Northerner and a disciple of the god Enki, brought his war hammer down on a Goblin about to skewer Gverth with a rusted sword.

"Thank you." Gverth quickly stepped away from the spreading pool of Goblin blood.

"Are there any more?" Sera looked around the cluttered room.

The sturdy buildings in the nuraghi had been there for centuries. These collections of ancient buildings were found all over Drakanon. Created in the distant past, they were frequently repositories of history and knowledge. However, the interior of this one was a mess. Goblins had strewn trash, boxes, and debris everywhere. Rough sleeping pallets lay along one wall, and a small fire burned in the hearth of the fireplace.

"I think we got them all," Hohan, the big man, said cheerfully.

"I love a man who enjoys his job." Ora swung his blade in a tight overhead arc. The momentum cleaned the blood from his sword.

"Nice trick. Where'd you learn that?"

"Oh that? I did a stint in the forces in Drounid long ago." Ora didn't want to mention just how long ago. "You don't always have a cleaning cloth ready, and it gets the blood off quickly."

"Any sign of the girl?" Sera looked around the room they were in.

"I'll search," said Ora.

"Gverth, collect the ears for our bounty." Sera motioned for Ora to get on with it. "If you please?"

Ora pulled Life Magic from his internal life energy using a technique called Shimmershield. Life Magic could be used to have positive or negative effects on anything living or that had once been alive. Using it, Ora could enhance his strength, speed, or senses. This time he focused on his sense of smell. The smell of death and unwashed bodies made him gag. Ora pushed those aside, like shoving through a crowded room, until he found the distinct fragrance of the Human girl. He pointed at the back door.

"They took her out that way." Ora fished in his pouch for a small cloth bag filled with fragrant herbs. He held the bag up to his nose and inhaled deeply, and basil and rosemary replaced the smell of slaughter.

The quartet exited the barracks and shifted around the enormous building in the center of the ancient nuraghi. It was wide and very much like a castle's keep, without the castle. Instead of walls, the perimeter comprised a series of outbuildings. These all seemed to have functions like storage and workshops and weren't laid out for families.

Ora led the group of four into the side gate. An unknown force had long ago pulled the portcullis open. Like something large had pushed its way through the middle of it, bending the bars outward.

"Watch for Goblins. There will be more." Ora proceeded down the hallway. Dim light gleamed up ahead from torches he could only assume were from the Goblins.

One by one, the four of them crept down the hallway. At the end of the passage, it opened up into a larger room. Ora spotted a Goblin in rough, cured hide armor, a wicked curved sword grasped in his left hand, the blade resting on his shoulder pauldron.

The slavering Goblin's mouth turned upward into a slow grin that revealed rows of pointy teeth and it snarled, *"Kharbazh!"*

Goblins attacked them from everywhere. It was only reflex that got Ora's sword up in time to block a crude trident thrust at him from the shadows to his right.

"Attack!" Sera said from behind him, engaged with two spear-wielding Goblins of her own. The golden-haired warrior spoke a phrase in a sibilant language. The air next to her shimmered and thickened in time to block one spear thrust. She slapped a second thrust away with her gauntleted left hand and stabbed the second Goblin through the chest with her rapier.

The Goblin thrust at Ora again, this time twisting the short sword out of his hand with the tines of the trident. Another

Goblin rushed at Ora with a wickedly curved little sword. A firm boot to the chest sent the trident-wielding Goblin sprawling across the marbled floor, and Ora got his long sword around to decapitate the other.

He picked up the Goblin's short sword, then turned to where Sera was still fighting. The Goblin she had stabbed still clung to her left hand, pulling her arm outward while the other Goblin circled to strike with his spear.

Ora threw the Goblin's blade. Unfortunately, it was not balanced for throwing and just slammed into the back of his target, but that knocked it off stride. Ora bent and retrieved his short sword.

Sera backhanded the off-balance Goblin, then stabbed deeply into its side before whipping her rapier around her head to scrape the other off her.

Beyond her, Gverth lifted a hand and brought forth a searing beam of fire that lanced into the nearest Goblin, igniting it as if someone had dipped it in oil.

The flaming horror screeched and ran straight for Gverth.

Gverth flinched and toppled ass over teakettle trying to get away.

Hohan swung his war hammer in a tight arc, crushing into the chest of the flaming Goblin and launching the humanoid backward into the wall. It lay still and smoldered. The stench of burning Goblin flesh permeated the air.

A broad smile lit Hohan's face, and beads of sweat made his ebony skin shine in the firelight. "That was quite the incendiary endeavor, my friend. You might try something that won't get them to rush at you like that. I daresay you may be more flammable than he was." The room was quiet except for their heavy breathing.

"Anybody hurt?" Sera asked.

Ora picked up the Goblin sword he had thrown and grabbed the scabbard off the dead Goblin, then tucked it into his belt. "I'm fine."

Gverth and Hohan echoed him.

Sera picked up one of the better-crafted six-foot spears and hefted it. Ora raised his eyebrows. She gave him a fierce grin. "I forgot how much reach they had until that sack of dung tried to skewer me. My turn now."

"This looks like a banquet hall or some sort of greeting hall," Gverth said, looking around as he collected ears from the fallen Goblins.

"You can admire the architecture later." Sera peered down the hallway that branched off into too many corridors to easily discern where they took the girl. "Ora, can you tell where the girl went?"

Ora concentrated and pointed to the rightmost corridor. The hallway ran to what appeared to be a study or library.

They held their weapons at the ready, and stepping carefully so as to not make noise, they advanced into the passage, watching the shadows for additional Goblins.

They were almost at the end of the corridor, about to enter the study, when Hohan whispered softly to them, "Hang on. I think this is a door."

They turned back to see what he was pointing at. Next to him on the passage wall there was a slight line and the barest of scuffs on the floor.

"Do we spike the door closed or open it?" Hohan whispered.

"Open it. I don't want more Goblins making noise or jumping us from behind." Sera looked at them for any disagreement.

They gathered around to see if they could find a catch or latch or something that might indicate how to open it.

Gverth rubbed his fingers along the wall, mumbling, eyes closed. Then they heard a click. He opened his eyes and gave a smug look. "I found it." He stepped back, letting Ora and Sera step in front of him.

Ora reached out a hand to pull the door open. Sera gave a nod that she was ready. Ora yanked the door open to see nothing in the pitch-black darkness beyond.

Gverth whispered, and his right hand burst into a soft yellow flame, lighting the area for them.

Sera entered the passageway, with the rest of them close behind.

Hohan pulled the door closed after them. "I don't want to make it easy for them to find us."

With multiple nods, they continued down surprisingly large stairs. A normal stair was about a hand length tall. These were easily twice that. It made the going awkward.

From the dust on the floor, it was apparent that no one had been down this passage for a very long time.

At the bottom was a double-door etched with a giant, stylized dragon across the both of them. A heavy, metal disk in the center locked them.

When Gverth brought his lit hand towards it, the disk seemed to absorb the magical light, and after a few moments, runes on the metal seal glowed. The disk was made up of several concentric, glowing rings with rows of runes around each circle.

"How do we open it?" Sera asked.

Gverth studied it for a moment. "I think it's a puzzle lock. I guess we have to align the runes in a specific pattern to open it."

"Let me try something." Ora spun the outer disk to the right until a triangular rune was at the top. "This is the symbol for 'Open.'" He then spun the next circle to the left until a similar triangular rune was just below it.

Sera whispered, "It can't be that easy."

Ora just smiled at her and twisted the center ring until the triangular rune on it lined up with the first two and a seam appeared in the door.

"By all the Holy Giants! I can't believe it," Gverth said. "How did you know?"

"I've seen something like this a long time ago." The other three looked at him skeptically. He just shrugged. "Shall we see what is on the other side?"

Just as they had for the door above, Ora got ready to open the door, Sera readied her spear and shield, and the two others braced themselves behind, ready for anything that might leap out at them. Ora gripped the edge of the left half of the door and pulled it open.

Gverth held his flaming fist high in the air. It was lined floor to ceiling with shelves. It was empty, except on the top shelf, there rested a cloth-wrapped bundle.

"Should we touch it?" Sera asked.

Before they could reply, Ora grabbed it and pulled it off. He unwrapped the blue, shimmering cloth, revealing a leather-bound book easily a hand thick, three hands long, and two wide.

Everyone stared at him.

"What are you doing?" Sera asked in a tight voice. "That could have been trapped."

Ora just shrugged again. "Things like this aren't trapped if they're behind a seal... so I've been told."

Sera squinted her eyes at Ora. "How do you know this?"

"Like I said, I've studied." Ora looked at the latch holding the book closed and begrudgingly admitted, "Now, this might be trapped." He held the book out to Gverth.

The mage peered closely at the latch and rubbed his fingers in the air about an inch from it, concentrating, eyes closed. "I detect nothing on it, but let's study it later."

Ora shrugged off his pack and stuffed the book into it.

Gverth looked around the inside of the closet. They saw nothing else, so they closed the doors. Ora spun the rings on the seal, and they headed back up.

Upstairs, their Goblin foes' bodies still lay on the floor. They listened for a moment to see if they had drawn any other Goblins to the noises of the earlier fight. Nothing stirred.

Ora pointed the way they had been going before they found the secret door. The doorway to the library was just ahead. They readied their weapons and stepped through it.

The room was enormous, easily fifty feet across and three times as long. The ceiling was lost in the darkness. Empty shelves lined both walls. At the far end stood a fireplace. In the corner, elevated several feet off the floor, was a square cage made up of lashed-together strips of rough-cut wood and branches. Inside was the girl they'd been sent to rescue. She cowered in the corner, arms holding herself as she rocked side to side.

Near the cage stood six Goblins. One of the them threw a rectangular object into the fire. Gverth hissed. Another two were off to the side hunched over working on something.

"They're burning books."

Hohan peered at the vacant library. "I think that was the last book."

Gverth, eyes drifting across hundreds of empty shelves, choked at the destruction of what would have been a priceless collection of knowledge.

Sera said softly, "Ora, I need you to take the one closest to the girl and shield her. Gverth, can you make the fire explode on the Goblins on the far side?" At his nod, she continued, "Hohan and I will work our way from Ora to whatever is left standing." She looked around. "Good?"

They all nodded assent.

Ora pulled on Shimmershield and energized his legs. He sensed a similar energy from Hohan.

"Go!" Sera said. Ora and Hohan ran for the Goblins. Enhanced by magic, the pair of them covered the one hundred twenty feet in less than half the time a normal person could.

Ora slid into the Goblin closest to the cage, blade first.

Hohan wasn't nearly as subtle as he plowed right into one Goblin, catapulting him into his fellow in a bone-crunching body slam reminiscent of bocce balls.

Sera arrived just as the other Goblins reacted. She skewered the next closest Goblin with her spear. The last two around the fire grabbed their weapons and screeched.

Tendrils of flame lashed each Goblin with a blazing whip. Their screeches of anger turned into howls of pain as they thrashed and writhed at the flaming touch. Sera and Hohan dispatched them both.

The two Goblins who'd been away from the fire attacked. The first fired his short bow at Sera. She twisted, but the arrow ripped along her arm.

The second ran at Hohan, swinging its sword wildly. It opened up Hohan's thigh with a vicious slash.

Gverth pointed his hand at the one with the bow. *"Pir."* A blazing bolt of fire shot past the Goblin, only singeing the creature's side. It laughed at Gverth and aimed its bow at the mage.

Hohan backhanded his war hammer, catching his Goblin in the side of the head.

Sera conjured an ice blade, and with the flick of her wrist, sent it streaking at the Goblin archer. The spike of ice sank into the Goblin's throat with a wet *thock*.

Ora turned to the little girl. She huddled, whimpering, in the back corner of the cage. He deftly sliced through the rough rope fastening the cage door and pulled it open. He called to her soothingly.

"It's all right, Mirella," he said in a calm voice. "Your parents sent us to get you." Her tear-streaked face lifted at the mention of her name. "Are you hurt?"

"No…" she whispered.

He held open his arms. "Let's get you home to your parents."

She leapt into his arms and buried her face in his neck.

Hohan gave the pair a wide, toothy grin and Sera looked pleased. Gverth stared regretfully at the burning husk of the last book.

Their contract from the town council had been to rescue the girl and hunt the Goblin bands that had been running through the surrounding territory. The six in this room plus the others that they had killed would fetch a handsome bounty.

Sera gathered the tips of the ears to prove how many they'd killed and put them in a leather sack with the others they'd already collected.

Hohan pressed his hand to his thigh, holding his hammer to his chest, and murmured a prayer. The hammer glowed, and the wound stopped bleeding.

Outside, they made their way to the copse of trees where they had stashed their horses and pack animal. Waiting for them was Teer, a lad of fourteen from the town that they had brought along to watch the horses. Teer, bright eyed with sandy hair, sat on the back of one horse whiling away the time by flicking pine needles into a cup.

On their approach, he jumped down and dashed up to them. "Did you find the girl?" He flushed when it became apparent that Ora was carrying an exhausted little girl.

"We also found a band of Goblins." Hohan clapped Teer on the shoulder. "We've dispatched them into Enki's light."

"What about treasure? Did they have treasure?" Teer asked.

Gverth was about to respond, when Sera shook her head. "No, the Goblins had nothing. That place had been picked over, but we'll definitely be able to treat you to a nice dinner tonight from the bounties we collected." Sera held up the leather bag with the ear tips.

Teer flashed a grin. "Let me get the grain bags off the horses and we can go!" He rushed to pull the feedbag off of Ora's massive stallion.

The horse whinnied and lifted his head out of Teer's reach. Ora chuckled, remembering his son years ago, trying the same thing. Coupled with the little girl in his arms, it brought back memories of both of his children. He smiled for a moment, then passed the sleeping girl to Hohan.

The Northerner, a gentle giant of a man, held her gingerly, whispering a prayer to Enki over the girl.

Ora soothed the horse so Teer could remove the bag, mounted up, and took the girl back.

Remembering the Goblin sword he had taken, Ora pulled it from his belt. "Teer, I brought you something." Once the lad had turned, Ora tossed the short sword to him.

Teer immediately pulled out the blade and held it up to the sun, face shining.

"Really? You're giving the boy a sword?" Gverth gaped in surprise.

Hohan laughed. "He's not that much younger than you, my friend. Besides, I got my first sword at seven. He's overdue."

CHAPTER TWO

ORA EARL

he trip from Fagan Nuraghi to Somerville took two days, then several more to the city of Dracopolis. The city, usually called Draco by those who lived there, was the seat of the High King of Drakanon.

It was also the best place for those such as Sera and her band to get contracts as problem solvers. With their particular blend of skills, they usually picked up caravan escorts and monster extermination gigs. After Ora joined the group, they were able to take on larger, more complex contracts like this one, hunting down and removing the band of Goblins that had been terrorizing the surrounding area.

Once back in Draco, they returned to the Dragon's Cup. Though located in a rougher section of town, the tavern was well maintained and the preferred establishment for those willing to take on honest contract work and bounty collection jobs.

They sat in their alcove, a dining area set off the main room. A series of sliding panels could be pulled over to block out noise and prying eyes of the other inn-goers. There were several such semi-private rooms around the main area reserved for when other groups were in town.

"We made a pretty good haul from saving that little girl." Sera put the last few coins into four modest piles on the table.

Hohan set his heavy mug on the table and belched loudly. "The bounty from the Goblins didn't hurt either."

"But, these coins will set us up for the next month. What do we want to take on next?" Sera handed out the shares.

Hohan pocketed his. "Enki blesses you." He frowned at Gverth who was lost in the book, hunched over the tome that they'd recovered. Gverth had a sour expression on his face as he thumbed through the pages and tried to make heads or tails of the writing. Hohan grinned and reached for Gverth's stack.

"Leave him be." Sera sat back in her chair. "Several offers for contracts came in while we were out." She held up several pieces of paper. "The first one is something about an Orc raid—"

"Bah!" Gverth slammed the cover closed in frustration and pushed the tome away from him. "You'd think with as much time as I spend studying, I could make something out of this." He stood up.

Ora had been biding his time. He looked at Gverth. "Do you mind if I take a try?"

When Gverth held up his hands, Ora picked up the book and opened it up to a random page.

Ora recognized the script immediately, though he didn't let on how well he knew it. However, though he'd spent several hundred years going through scrolls, letters, and books recovered from various nuraghi with similar writing, he could only make out *some* of the words. The Old Akkermenian in this book was slightly different from the other artifacts he had studied. The nuraghi had been built more than two thousand years ago. The scrolls and books that had been recovered from them were old, and not everyone knew how to translate them well.

Ora pointed out one passage. "This says that 'the meeting was disrupted.' I don't know this word. 'And they were'—something— can't make that out either—'at the Solstice.'" He looked up.

Sera stared at him with a quizzical look. "How is it you know so much about this and you're not a Reader?"

He shrugged. "You don't have to be a member of the Readers to study our history. It's one of those things I was interested in. When I was younger, I had an opportunity to talk with people who were very well-versed in this."

Her eyes narrowed, but she didn't ask or press further.

Gverth knocked on the table to get their attention. "My mentor at the college might be able to decipher the book. He's a Reader. Do you want me to see if he's available?"

Ora didn't say anything. He really didn't want to meet with Readers in this city for fear that they might recognize him, but the others seemed to like the idea.

Sera nodded.

"Right, then I'll go make arrangements." Gverth headed out.

Ora sat back and watched Sera and Hohan discuss the tome and what they were going to do next.

Sera was a young woman, powerfully built, yet still feminine, with long, blonde hair pulled in a tight braid that started at the top of her head and ran down her back. She had pale skin and blue eyes. Her accent was from one of the northeastern kingdoms. The way she absentmindedly played with her hair while she was thinking reminded Ora of his daughter.

Hohan was the opposite. Where Sera was soft-spoken and articulate, Hohan was blunt and loud. However, he was quick to laugh—a deep, hearty laugh that got everyone smiling with him. Sera had recruited him from the temple when the band lost their other healer to a rival group with the lure of bigger, more lucrative contracts.

Sera gathered up her things. "I'm going to go get cleaned up. Let me know when Gverth gets back." Ora nodded.

"I'm getting more drink. Want anything?" Hohan asked.

Ora nodded. "Can you get me some mulled wine? And ask if the stew is ready? I want to see if I can make out any more in this book."

Sera shook her head and left. Hohan followed her.

● ● ●

Gverth took a seat next to Ora. By then, Sera had changed, and the remnants of dinner had been cleaned up. Hohan lounged with his feet propped up on another chair sipping on his ale. "My mentor, Te'zla, has agreed to meet with us tomorrow, first thing."

A shock of recognition went through Ora. He'd not only met the man, he'd interacted with him numerous times when Te'zla was younger. A ball of fear grew in Ora's belly. *Even though that was a hundred years ago, what if he recognizes me?*

Sera clapped Gverth on the shoulder. "Great job. How did you get him to agree?"

"That was what took so much time. Master Te'zla had been in meetings. But he sets time aside for working with students. Something about the youth being the hope of the future." Gverth raised his hand to get a server's attention, then turned back to Sera.

"I told him that we had found a tome written in Old Akkermenian. The Readers preserve knowledge, so he agreed to see what we have." Gverth had a satisfied smile.

Ora was impressed despite his inner turmoil. Sera and Hohan seemed excited about the meeting, which made sense. It wasn't every day that a normal person got to interact with a Reader. They were going to have to be careful despite Gverth's relationship. The Order of Readers tended to gather information, not disseminate it.

Gverth turned to Ora and peered closely at him. "Are you all right?"

Ora nodded grimly. "Must've been something I ate."

● ● ●

They set out for the Reader's Library the next morning.

At this time of day, the city was just getting into stride, with merchants setting up tables and opening shops. The smells of cooking permeated the length of their trip, fresh baked bread and pastries mixed with the spicy aroma of grilled meat. Too quickly, in Ora's mind, they were in front of the Reader's Library. Its large, multi-storied, stone building framed in sections with a dark-stained wood. Until the Grand Imperial Library had been built, this building had been the primary repository for knowledge in Dracopolis. Ora could only guess at what mysteries were housed in these walls.

Gverth addressed the attendant. "We are here to meet with Te'zla. If you would be kind enough to let him know that we are here."

The Reader, a young woman in flowing robes, pointed to her left. "You may wait in the entry area." Inside were several upholstered chairs.

After a few minutes, the attendant appeared again. "You may come with me." She led them further into the hall and up a set of stairs to an office.

Ora hung back—letting the others enter the room first—and took stock of the man inside. Te'zla was a thin man with gray eyebrows and a wild mane of gray hair that stuck out every-which-way. *It's the same man*, he sighed to himself.

Te'zla's study was appointed in dark woods beautifully carved with symbols and animals. Books and scrolls of all manner occupied every space available. Hohan immediately began to explore some of the artifacts along the back wall. Ora stayed by the door.

Gverth bowed to the man. "Master Te'zla. May I introduce you to our leader, Sera Demott."

Sera stepped forward and extended her hand to him.

Te'zla shook it. "Welcome, my friends," Te'zla gave a grandfatherly smile. "I appreciate you coming to me with this ancient tome. May I see it?"

Gverth placed the wrapped book on Te'zla's desk. Reverently, he unwrapped the cloth from the book. Te'zla opened up the cover, tracing the script with a finger as he read the first few pages.

Then he read some more.

Sera coughed politely into her fist. "Master Reader, surely you aren't going to read the whole book while we're here, are you?"

"This book is amazing," Te'zla told her, flipping through the various pages. "Where'd you find this?"

"Fagan Nuraghi."

"Amazing. It relates some of the stories of the old Giants in their struggle with mankind. And most fascinating, this section here details how different tribes of men were set in the different regions to harvest resources. Foods, trees, and specific woods. This section here talks about how one particular group, down on the coast, would harvest ocean animals. Another section talks about the Corvis, a birdlike race used for tasks such as sending messages."

Hohan harrumphed. "Surely the book mentions the gods and how they struggled to bring light and food from heaven to care for Humans. I don't know what this Giant stuff is, but it just obscures Enki's message."

"You surely aren't that dimwitted, Hohan. Giants and gods coexisted," snapped Gverth. He turned to Te'zla. "This is Hohan; he's a priest of Enki."

Te'zla nodded. "So you don't believe in Giants?"

Hohan scowled. "Enki is the—"

Sera cut him off. "This isn't the time for that."

Te'zla winked at her, then glanced up at Ora benignly. "You sir? What is your name?"

"He's Ora Earl," Sera exclaimed. "He joined our band almost a year ago. He holds his end up as a fighter and has some passing familiarity with Life Magic."

Te'zla sized Ora up. "You are too old to be named after the current king. You must have been named after Ora Earl, the Lightbringer himself. Are you from this kingdom?"

Ora peered closely. There seemed to be no hint of recognition. "No, Master Reader. I was born in a kingdom far to the south. It's been many years since I've seen home, but I was very happy to get hired on by Sera and her band."

Ora pointed at the open page in the book. "This word here, this symbol means dragon, doesn't it?"

Te'zla glanced up quickly, then nodded. Ora squinted at him. *He's not telling us something*, Ora thought to himself.

"Did you say 'dragon'?" Gverth leaned toward the book.

That seemed to startle Te'zla. "Yes, this book talks about the Giant clan that occupied this continent, this region of Eldros." He flipped to a drawing of a stylized dragon.

Sera gasped. "That's just like the—"

"Ah, the symbol of the dragon on the door," Gverth blurted.

Sera leaned in. "Master Reader, can you tell us more about these dragons? What else does it say?"

"Well, it will take a bit. If you're willing to leave this book with me, I can provide you a better idea of what its contents reveal."

Gverth was quick to agree. "But of course, Master Reader."

"I don't think we need to leave it here." Hohan pointed at the books around the office. "I'd hate for it to get lost in all of this. Perhaps it would be better if we kept it, and the Master Reader could come visit us at the Dragon's Cup."

Sera looked back and forth between the two of them and then looked at Ora for his input.

Ora hesitated. He wanted to learn more about the book, but he just didn't know what to make of Te'zla. He thought of a compromise. "I think it would be all right for us to leave the book in Master Te'zla's capable hands." Ora turned to Te'zla. "Can we set a time to get a report or some periodic translations, so we can understand the progress being made?"

Sera nodded. "I think that's a good idea. We have other things we need to be doing. Is that acceptable to you, Master Te'zla?"

"Of course. When I have something more, I'll come down to the Dragon's Cup."

CHAPTER THREE

TE'ZLA HARDEN

Te'zla sent word for his protégé and sat down with the tome. It was in fantastic condition. He slowly turned the pages. The Old Akkermenian was like an old friend. He hadn't wanted to let on to Gverth's band how easily he read it. Afterall, it was a large tome and would take time to get through it. He ran a finger over the dragon symbol. He thrilled with seeing it.

He murmured to himself, "The Giants are being revealed. It can't be long before they are back in the light for all to see."

Anya Scany entered Te'zla's study. As usual, she'd pulled her long, brown hair into a tight braid, making her face seem stretched.

"Thank you for coming, Anya. I've just had a very interesting meeting where an adventuring group brought me this." He indicated the book. "It details early Drakanon history, chronicling the start of the insurrection against the Giants."

Anya's eyes widened, and she came around to look at the book. "Where did they find this?"

"Fagan Nuraghi." Te'zla had opened the book to the symbol of the dragon. He saw that Anya recognized it.

"The old symbol of Drakanon." Her eyes shown with interest.

Te'zla nodded, pleased she was making the connections. "And they know something more about the symbol. They've seen it in the nuraghi."

Anya looked up quickly. "Did they find one of the portals?"

"A thuros? I doubt it. They might've seen an emblem or even possibly a plunnos, but that's not the best part," Te'zla said with a smile.

"Oh?" Anya asked, motioning with her hand for him to continue.

"A hundred and one years ago, when I first started as his protégé, my master, Baagrem, introduced me to Ora, the Lightbringer. Guess who was in my office today?"

"You aren't serious, are you? Are you saying that *the* Ora Earl was in your office? How did you know it was him?"

"He looked the same today as he did when I first met him." He chuckled. "He even goes by Ora Earl."

Anya waived her hand dismissively. "There are a hundred children in this city named Ora Earl. But I'm confused. How could he be here? I thought he died of old age?"

"My dear, Ora Earl has lived for a thousand years, and even before he became the Lightbringer, he had some mastery over Life Magic."

"But he can't use that to extend his life for a thousand years, can he?"

Te'zla sat in his chair and motioned for her to take a seat opposite him. "No, Life Magic in and of itself can't keep a person alive that long. However, this is only known to a few Readers who have access to the Special Archives. When he killed the Demon, he was imbued with some essence that's kept him alive."

Anya had a quizzical look on her face. "He can't be killed?"

Te'zla shook his head. "No. He cannot age or die of natural causes, but if you run a sword through him, he'd probably die."

Anya was puzzled. "But I went to his funeral. He was old. I saw his body lying in state."

Te'zla chuckled. "My dear, like I said, he has a mastery of Life Magic. He'd been planning his death for the better part of a hundred years. That's how long ago I met him. And here's the bit that cannot leave this room. "Baagrem felt that Ora needed a push in the right direction. He wove Lore Magic to get Ora out of the castle, and I helped with the ritual. Not just helped, I kept the magic going after Baagrem passed."

She tilted her head quizzically. "To what end?"

Te'zla steepled his fingers. "For Ora to become a force of good out in the world again. After he abdicated, eight hundred years ago, he sequestered himself. He studied tomes, manuscripts, maps, and legends, basically avoiding the outside world. We needed Ora out of the castle to interact with what we know is coming. When the Demon horde rampaged across the land a thousand years ago, he stepped up into that void to save all of us. If he is out in the world, he will be in a better place to be able to do it again."

Anya opened her mouth as if to protest, but Te'zla raised a hand. "You need to read the Chronicles in the Special Archives. Our order carefully documented what happened during that period, and there are things you need to know. Things that I need to show you." He tapped the tome on his desk. "The discovery of this book means we need to do it now."

CHAPTER FOUR

ORA EARL

I have three possible contracts." Sera arrayed three pieces of paper on the table in front of them as they sat in their alcove. They had the panels slid back to take advantage of the slight breeze flowing through the inn. "This first one is for an Orc raiding party that's been attacking mining settlements up in the mountains. It has a contingent reward offered by the Delvers in the local Human outpost.

"This second one is for us to guard a float barge going downriver to one of the southern kingdoms." Nobody looked thrilled about that one.

"This third one—"

The door to the inn slammed open, and a man ran in shouting, "The king is dead! The king has been murdered!" He paused for a moment and shouted again, "The king is dead!" He then fled back out into the street, shouting as he went.

The group stepped out into the main room. Everyone in the inn started speaking at once. Chairs were upended, and one large man in the back flipped his table over, sending drinks and plates everywhere. A couple of people even cheered the news, but were quickly quieted—one with a fist to the mouth. Ora sat, shocked. It was his great-great-grandson several times removed, though he'd never interacted with the man.

How could he have been killed? How did they get past the guards? Who could have done it? A myriad of thoughts ran through Ora's mind that sent him reeling. The conflict of emotion threatened to overwhelm him. He stared blankly at Sera.

While the inn was in chaos, Sera pulled a chair over next to him. "Are you all right? I had no idea you were such a royalist."

Ora just stared at her.

She caught the attention of a passing barmaid. "Bring us two ales." She looked backed at Ora. "Actually, bring us rum."

The maid hurried off amid all the exclamations and shouting. Hohan moved around the main room as the voice of reason. Several patrons gathered with him as he led a prayer to Enki. Gverth sat in the room and watched the pandemonium with interest.

Sera turned her chair toward Ora. With kind eyes, she put a hand on his arm to comfort him. "Ora, it'll be fine. It can't be dark all day."

That phrase snapped Ora's head up, and he stared at a time long past.

CHAPTER FIVE

ORA EARL

A constant torrent lashed down from dark gray skies. The violent storm had been pounding the keep for the better part of three days. Ora changed out of his wet riding gear and heavy cloak and headed up to his family's apartments. He tapped gently on his daughter's door.

"Rella?" He opened it gently and saw her sitting on a large, stuffed chair watching the rain pelt on the glass.

"Rella, I brought you something."

She didn't turn but in a flat voice asked, "What is it this time?"

"I brought you something from my expedition. You like trinkets." That evoked a response from her, but not the one he'd been hoping for.

"A trinket?" she hissed. "You brought me a trinket?" She looked away. "Another trinket. Is that all I am to you? The keeper of your trinkets?"

She shot to her feet, back stiff, and waved a clenched fist at the shelves of various items that Ora had brought her from all his trips. The tight braid of her golden hair whipped about as she talked.

In a low voice tinged with anger, she continued, "I can't believe you brought me a trinket, a measly trinket." Her vehemence caused him to take a step back.

He held up the ornate, silvery bracelet with a moonstone set in the middle, and in the light it barely glowed. "But—"

"Just put your trinket on the shelf and go."

"But Rella, I wanted to... I wanted to talk with you. I want to know... I thought you would like this."

She stepped up to him, her blue eyes blazing. "No, I wanted a father when I was six. Where were you? You were on a trip—" She poked him in the chest. "You were visiting a kingdom—" She poked him in the chest again. "You were doing anything but being here—" poke "—and being with us, being with Mother—" poke "—or me—" poke "—or my brother.

"If all my relationship is to you are these trinkets, you can have them. I don't want them!"

She stormed out of the room, her heels echoing loudly as she stomped down the corridor.

Ora went after her. "Rella, wait."

The very act of calling her name goaded her on, and she began sprinting down the hall, out of sight.

He looked down at the bracelet that he had fought hard to get as they had explored the nuraghi. He *had* been on numerous trips, but he was the High King. He had to go on those trips. She knew that, surely. She would understand and come around. With another heavy sigh, Ora set the bracelet on her shelf and left her room.

The next day, Ora went looking for his daughter. Not finding her, he asked his steward if he'd seen her.

"My lord, the Lady Rella and her attendants left for the Estate with a section of the guard at first light. I thought you knew!"

"Do you know when she'll be back?" Ora asked.

"My lord, they will be gone for the month. Should I send for the guard to bring her back?"

"No, I'll talk with her when she gets back. We'll have to take care of kingdom business before then so that I can have a clear schedule and spend time with her. We have some long days ahead of us. Get the staff together."

"Very well, Your Majesty, we'll make it so." The steward bowed again and left to make arrangements.

Three days later, a fast horse galloped into the courtyard. The horseshoes on the cobblestones echoed loudly, capturing everybody's attention. The guard threw himself from the mount and ran into the palace. Soon enough, an entourage of functionaries and guardsmen flowed into the sitting room where Ora had been going over reports with the Exchequer.

The rider braced to attention and saluted. "Your Majesty, I bear grave news."

Ora looked up worriedly. "What?"

The rider stared slightly above and past Ora, face set in a dispassionate mask that sent a chill down Ora's spine. "My Lord, Princess Rella's caravan was attacked."

Ora sat up straight. "And Rella? The others?" he asked, his heart quivering in fear.

The guard exchanged glances with the steward. "Your Majesty, they've all been killed."

Ora stood stock still, eyes wide. His pulse hammered in his ears, and he let the sheaf of reports fall to the floor.

Queen Daphne came into the room. "What is it? I heard it was Rella's retinue." She saw the look on Ora's face. "What happened?"

Like his heart had been ripped from his chest. Ora turned to face his wife. "Rella's gone. They're all dead."

CHAPTER SIX

ORA EARL

re you all right?" Sera asked.

Ora blinked, coming back to the present. He looked around the room at the uproar in the Dragon's Cup.

"Here, drink this." Sera handed him a glass of clear liquid.

He took a deep breath and knocked it back.

"You didn't answer me. Are you all right? You know it can't rain all the time."

"I know. The death of the king just hit me hard. I didn't expect it. We haven't had anything like an assassination in a long time, longer than I can remember."

Sera handed him another beverage. "It's one thing they said about Old Ora. He was able to get the peace and keep it. His descendants were able to keep it going. I'm wondering if this is because he finally passed away last year? If political enemies are somehow emboldened to move against the High King, of all people, all the other rulers of the different kingdoms of Drakanon better watch out. That's for sure."

Ora shrugged and knocked back his drink. The rum burned its way down to his belly. A slow warmth spread out.

She peered at him. "What gets me spinning is trying to figure out who would wait all this time to make a move? They've had at least a year. Possibly even longer if Old Ora had been on his deathbed. The Giants know that Ora IV was a degenerate who couldn't pass on a whore or a drink."

Not getting a rise out of him, she slid another beverage over in front of him.

He woodenly picked it up and drank it. Sera repeated the process several times until she decided to change things up. For his sixth drink, she put a darker rum down in front of Ora.

He raised an eyebrow.

She stared boldly at him. "It's a special rum from Stuitor. One of the kingdoms down south."

"They always did make good spirits." He sniffed the smoky liquid. It possessed a slightly spicy aroma, and he knocked that one back too. "Whoo! That one's got some kick."

Sera waved three fingers at Deirdre, the barmaid, and slid closer to Ora on the bench. "So, are you feeling a little better?" She smiled at him.

"I'm feeling pretty good." The pain from his memories of his daughter and the assassination of his great-grandson—however many "greats" that might be—felt as if they were wrapped in cotton.

Sera plied him with more drafts of rum and an occasional ale for the next couple of hours.

I must be more in my cups than I thought, he mused to himself. He looked at Sera, blonde hair loose now.

She smiled at him, her blue eyes sparkling.

He reached for the mug in front of him, but didn't quite have the distance and knocked it all over. He stood up, and his head spun. "Oh! I'm sorry, Rella." He sat back down quickly.

Sera jumped up quickly to avoid the spilled ale. Her eyes narrowed as she realized what he had said to her. "Who's Rella?" she asked with an icy edge to her voice.

He stared dumbly at her.

Sera looked at Hohan. "Get this idiot up to his room."

The burly Northerner laughed and grabbed Ora's arms.

"Hohan, my friend, are we going on a trip?" Ora slurred.

"Yes, my friend. You are going on a trip to the Slumberland, where these angry dreams of yours will hopefully be drowned in your ale."

Ora smiled. "You're a good friend, Hohan."

The next morning Ora slunk down to the common room, head throbbing. He could use his Life Magic to get rid of the hangover, but he thought he needed a little reminder to not get in his cups that far. Gverth, Hohan, and Sera were already at the table when he sat down.

"Well, if it isn't Lord Party-boy," Sera said with a bit of flint in her tone.

The barmaid set a bowl of gruel and an ale in front of Ora. He squinted up at her. "Deirdre, my love. Could you bring me some cold milk if you have it? And take the ale away?"

Deirdre laughed with an impish grin. "Oh, I saw you last night. I wasn't sure if the hair of the dog would help you. I'll go get you milk." With that, she left, and Ora turned back to the trio at the table.

"Good morning to you." Sera sniffed.

Ora addressed her. "Miss Sera, did I happen to do or say something that might offend you?" he asked with his best attempt at an innocent expression. "As you well know, I was in my cups, and if I did or said anything inappropriate or offensive, I do apologize."

Gverth snorted. "I've never seen you that drunk before. Hohan had to carry you to bed."

Hohan clapped Ora on the shoulder with one of his very large hands, causing Ora to wince. Sera leaned in, fixing Ora with a cold glare.

"Who's Rella?" she asked.

Her tone set off a warning bell in Ora's mind, but he was too surprised at the name to heed the warnings, and before he realized it, the words came out of his mouth.

"She's my daughter."

Gverth spat his wine out on the table.

"*You* have a daughter. How is that possible?" Sera asked.

Hohan looked on with interest. "Where is she?"

Gverth wanted to talk but coughed on his wine, spluttering and getting it all over himself.

Ora sat at the table and stared at his hands. His heart felt as if a fist clenched it in his chest. He spoke in a soft voice.

"She *was* my daughter. She was killed." He sat quietly, head down.

When he looked up, his eyes shone with unshed tears. "She was going to visit her grandparents. Raiders attacked and killed her and everyone in the caravan." He took a large, shuddering breath.

"I'm sorry for your loss." Sera reached a hand out to comfort him.

Ora looked up at the other three sitting with him at the table, concern plain on their faces. He took a deep breath and stood up.

"I'm going to head to the castle and see what I can find out about the king's murder."

That surprised the others. Sera looked at Gverth and Hohan. Neither of them seemed to want to go.

She stood up. "Fine. I'd better go with you." Ora glanced at her sharply trying to discern her motives. She must have seen his expression as she quickly added, "To keep you out of trouble."

He pushed back. "Well, I don't need you to nursemaid me. I'm gonna be all right."

Sera shook her head. "That isn't what this is about."

Ora watched her for a moment then nodded. "Let's go then."

They stepped out onto the cobblestone street. Ora turned right and headed towards the castle. Over its two-thousand-year history, the city had outgrown the original walls. This created a dividing ring from the old city to the new city. The pair had to pass through the buildings of the Old City. They passed mostly merchant shops, staging warehouses, and residences.

Sera kept pace, matching Ora's long stride step for step. "I like you, Ora, and we need you for these contracts." She looked up at him and then dodged a merchant coming out of a bakery shop.

He quirked a smile and glanced at her. "You mean, you need me."

She elbowed him as they walked. "Yes, I need you. Your fighting skills. And, Gverth and Hohan look up to you. You're like their big brother."

"What about you?"

She stumbled slightly, but managed to keep her feet. "We've completed more contracts since you joined us."

Ora nodded, letting her talk.

"And you are handy with a sword, though not as good as I am."

"All that and modest too." He chuckled.

"You know what I mean. We've been very profitable. And you know, I just want you to know that you're appreciated."

Ora stopped. "Look, Sera. I'm not going anywhere. I'm not quitting the band. I just want to find out what's going on."

She squinted at him. "Are you sure? No other offers?"

Ora laughed and started walking again. Just on the inside of the gate, they passed a series of merchant houses where goods were kept and prepared for either shipment out of the city or for consignment at shops within the city. However, there weren't many people, which was odd for this time of day.

"I wonder if everybody's at the viewing?" she asked.

"The viewing?"

"They're displaying the body of the king in Draco Plaza."

"In that case, we'll find out here in a moment."

Turning a corner, they easily saw the raised platform. Three sides were surrounded by dark blue curtains. On the center bier, the body of the king, wearing robes of state, lay with the crown resting before his chest.

A large crowd watched, and they were more subdued than Ora expected. Several glanced around the crowd nervously.

Others shifted back and forth on their feet. Families grouped in tight knots. The conversation, if there was any, was in hushed whispers.

"They're terrified," hissed Sera.

"Yes. What's going on? There's a lot of fear, more than I've ever seen here."

"Ora the Fourth wasn't a popular king," she said. "He was more interested in chasing women and gambling than he was taking care of the people, but still, I don't understand it either."

They had worked their way up to about halfway towards the dais when a couple of people exclaimed, and five Wlewoi came out from behind the curtains around the viewing platform.

The Wlewoi, catlike humanoids, made their way around the bier and arrayed themselves along the front edge of the platform. Glancing behind them, Ora noticed that several people in the crowd had started to leave the Plaza. Most slowly made their departure, but a few moved with haste, pushing their way through the crowd.

Ora turned back to the Wlewoi on the platform. They wore the uniform of the Esroi, the guards of the High King. When he'd abdicated, they swore to protect the king now and forever, and ever since, they'd never failed in their duties.

Until now.

Four Wlewoi dropped down off the platform and began harassing the crowd. He hadn't seen where the other one had gone.

Ora heard their words over the crowd. "Get your look and move on."

Sera nudged him. "Are you all right?"

"The uniforms didn't used to be that ostentatious." Ora squinted a bit. "I don't recognize their clan markings."

Sera looked at him sharply. "Have you had dealings with the Blood?"

Ora shook his head. "No, not with these."

"But you've been around Wlewoi enough to recognize clans?" She didn't look amused.

"It was a long time ago," he said softly.

Ora felt the weight of Sera's gaze on him.

"Let's get out of here," she told him.

Ora thought for a moment and then nodded.

Sera turned and headed out through the crowd.

What had gone so wrong that his lineage had devolved into gambling and whoring?

He was so lost in thought that he didn't notice that Sera had come to a stop. He barely caught himself in time to avoid colliding with her. He peered around her to see the fifth Esroi blocked their path.

The Esroi boldly looked Sera head to foot, gaze resting on her sword and dagger. He sniffed at the air. "What is your purpose here?"

Ora turned slightly, interposing the edge of the hood on his cloak so it would help hide his face. Hoping he wasn't too late, he used his Shimmershield to mask his scent and aura from the Wlewoi.

"Well?" the Wlewoi demanded. "Do you need to see the inquisitor?"

Ora felt Sera shudder at that. *An inquisitor? What in Giant's name is that?*

"We were just viewing the king. We've done nothing," Sera replied meekly.

"I'll be the judge of that. Do you live in Draco?" he asked.

"Yes, we work contracts down on the lower tier."

The guard turned his attention to Ora. "What about you? Do you hide behind this *female?*"

"It is as the lady said. We were just paying our respects to the king. We aren't here for trouble." Ora held his hands up, palms out.

Something didn't feel right with this Esroi. He couldn't put his finger on it, but this guard wasn't like the others Ora had known. His clan markings, the patterns in the Wlewoi's fur, along with his coloration, were like none Ora had ever encountered, and he'd grown up around Wlewoi. Even the guard's harness, up close, looked like a gaudy imitation of a true Esroi harness.

The guard sniffed at Ora. His eyes narrowed, head tilted to the side, as if he were evaluating prey. Shouting off to his right caught his attention. "All right. Be on your way." He stepped out of Sera's path and strode into the crowd, which parted before him and closed up after he had passed.

"That was close." Sera took a relieved breath.

"The Esroi just protect the king," Ora asserted. "Right?"

"The Blood. You know that's what they're called, not Esroi." The way she said it dripped with venom. "The Blood. That's street slang for the king's enforcers, and the people who get taken by them are never seen again."

Ora was horrified. Surely his descendants hadn't used the Esroi like that. The royal guard, Esroi, were people of honor, people originally from his homeland. And then it clicked. Those Wlewoi were no Esroi. He didn't feel the bond with them that he had had with every Esroi who had protected the king for the last thousand years.

Sera and Ora made their way back to the Dragon's Cup. They entered the inn and headed to their alcove. There they found Gverth and Hohan sitting and chatting while picking at a plate of cheese and smoked meats.

"Well, how was the viewing? Is the king dead?" Gverth asked with a sardonic smile.

Ora looked at him sharply.

"What?" Gverth shuddered. "Looking at a body is creepy."

Sera put her hand on Ora's arm. "Why don't you have a seat, and I'll get us some wine."

"Yes, we saw the king. Yes, he's dead," Ora said somberly.

"I meant no offense," Gverth said.

"We ran into the Blood." Sera put down a bottle and a set of glasses and began pouring.

Both Gverth and Hohan sat up straight.

"Any issues? Do we need to—" Hohan started.

"No, they were just looking for agitators in the crowd," Sera explained, passing a cup to each person. "Apparently, our friend here," she indicated Ora, "has never encountered the Blood."

Both men looked at Ora in shock.

"How long have you lived in the city?" Gverth asked.

"I've been here a long time, and I've never seen their like. Maybe I move in different circles." Ora shrugged.

"Were you able to find what you were looking for?" Hohan asked.

Ora sighed. "No, I was hoping to get access to the keep. Maybe talk with someone who had been there that night, or to find a clue. Something of why someone might want the king dead. But the viewing and the Esroi…"

"What kind of clues?" Hohan leaned in, clearly interested.

"It's not important right now." Sera sat down. "What have you two been doing while we've been gone?"

"I just got back from the temple," Hohan explained. "And there's a big event up north that called the head of the temple up there."

"Is that unusual?" Sera asked.

"For the local matriarch to get called away, it has to have been something significant."

"You have duties at the Temple of Enki, yes?" Ora asked.

Hohan nodded.

"Do they still have a library there?" Ora asked. It must have been three hundred years ago that he had donated architecture diagrams of Draco Keep along with some of his work on nuraghi to the Temple of Enki. They included a translation guide that he had copied to go along with a set of documents he had found describing the rise of Enki on Drakanon.

When Hohan nodded, hope blossomed in Ora's chest.

"Do you think you could arrange a tour of this library?" Ora asked.

"It's possible." Hohan tilted his head. "We'll have to ask the curate that's in charge, but I don't know why she wouldn't let you. When would you like to?"

Ora surprised him by shooting to his feet. "Now."

"Easy, Ora," Sera said. "It's late. Let's do this first thing tomorrow."

Ora slid back into his seat. "Tomorrow should be fine." He tried to tamp down his disappointment.

"Excellent. Now that that's settled..." Gverth held up a small throwing knife. "Who wants to throw for the next round of drinks?"

Hohan held up his hands and gave a toothy grin. "Not me. The Land Mage cheats."

Gverth sputtered in protest.

Ora smiled at their antics. "I'll give it a go." He pulled out his own throwing knife and danced it across his knuckles.

Gverth hesitated as he watched the display. "Um, no magic, right?"

CHAPTER SEVEN

SANKARA MURCHALA

It was a cool day on the edge of Kinderkesh, one of the western mountain districts of Amaranth, the jewel of Lathranon. Sankara Murchala, the seventh son of the ruling prince, sat in the main room of his suite of rooms in the House of the Floating Lily.

Cushions covered in fine silk fabric lay around the low-carved table that bore a tea service. He steeped the tea sifter and inhaled the rich aroma of his favorite blend from Sratapanara. His room was on the ground floor and opened to the lush gardens overlooking a bathing pool where many young maidens lounged by the pool and giggled at whatever might pass their fancy.

He leaned back on the cushions, relaxing from a hard day on patrol. Sankara was the military leader of this district. Periaslavl, the neighboring realm, had no desire to invade Amaranth, which was why the seventh son commanded here and not someone deemed more important.

A gentle bell rang.

"Come," he said.

A young woman entered. "Lord Murchala, you have visitors."

"Send them in." He sat up a little straighter, wondering who might be here to visit him. The House of the Floating Lily was his refuge, his place of rest and recuperation, and no one bothered him here unless it was urgent.

The young lady ushered in two people. The man had a medium build, dark hair, slightly gray at the temples. He wore robes of the latest styles from Sratapanara.

Sankara's breath caught in his throat at the sight of the woman. She possessed an otherworldly grace as she moved into the room. She was tall, possessed angular, violet eyes, and had her blonde hair pulled back to where he could just see the tips of her strangely pointed ears. Her dress, though cut modestly, revealed a fantastic figure underneath.

It almost pained Sankara to tear his attention away from the woman, but he inclined his head. "What brings you here?"

The man bowed. "Lord Murchala, my name is Houshkulu, and this is Lavinia."

Sankara thrilled at hearing her name. He focused back on Houshkulu.

"We have a proposal that I would like to discuss with you if you're open to new opportunities."

Sankara pointed at the cushions opposite the table. "Please, be seated."

"My lord, it was your reputation that brought me here. Word of your competence—" Houshkulu emphasized the word "—has reached us, even in the capital, and that intrigued me. I would like to discuss a venture. There is a land that could use a competent and strong ruler like yourself."

Sankara tilted his head. "I have responsibilities here. Obligations to this district, protecting the border, and ultimately, as the son of Rao Sahib, I have a responsibility to the principality."

Houshkulu nodded his head as if he were agreeing with everything Sankara had to say but then looked him in the eyes, piercing Sankara to the core.

"Lord Murchala, we are alone, so we can be frank and open. You don't know me, but I know you very well. The seventh son of the prince with six very healthy brothers between you and any chance of the throne."

Sankara was about to speak, but Houshkulu put his hands together in front of him, palms together. "Please, let me continue. You and I both know that your reputation here is what brought me. You've reduced crime. Incidents amongst the troops are at the lowest they've ever been. The people respect, if not revere you."

"Your compliments are nice," said Sankara, eyes wary.

"Of course, your successes have made others in the kingdom jealous. And second, it has awakened desires in the districts around here. Desires might not be the right word. Maybe, envy of the success that you have forged out of this district would be better. Merchants come *here* first, goods are flowing, and your district is prosperous. Is that not so?"

"Yes," Sankara agreed. "An old woman with a bag of coin could walk unescorted across this district without fear for her safety."

Sankara shifted on the cushion. "If you know this much about me, you know that, in my family, we don't kill each other. Not for the last three hundred years. Those are the rules. So, good sir, what are you proposing?"

Houshkulu sipped his tea, a slight smile on his lips, and set it back down. "My Lord, I am not proposing we move against your family. I'm proposing another land. What if I were to tell you I could transport you to a region lacking strong leadership? A region with few warriors. It's ripe for someone like you to take over."

"Where is this region?"

Houshkulu said, "All in good time. But first, does my proposal intrigue you? Does it seem like something you might like to go after?"

Sankara thought for a moment. "In principle, yes, but I need to know more details. I want to know where this is. And more specifically, what's in this for you?"

Houshkulu flicked his hand dismissively. "It would open up trade that has been… resistant. It would benefit me to have a friendly ruler in place."

Sankara nodded.

Houshkulu continued, "I will return in two days and show you specifically where we're talking about. Would that be acceptable?"

Sankara looked at the man, trying to discern a trap. *Is he with another branch of the kingdom? Or was he sent by one of my brothers?*

"I am not playing a game. I am very serious," Houshkulu said.

Sankara shot a quick glance at Lavinia and found her studying him with those perfect, violet eyes. His heart thrilled as they made eye contact. She nodded slightly.

Staring at her, Sankara found himself saying, "Yes, I feel that this would be acceptable." He broke eye contact with her and addressed Houshkulu. "Two days. Let's have a better discussion then and see what you're about."

Houshkulu and his assistant both stood up. They bowed simultaneously. "My Lord, two days and we will return by your leave."

Sankara nodded and bade them farewell. He watched them leave, his mind awhirl. If what Houshkulu was offering was real, there was an opportunity. One of the things Sankara longed for was to redeem himself in his father's eyes. After ten years, he still blamed him for the last failed excursion into Periaslavl.

It irked Sankara that he shouldered the blame and hadn't even been in charge of that raid. Despite the fact that Sankara had been successful in every military action he had been directly in command of since then, his father refused to look past that one incident and acknowledge that Sankara was a capable leader. And that disappointment just became fuel for his other brothers, who treated him with distaste and scorn to curry favor.

He sipped his tea. *Perhaps it is time for my brothers to envy me for my success.*

CHAPTER EIGHT

ORA EARL

The Temple of Enki was within the wall and near the garden just south of the keep. While Enki was predominately worshipped in the south and west of Drakanon, he was one of a pantheon of gods. Enki was the god of water and knowledge.

As they traveled through the city, the glittering metallic dome of the temple stood above the surrounding buildings. It didn't take the four of them too much time to get there, especially since there weren't many people out at this time of day.

Hohan bowed to the curate in the antechamber of the temple. "Mistress Joane, my friend here is a scholar and asked if he could research in our library."

She looked Ora over, then pointed at his sword and dagger. "He looks more like a degenerate than a scholar."

Ora flourished a bow. "Curate, if I may, the weapons are for defense. Many, as you know, are willing to set themselves upon the scholars who strive for nothing but knowledge. Would you begrudge me my ability to mount a solid defense?"

She smiled slightly at that. "You're a charming one, aren't you? I'll tell you what, I need a task performed. If you accomplish this task for me, I will grant you complete access to our library. What do you say?"

"Gracious curate, I accept. Tell me about this task. Tell me what it is, that I may accomplish it and revel in your library."

She smiled. "There is a container down at the docks. The ship factor, whom we have already paid, is holding it hostage, wanting twice the payment that we agreed upon. If you could persuade him to accept our original contract, I would be eternally grateful."

Gverth stepped forward. "Mistress, do you have a copy of this contract?"

"Wait here." The curate went inside for a few moments, then returned, extending a scroll to Hohan. "Is there anything else?" she asked.

"No, Mistress. We will be about fetching your crate and will return with your goods. If you will permit us your leave." Ora bowed again.

On the steps of the temple, Ora halted. "Let's see that contract."

Gverth extended it to him.

"Says here that it's being held by the factor Tamaroa down by the docks. Have any of you heard of this guy?" he asked. A trio of no's came out of them.

"But we can find out," Sera said firmly.

CHAPTER NINE

SANKARA MURCHALA

The servants poured a bath for Sankara. The aroma of sandalwood reminded him of home.

He was soaking in it when his favorite courtesan, Giuliana, brought him a bowl of sliced, fresh fruit. As she extended the bowl towards him, her eyes opened wide in shock.

"Giuliana?" He sat up.

Her eyes rolled back in their sockets, showing only the whites, and blood ran out of her mouth. She fell forward limply into the edge of the tub, revealing a dark-clad figure behind her holding a wicked, curved blade dripping with her blood.

Sankara didn't hesitate. He flung the bowl at the man's head. The assassin had to raise the knife to block it, and Sankara dove out the other side of the tub away from the man.

On the opposite side of the tub, away from the intruder, was a small table with a decanter of chilled wine and several goblets. Sankara caught movement out of the corner of his eye as he grasped the decanter and spun, swinging. Whether it was by skill or happenstance, he smashed the edge of the decanter into the assassin's temple, knocking his head to the side and throwing the knife thrust wide. Sankara grabbed the stunned man's arm and shoved him headfirst into the tub.

"Guards!" Sankara shouted as the assassin thrashed about, trying to lift his head out of the water. Sankara leaned his full weight into the man's torso, forcing his head into the bottom of the tub. "Guards!"

Two of Sankara's guards burst into the room and moved for the assassin.

With a final blub of air, the assassin went still. The guards pulled him out of the water, pinning his arms and throwing him back onto the ground. The assassin retched and threw up the contents of his stomach, clearing his mouth and lungs of water, heaving with fits of coughing.

Sankara retrieved his sword from the stand and held it at the assassin's throat. "Who sent you?"

The assassin glared at Sankara, hatred boiling in his brown eyes. "I can't say."

Sankara pressed the sword into the side of the man's neck. "Who sent you?"

The assassin kicked the guard holding his right arm, forcing him to let go of his arm or fall. As soon as his arm came free, he grabbed a dagger concealed in his sleeve and threw it at Sankara.

From sheer instinct, Sankara batted the blade out of the way and swiped his sword across the man's neck, causing a gush of blood. Realizing what he had done, Sankara knelt next to the bleeding man.

"Who sent you?" he asked softly. "Tell me before the gods take you, and they will count this in your favor as they judge your deeds in the afterlife."

Sankara could see the life ebbing from the assassin, who whispered, "Priya."

Sankara rocked back on his heels, stunned. He had witnessed Priya's heavy hand in dealing with the other noble houses. Insult or opportunity brought out the worst in her. Seems his third brother's wife, Priya, was no longer playing by the rules. And if the rules no longer applied, and Sankara was to ever get back into his father's favor, it became more likely his brothers were going to try to put an end to him. He looked down on the dead assassin. Worry and anxiety settled into resolve.

He stood up and wiped his sword on a cloth, sheathed it, and sat down in the chair. He stared at the courtesan's body in front of him. *Poor Giuliana.*

CHAPTER TEN

ORA EARL

Sera checked the scroll a third time for the address. "Well, I think this is it."

The warehouse was two-thirds of the way down the quay by the river. It boasted a massive door, easily fifty feet tall, spanning almost the entire height of the warehouse itself. Next to it was a smaller door.

Ora strode up to the man-sized door and rapped on it sharply. Nothing happened. After a minute, he hit on it harder.

He heard a muffled, "Hang on!"

The door opened, and a middle-aged man wearing serviceable workmen's clothes looked out. "Can I help you?"

Sera stepped forward, holding up the scroll from the curate at the Temple of Enki. "We have a shipment we're supposed to pick up."

The man squinted at the scroll. "Give me a minute. I'll get Tamaroa, the boss." With that, he stepped inside, closing the small door.

Sera glanced back at the others. Gverth just shrugged.

After a few minutes, a sound of a chain winding could be heard, and the massive door slid open, revealing a small group of people led by what looked like an octopus.

The creature glided forward on four thick tentacles, each as big and round as a grown man's leg. Instead of a head of hair, there were thinner tentacles, each the width of a finger. At the shoulders on his torso were two arm-like tentacles that ended in a series of six finger-tentacles.

"I'm Tamaroa. So, she sent you to come get the box, did she? Did you bring my payment?"

Sera shifted. "Good sir, I... I assume you're a he?"

The octopus man laughed at that. "Yes, I am a he. I take it you've never seen my kind?" he asked with a grin that revealed four needle sharp fangs and a mouth full of bright-white, wide, pointed teeth, much like a shark's.

Hohan spoke up from where he stood, "No. What are you?"

Before the creature could answer, Ora spoke up, "He's an Ohtovid."

Tamaroa was delighted. "Yes! I'm an Ohtovid. My consortium lives down around the southern Nid islands and operates in all the major cities, but all that matters for your purposes is that I'm the one with the cargo. Did you bring the money?"

Sera straightened at that. "You mean the money for the cargo that's already been paid for? The curate said you signed a contract—" Sera tapped the scroll "—didn't you?"

The Ohtovid spread the ends of a couple tentacles wide, mimicking the Human gesture. "Everything in life is negotiable."

"Not contracts you've already negotiated. You put your mark on this paper. They've paid you."

He shrugged. "My expenses were greater than expected in obtaining this cargo."

"I don't see anything here about a cost for additional expenses." Sera squinted at the contract, then glanced up at him. "Do we need to involve an inquisitor?"

That invoked a sharp intake of breath. "Let's not get hasty." He stepped close and placed a friendly arm around her. "I'm sure we can work this out."

Tamaroa glanced around, looking to regain the advantage in this conversation, and then smiled a toothy grin. "I don't see that you've brought a horse team and wagon."

She narrowed her eyes. "Just how big is this cargo?"

Tamaroa roared with laughter. His crew laughed with him.

"She didn't tell you, did she?" At Sera's headshake, he swept a tentacle back into the warehouse. "Let me show you, and perhaps we can come to an arrangement to get it delivered."

They stepped into the warehouse, letting their eyes adjust to the dimness inside. Tamaroa waved his tentacle-arms wide, gesturing toward an enormous stone box. It was the height of a man, equally as wide, and the length of two men if they were to lay down.

Hohan whistled. "That's quite the box."

Sera and the others circled it while Tamaroa's crew chuckled as they watched them.

Gverth tapped Sera on the shoulder and whispered something into her ear.

She nodded, then looked at Tamaroa. "Can I have a moment to confer with my colleagues?"

Sera and the others gathered together, and Gverth outlined his plan.

"Do you think it'll work?" Hohan asked.

"It's worth a try. Worst case, all we're out is effort," Ora said. "Besides, Ohtovids like betting."

Sera looked back at Tamaroa. "I hear your kind likes wagers. Would you be interested in a wager about this box?"

Tamaroa leaned forward in interest. "What do you have in mind?"

"We wager we can move this box out of here without assistance from anyone else, without a horse and wagon, just the four of us."

Tamaroa laughed. "Just the four of you? No horses, no crane, no tackle?"

Sera nodded. "If we succeed, we get the box."

Ora could see the greed in Tamaroa's eyes. "And if you fail?"

"Then we pay double your fee for you to deliver it."

"You have a deal. Let's see this miracle."

Gverth started for the door.

"Hang on, where's he going? You said just the four of you."

"I'll be right back," Gverth reassured him. "I need to get something, and no, it's not a horse and wagon." The group waited, and about fifteen minutes later, Gverth returned carrying a small pail.

"You think a bucket is going to save you?"

Tamaroa's crew laughed.

Gverth just shrugged and walked over to the container. Sera, Hohan, and Ora gathered next to him at the far end.

"Are you ready?" Ora looked at Hohan, who nodded back in reply.

Ora reached for Shimmershield and wrapped himself with strength and then branched it out to envelop Gverth at the same time. Hohan did the same thing to boost himself and Sera with mystical strength. The four of them reached up on the lip of the box and pushed with their magically enhanced might. The box held fast for a moment and then, barely, lifted up.

"Now, Gverth!" Ora grunted.

Gverth tipped the bucket over, spilling the pea-sized gravel that had been contained in it. Gverth used his Land Magic, pushing the gravel under the box.

"We need to lift it up a little more," Gverth gasped. "Push harder!" All four grunted and pushed it higher just a fraction of an inch. They were surrounded by a slithering sound as more pea gravel slid under the box.

"Pack it tight," Sera said.

"It's as tight as it's going to get. Let's go around the other side." Gverth relaxed and shook out his arms.

The four of them moved around to the other side of the box. They arrayed themselves along the end and repeated the effort, grunting with all of their Life Magic-enhanced strength. It took more effort this time, but they managed to lift the box up just enough for some pea gravel to slide under, pushed by Gverth's Land Magic.

"I think that's about it," Gverth said.

The four of them stepped back from the container. Tamaroa's crew looked on with interest, trying to figure out what was happening. Hohan and Ora let their magic dissipate for the moment. They shook out their arms.

"That's it?" Tamaroa said, laughing. "That was your show?" His crew laughed again.

"Just wait." Gverth smiled at them.

"Gverth, get up to the front and make sure the flow is smooth. Also, you're our guide," Ora said.

Ora stayed at the back of the container with Sera and Hohan. Once again, Ora and Hohan pulled Life Magic, giving strength, and they pushed the box.

The giant, stone container shifted forward a hair. Then a fraction of an inch. Gaining momentum, it started sliding forward at a very slow, constant rate. The heavy container rode on the river of rolling gravel with a rumble. As the gravel flowed out behind the box, Gverth directed it back toward the front, creating a loop of gravel that the massive container rolled over.

Astonishment painted the faces of Tamaroa and his crew.

After a few moments, Tamaroa rushed after them.

"Hang on!" he called to Ora and the crew.

"Keep pushing." Ora put a hand on his hilts. "I'll take care of him."

"I had to talk with you," Tamaroa said. "You are magnificent. Come work for me."

Ora blinked. "I appreciate your offer, Tamaroa, but I already have an employer." He hooked his thumb back at the crew.

"I'll hire you all. You did, in fact, best me with a bucket of gravel."

Ora shook his head. "We are in the middle of something—"

"A beverage! At least let me buy you all a beverage, and we can discuss it."

"All right. After we finish our task, we'll meet you for drinks." At Tamaroa's apparent delight, Ora held up a hand. "Not too fast. I'll send word when we are done."

"Done!" Tamaroa looked up the street. "It looks like your friends need your assistance." Tamaroa pointed at a struggling Sera and Hohan.

Ora dashed up the street, refreshing the strength in himself and Sera, and pushed on the stone.

"What did he want?" Sera grunted with effort.

"A date." At Sera's sharp look, he winked at her.

Sera shook her head. "Gverth, how are we doing?

"Oh, I'm fine. We might need to stop at some point and get more gravel."

"Where did you get the gravel from?" Hohan asked.

"I just pulled it into this bucket from the surrounding streets."

"Won't the city works get grumpy when they find out you've stolen their filler?" Ora laughed.

"Hopefully, they won't notice."

The four of them attracted quite a few stares as they pushed the stone container through the streets toward the Temple of Enki. Once they reached the front of the temple, they stopped and caught their breath. Hohan went in to get the curate.

She came out and stood at the top of the steps, hands on hips. With a severe expression, she surveyed the spectacle.

"I can't believe you were able to get it so quickly. Did they put up much of a fight?"

Ora stepped forward. "I don't think that really matters, at this point." He patted the container. "What does matter is you have your box and cargo. I believe we've fulfilled the terms of your task, and now we would humbly request access to your library."

❀ ❀ ❀

The library, while not as extensive as the Grand Imperial Library, was packed with more books than any reasonable person could expect to see. The polished lacquered shelves ran down both walls, arranged in two tiers with ladders interspersed. Reading tables were arrayed through the long room.

After checking to make sure they were alone, Sera turned to Ora. "We went through a lot of effort to get to this point. What are we here for?"

Ora gave a close-mouthed smile. "The old king donated a collection to the temple. It includes a translation guide for the old language. If we can find that, it will help us with that book."

"Just how do you know about all this?" she asked, arms crossed over her chest.

"It's complicated. But, trust me. If the works are still here, that guide will help us translate the tome." Ora glanced at Gverth. "No offense to your master, but I like to find my own answers."

"Trust, but verify. All right, I'll trust you—" she pointed a finger at him "—but you owe me a story." Sera turned to Hohan. "How do we find this collection?"

Hohan went over to a large tome residing on a lectern. "This should be an index of everything that's in this room, including any collections. If it's in this library, it will be in this book." He started turning pages. "How long ago do you think it was given to the temple?"

"About three hundred years ago." Ora peered at the book over Hohan's shoulder. After flipping through many pages, Ora pointed at one of the entries. "There."

Hohan read the description and looked around the room for the markers that were on each section of shelves. He indicated a section that was across the library. "Third from the end. According to this, it should be in that stack over there."

As a group, they all trooped over and started scanning faded and peeling labels from different archive boxes.

Gverth, squinting at labels on the bottom shelf, called out, "I've found it."

He pulled the archive box out and set it on the nearby table. Inside were all manner of parchments, scrolls, and a well-worn six-inch by nine-inch leather-bound book.

"That's it. That's the translation guide." Ora pointed. "Look at it. Am I right?"

Gverth opened up the book and nodded. "He's right."

"Here, let me look at it." Hohan leaned over the book.

While the others crowded around the book, Ora thumbed through the parchments and scrolls remaining in the box, looking for something specific. His eyes crinkled at the corners when he finally located it.

It was a long scroll, faded with age. He pulled it out, untied the ribbon holding the scroll closed, and spread it out. It was actually multiple sheets of parchment rolled tightly together.

Hohan looked over and whistled. "Is that the castle? Is that Draco Keep?"

CHAPTER ELEVEN

SANKARA MURCHALA

A guard ushered Houshkulu and Lavinia into Sankara's study. "Lord Murchala, I received your summons. On the way, I spoke with your guard, and I'm pleased that the assassin was not successful."

Sankara looked up at Houshkulu. "I appreciate your sentiment, my lord."

Houshkulu bowed his head. "Is there some way I can help with your response? Perhaps Lavinia—"

"No, I've sent a return gift. My brother Kanan should be finding his dead wife about now, and he will blame my second brother, Ramesh. But that's not why I asked you here." Sankara leaned forward. "About this proposition you have, I accept your offer. What do we need to do to move forward?"

Houshkulu looked pleased. "I made arrangements in the hope you would accept, my lord. When would you like to start?"

"I can have two hundred men ready immediately. Any more would require a conversation with the Regional Commander, as I would have to empty the garrison, and that could lead to an uncomfortable conversation before we even started." Sankara laughed, feeling suddenly unburdened by this decision. "In this instance it is easier to ask forgiveness and have something to show for it."

Houshkulu smiled. "Excellent thought, my lord. That's a sizable force for where we're going." He looked at Lavinia. "Make arrangements for two hundred arms and armor." He glanced at Sankara. "We wouldn't want to be accused of stealing from the prince. What about the horses?"

Sankara shook his head. "My men own their own horses. It was part of the arrangement for joining the cavalry."

"Very well. I'll arrive mid-morning and guide you. We will take our leave." Both Houshkulu and Lavinia sketched a bow and left.

Sankara called for the guard. "Please find Risaldar Marchandani and have him come here." While waiting for his second-in-command, Sankara busied himself with writing out letters of authorization and instructions for while he was away. He had finished the last of them when Risaldar Rajan Marchandani arrived.

Rajan saluted crisply. "You wished to see me, Commander?"

"Ah, Rajan. Please come in." He rose from the desk. "Please join me." They both moved over to the cushions.

The servants brought in a tea set, poured each a cup, and withdrew, leaving the pair alone.

"Rajan, I've accepted an opportunity that could benefit me, but also has opportunities for my officers." He leaned forward. "For you specifically."

"Sankara, I've been with you a long time. I go where you go."

Sankara leaned back. "This is the opportunity I have been waiting for to prove myself to my father."

Sankara's enthusiasm was contagious, and Rajan grinned. "And to put your thumb in your brother's eye."

"Exactly." Sankara sobered. "I need you to get the First and Second Sowar ready to move tomorrow morning. Personal equipment and horses only."

"No armor?"

Sankara shook his head. "It is to be provided."

"Very mysterious. Where are we going?"

The corner of Sankara's mouth almost turned in a smile. "We find out tomorrow."

❦ ❦ ❦

The next day, Houshkulu and Lavinia led Sankara and his troops up into the mountains. They started on one of the roads, then left that for a game trail. Eventually, they dismounted and traversed a narrow path up to a small plateau barren of scrub and trees that abutted the foot of one of the mountains. It was so inhospitable even birds didn't fly over it.

Houshkulu led them to the granite wall at the back of the space.

"Where are you taking us, Houshkulu?" Sankara asked.

Lavinia stepped close to him. She smelled of sandalwood and spices. "Patience, my lord. I think you'll appreciate the outcome."

Houshkulu put his hands to the wall. There was a click, and a portion of the wall pivoted to show a large passage into the mountain. "I hope this eases your doubts, Lord Commander."

Sankara watched as Lavinia strutted past, leading her horse into the cavern beyond. She smirked at him from over her shoulder. "Are you coming?"

The initial passage widened into a large, well-shaped storeroom holding racks of exotic armor and weapons. Sankara had never seen anything of these designs.

Rajan picked up a vest made of small, interlaced plates. "This is incredibly light. How will they hold up against arrows and spears?"

"My people have learned forging techniques unknown to your smiths." Lavinia's smile brightened the room. "They are indeed light, making them easy to move and fight in, but you will have no cause to regret wearing it."

"Commander?" Rajan looked at Sankara.

"Have the men draw arms and armor as they enter."

Rajan nodded. "As you command."

"While they are doing that, Lord Commander, I wish to show you something." Houshkulu led him out of the makeshift armory, along some passages, and ushered him through a doorway boasting two huge, ironbound, oaken doors with strange hinges.

Sankara's head started to hurt. The pattern of the hinges seemed to twist in ways that made no sense. *There's something wrong with those.*

Before he could figure out what was off, Houshkulu opened the door and ushered him inside.

The hall was huge, but that wasn't what took Sankara's breath away. Gemstones as large as his head glittered in large lightstones set in the ceiling. They illuminated immense murals that covered the walls, showing scenes that seemed familiar. He was no pujari, but he recognized many tales included in the Ganeshian mythology of Amaranth.

The artists who'd painted these had been incredibly skilled and detailed, using gems inlaid into the art for accent. For a moment, Sankara thought the murals moved. He shook his head. "Must be a trick of the light." He hurried to catch up with Houshkulu.

Huge columns rose to the ceiling. These had been carved into twisting patterns. He turned from them as the patterns, like the hinges, made his head hurt.

And there, at the end of the room, was a staircase of large steps leading up into an archway. Rune-covered pillars supported the arch, but that wasn't the amazing thing.

In the arch itself, there was a swirling, roiling pattern of light.

"What is that?" he murmured, stepping closer to see the roiling light better.

"That, my Lord Commander, is a thuros, and it will lead you to all I've promised and more."

CHAPTER TWELVE

ORA EARL

O ra sat at the table in their alcove at the Dragon's Cup, tracing his finger along a sketch he had made of the drawings in the library, especially the secret passage in the foundation of Draco Keep.

While he had been the High King, Ora had gone to great lengths to resolve inter-kingdom disputes. The two hundred years he sat on the throne had been hard at first. But through trade and beneficial road works, commerce improved, money flowed, and neighbors became business partners.

All of that effort laid the foundation for eight hundred years of peace and mutual respect. Shattered in an instant with the assassination of the High King. *I have to find out who could orchestrate the assassination.*

If the guard were corrupt, or replaced. Ora shuddered at the thought of who could overpower the Esroi without open warfare. They were tough fighters from a fierce race.

Maybe if I could get into Draco Keep, I might be able to find a clue?

A mug thumped down next to him. He looked up to see Sera and the others joining him.

"What are you working on?" Hohan asked.

"Just organizing my thoughts." He closed the journal, tied the leather cord around it, and put it back into a pocket.

"We wanted to talk about what we should do next," Sera said.

"What contracts do we have lined up?" Gverth shuffled into the alcove with a bowl of stew and mug. The aroma of spiced meat set Ora's stomach rumbling, reminding him he hadn't eaten anything in a while.

Sera unfolded a piece of paper and smoothed it out on the table. "We still have the three offers: The mining camp protection deal. The river guard gig. And the last one is—"

There was a polite cough at the entryway to their alcove. Satya, one of the Cup's waitresses, stood there. "Miss Sera, there is a person here to see you. Shall I show him back?"

"Yes, please. And thank you."

Satya led Deveris Develin, factor and contract negotiator, to their little room. He was an overly dressed, slender man, pale, as if the sun had never shone on his face. He was the factor who had found them the Goblin contract near the nuraghi. Sera had been working with him for as long as Ora had been involved with the band, but Ora really didn't like the man. Something about him was off-putting. He was too pretty, too soft, and too greedy.

"Good. I see all of you are here. That was excellent work on the last contract." He pulled a handkerchief out and wiped the chair seat before sitting down. "I have a new contract for you. Just came in, and they requested you, specifically." Deveris's brown eyes almost gleamed with avarice as he held out a scroll to Sera. "Your reputation is growing. This contract is very lucrative, I must add."

Sera read the contents and whistled. "This *is* a lot of money, and it says that it's just to stop Gnolls that are attacking sheep on a ranch?" Sera looked sharply at Deveris Develin. "This is dragon-hunting money. What's the deal?"

Deveris gave a wry grin. "They want this to happen quickly."

"All right." Sera shook the scroll. "How much time do we have to make a decision?"

"I need to know now. They want you to get out there and get this problem solved."

Gverth leaned forward. "What's the urgency?"

"I don't know. Some relative of some minor noble here in the city. You know how that goes." Deveris shrugged.

"I need some time to talk this through with my crew," Sera said. "If you would be willing to wait, that'd be fine. Or I can send a messenger to you after we have our conversation."

"Send me a messenger. I have a couple of other people that might be interested in this. I'll go check on them. You can find me at the Sun and Crown, and we'll see if it's still available." He turned to leave.

"What aren't you telling me, Deveris?" Sera watched the man's face. Ora and the others sat up at her tone, firm with a hint of violence.

The smarmy grin fell from his face. "I swear, this was brought to me by a trusted contact."

Sera leaned back in her chair, but her tone didn't warm up. "Don't mess with me on this Deveris. We've made you a lot of money. You know we get it done. Please don't add yourself to our list."

Deveris ran a nervous hand through his short, sandy hair. "By the Giants, Sera, I've never given you anything but quality contracts."

Sera looked around at the others. "Thoughts?"

Ora crossed his arms and stared at the man. "We take him at his word."

Deveris gave a weak smile and nodded. "I'll take my leave then." He hurried out of the alcove.

Gverth took the scroll and spread it out on the table between him and Hohan.

"This looks pretty straightforward," Gverth said. "But I don't understand why the bounty is so large."

Sera glanced at Ora. "And you?"

"I don't know." Ora patted the journal in his pocket. "The contract seems too easy, and I really want to figure out who killed the king."

"Why do you care so much about some noble who has never given a crap about any of us? Now he's dead. Get over it," Sera snapped.

Ora looked down, weighing his options. He'd been with this crew for a year, and he trusted them as much as anyone. He decided to tell them. He looked up. "I care about the assassinated king because he was a relative of mine."

For a moment, no one said a thing. The silence drug on for several moments, and then everybody started laughing.

Gverth chortled. "Sure, and I'm the Duke of Sabinia."

Ora stood up, knocking his chair back, and stormed out of the room. He made it out the door of the Dragon's Cup and started up the street. That was when Sera caught up to him.

"Ora, wait." Sera grabbed his arm. "We're sorry we were laughing at you. It's just what you said was so outrageous. You weren't serious, were you? You're related to the king? Are you some sort of noble?"

Ora stopped and turned to her. "Look, I didn't want to let you all know, but there's a lot you don't know about me. About where I came from and who I really am."

Sera's cheeks flushed. She took a deep breath.

"I understand. I'm sorry, and I'm willing to help, but you've got to meet me halfway." She searched his eyes and gently squeezed his arm. "I want to know more about you, I do."

Ora's heart thumped loudly in his chest for a moment, then she broke his gaze and looked up the street. "What's your plan?"

"I want to head to the keep. From the drawings I found in the Library of Enki, I know a way into it that will bypass the guards. I think we need to explore it."

"All right," she said. "But we weren't able to get near the keep last time because of the viewing. What makes you think this time will be any different?"

"Well, the king isn't laying in state anymore. Plus I have a plan for waiting until all the merchants and shoppers go home for the night."

When Sera cocked her head questioningly. He pointed behind her. "The Stag and Hounds." He guided her toward the entrance.

The establishment was well-appointed and maintained and had been old when Ora had first come to Dracopolis. He remembered that day so long ago. He'd rode in with a troop of soldiers. They had traveled almost directly from the battle with the corrupted forces on the plains of Arlene.

The trip to the big city had been a whirlwind boat ride up the river, then entering the largest city he had ever seen. People of all races and places walked past tall, beautiful buildings, and you could get anything you dreamed of in Dracopolis. Even Fadri, the capital city of Drounid, was nothing but a village in comparison.

Inside the Stag and Hounds, he found a table for the two of them to sit at, and held out the chair for Sera, who smiled but rolled her eyes at the gesture. He took a seat opposite her. "I figure we have a couple hours before the sun sets and it gets dark. That gives us some time to talk."

The waitstaff brought two of the winter ales that the Stag and Hounds was famous for. Ora studied the beer, remembering absent companions.

Sera tapped Ora's foot under the table.

He started. "I'm sorry. I was lost in my thoughts. Did you say something?"

"I did." Sera looked amused. "I asked what brought you to the capital city."

"Well, actually, a horse." Ora laughed. He stopped when he saw Sera wasn't laughing. "Ah, seriously, I'd been offered up a position here in the city, working in the keep. And it was my first trip to a city of any size. What about you? What brought you to Draco?"

Sera picked up her tankard and took a long pull, avoiding answering the question.

He continued, "I heard that you were involved with the mercenary companies. Was that down in the Nid Islands or Ikriledian?"

Sera choked a bit on the beer, put down the tankard, and wiped her mouth. "Where did you hear that?"

"I asked about you before I joined your group. I wanted to know what I was getting into." At the sharp look she gave him, Ora held up both his hands palms out. "A guy can't be too careful. Especially when you were asking me to go off into Giants-only-knew-where to kill creatures. I wanted to make sure I was going to make it back."

"Fair point. I also asked around about you, but I wasn't able to find out anything. Not too many people around here knew you when you came in, made me wonder if you were fresh off the boat or…" She shrugged.

"I'd been here working indoors. Nothing too public. That's one of the reasons why I wanted to get out and do something different. Something that made better use of my skills. You got your start in the mercenary companies?"

"I'm originally from Grules. That's where I attended a Martial Academy. My father was a pretty successful wool merchant." She took a long pull of her ale. "I have six brothers who worked in the business, and after spending my summers dealing with all of that, I really had no interest in anything to do with sheep. I hate wool so much, I'll even pay extra for cotton. What about you?"

The pair exchanged questions and answers for the next couple of hours until the sun was well down. When the Lamplighter made her rounds around the Plaza, igniting the various lamps, and then moved off down the Boulevard of Gamesh, Ora settled his tab.

"You ready to see if we can get into the keep?" Ora asked.

Sera took his arm in hers as they head out of the Stag and Hounds. She looked at the dark wall of the keep. Reinforced footers spaced out evenly along the unbroken wall provided a border to the Plaza. "So how do we do this?"

"We are going to walk along the shops looking in the windows and make our way around to the far side of the Plaza. Once we reach the keep, then it's just a matter of finding the right spot in the foundation."

On the far side, they stepped into the shadows, away from the lit streets. Ora started pacing out the distance between the foundation points.

"And this is thirteen." He took two strides to the next point. "Fifteen, and it should be about here."

He stopped and looked around to see if anybody was watching and stepped into a fold between the foundation footers.

Sera inhaled sharply in surprise. "Ora?"

Ora reappeared. "Shhhh. We don't want anyone to hear us." He reached out a hand, which she took, and pulled her into the darkness.

In what should've been solid wall there was a gap in the stones between the wall and the foundation footing, just barely wide enough for them to turn sideways and squeeze through.

She whispered, "How did you know this was here?"

"The paper. Remember the trip to the library?"

"I meant, did it describe this particular feature? I thought it was just a drawing of the keep foundation itself?"

Ora chuckled. "Well, I might've had a little extra knowledge. I just didn't remember exactly where this particular exit was."

He kept moving forward and reached a bend where the gap narrowed. Once they squeezed through, the chamber beyond was slightly wider.

"What now?" Sara asked.

"Now, we find the hidden door that gets us into the keep."

"How are we going to find anything?" she asked. "I can't see a thing."

"Sorry about that. Close your eyes." Ora lightly touched a finger to each eyelid. "Open them now. Can you see anything?"

"I can see like it's daylight."

"Shimmershield lets me give you the ability to see in the dark. It doesn't last very long, but hopefully long enough for us to find whatever mechanism it is that opens this passage. Look around."

"What am I looking for?" she asked.

"It'll look like a rock or some stone that's out of place, just like back at Fagan Nuraghi. Look for loose mortar. It'll be disguised. The builders wouldn't have wanted people to come in this way."

They spent several minutes poking and prodding at every crack, crevice, small stone outcropping, pebbles—anything that might look to be the opening mechanism—until Sera finally exclaimed.

She reached up under a small split in the stone. She pushed something, causing an audible click, and a seam appeared in the wall.

"Excellent," Ora said. He gripped the edge of the door and pulled.

The smell that came out from the door was overpowering, causing both to gag.

"I know that smell," Sera said. "That's death."

Ora pulled the door open wider, and they both peered into the blackness. Even Ora's magic-enhanced sight couldn't penetrate that darkness.

"We're going to need a light. Let's go on cautiously."

They stepped into the passage beyond, and Ora pulled the door closed behind them.

Ora heard Sera draw a dagger and speak in a sibilant whisper. Green flame sprung along the blade of her dagger. She held it up to light the passage. Just ahead of them, two shapes lay on the floor.

"Bring that light closer." Ora's heart caught in his throat. He could make out the uniform of one of the Esroi wrapped in his own cloak. Ora lifted the cloak off the body and could see that the Wlewoi had been stabbed repeatedly in the back. He gently touched the patterned fur on the side of his head. "Rest easy, loyal warrior."

Ora glanced up at Sera, then shifted over to the other form, who was also wrapped in a cloak.

Anger replaced the sorrow in Ora. "This is one of the king's personal attendants. I can tell from her uniform." He put a hand on her shoulder. "Rest, little sister. May Utu aid us in finding your killer."

"What do you think happened here?" Sera asked.

Ora straightened. "I'm not sure."

"Why haven't they been found? They've been dead a while."

Ora pointed. "If you keep going down this passage, it comes out into one of the cellars for storing produce and other goods. Anyone who came down here would probably have thought a rat died or a cat or something. No one would've suspected that there were two bodies hidden in this secret passage."

"How many people might know about this passage?" Sera asked.

"I only found it by accident, and that was after I started working here. I'd had quite a few restless nights and just wandered the keep. I found the entrance when I was exploring the root cellars."

Ora stood up. The flickering green light gave his face a ghoulish cast. "I think whoever killed the king came through here, killed the guard upstairs, then attacked the king and the attendant. Then they brought both bodies back down here to make their escape. These two take the blame as they have disappeared."

"Seems plausible, but how do we find out for sure?"

Ora glanced down the passage before them. "That way. The door into the cellar should be just ahead."

They moved several yards down the corridor. Ora ran his finger along the wall until he finally found what he was looking for. He pointed; she brought the green dagger closer. The light from the flames illuminated the catch.

"Put the light out and I'll open the door," Ora told her. After she had, Ora pulled on Shimmershield to enhance his hearing and pressed an ear against the wall. "I hear muffled voices. Let me open it a crack."

He triggered the catch, and the door released. He pulled it slowly. As soon as he opened the door just a hair, he heard distinct voices in the cellar.

"You have to dispose of the bodies in the passage." That voice definitely belonged to a Wlewoi, most likely one of the Blood.

"What's the hurry?" asked a gruff, older Human voice.

"Can you not smell the bodies?

"Yes, but why do we have to do it now?"

"Because I told you to," came the soft growl.

A third voice, a little younger than the second one, asked, "How did you explain their disappearance?"

"They ran off together." The second man snorted derisively. "Love."

A muffled voice called from somewhere deeper in the keep. Ora could not make it out.

The Blood spoke, "Get it done, now."

Ora whispered to Sera, "We need to get out of here."

"Can we make it into the storeroom without being seen?"

Ora put an eye up against the crack, looking to see where the people were and if there was anything that could provide cover. "No, we'll be caught."

"Then we have to head back."

Ora gently pushed the hidden door closed until the latch caught.

As soon as the door was closed, Sera ignited her dagger in the green flame. They both turned and moved as quickly as they could. Just as they passed the bodies, the door leading back outside opened and a man stepped in, holding a lantern.

He was dressed in black clothing with a tight-fitted, leather vest. His skin was a burnished gold hue, much like the people of southern Stuitor or the island of Brouhan. From the look on his face, wide-eyed and slack-jawed, he didn't expect to see Ora and Sera rushing at him. He fumbled for a dagger.

Ora poured strength and speed into his legs and rushed the man. Ora pushed up and out when he connected with him, shoving the man back through the door, splitting his head open on the doorframe and splattering both of them with the man's blood.

They heard a shout in the passage behind them. Ora turned to see two other men dressed in keep's livery rushing at them.

"Quick, close the door," Ora grunted.

Sera quickly pushed the hidden door closed. The latch caught with an audible click. Ora wedged the body of the man against the door in such a way that it would be difficult to open. He grabbed one of the man's daggers from his belt and stabbed it into the door seam.

"That should buy us some time. Let's go." He led the way through the narrow opening in the keep's footers and stepped out into the Plaza.

Ora pointed away from the street they had come from. "Let's take the scenic route. No sense in leading them back to where we sleep." The pair took off through Old Town towards Sun's Rise, the section of town on the east side of Dracopolis.

After a few minutes, they slowed to a normal stroll. Arm-in-arm like a couple out for an evening walk. Ora used his Life Magic to obscure their scent trail in case that Blood got involved. They paused every few blocks, leaning up against the wall as if for a kiss, to see if they were being followed. No one seemed to be following. They stopped at a fountain and cleaned off the blood and grime as best they could. They were just a few blocks from the inn when a noise warned Ora. He turned to Sera—

The air in front of Sera's chest thickened with a flash, her magical defenses activating. An arrow shattered on her armor. "An ambush!"

Ora's head whipped back to find the shooter. He was just in time to see four men step out of the shadows on either side of the street.

Sera pulled her sword from its sheath. In an instant, green flame licked the length of her rapier.

The four men split into pairs and separated. Having a few moments to watch them, Ora realized they were dressed the same as the man in the secret passage. As they moved, it was obvious to Ora that this wasn't the first time they had ambushed someone. Then they each drew out two long knives, and Ora had to re-evaluate his assessment of their skills. Fifteen-inch knives were a poor weapon against his thirty-two inches of fine, Delver-wrought steel.

"Get ready for them to rush." Ora drew his swords.

"Let's go right," Sera said softly. "Make them work to approach us."

He pulled on Shimmershield to quicken his and Sera's actions. Sera shivered as the magic coursed through her.

"Go!" She stepped quickly to her right. Ora kept tight on her left side, a benefit of working together for the last year.

The left-most pair rushed at Ora to close the gap.

Ora thrust at the closest opponent. He was surprised as the man flicked his sword away with the blade in his right hand. The man spun in place and stretched his left hand out to attack Ora. Ora barely got his short sword in place to deflect the dagger.

He took a half step back and twisted as he pulled his long blade across the attacker's exposed back. He could tell from the scrape, the man wore armor under his robes.

"They have armor." Ora kicked the back of the first opponent's thigh and brought his blades around to block the second opponent. Ora heard a pain-filled yelp and smelled burning meat.

"Doesn't stop magic though," said Sera.

Ora attacked his two opponents. For a moment, it sounded like an array of bells as their blades rang on each other from attack and defense. He could feel his magic ebb. He needed to do something soon, or he and Sera were going to be skewered.

High-low, Commander. A voice from Ora's distant past sounded in his head. The long-dead voice of one of his men in the Drounid Legion.

"You're right," Ora said out loud.

"What's that?" Sera asked.

Ora ignored her for a moment, redoubling his efforts. He slashed and thrust at both men's heads and necks, pushing them back a step with the ferocity of his attack. Then he stabbed at the lead foot of the left attacker. With all of his attacks high, their defenses couldn't react fast enough to the low-line attack. Ora's blade bit into the top of the foot. His opponent screamed with the pain.

As soon as the attacker quieted, Ora could hear the even tromp of boots and the jingle of armor. "The watch!" Ora exclaimed.

One opponent turned to spot the oncoming danger and shouted at the others. They disengaged and fled.

Ora enhanced his senses to capture their scent.

When the city guard approached Sera and Ora, they both kept the points of their swords down. Sera had extinguished the green flame on her rapier's blade.

One guard stepped forward.

"Sergeant," Ora inclined his head.

"What's going on here?" the sergeant asked Ora. "Dueling in the city limits is illegal."

Sera stepped forward. "I am Sera Demott, Captain of the Renegade Rogues mercenary band. Those men set upon us as we were returning to our quarters."

Recognizing the tone of command in Sera's voice, the sergeant stood straighter. "Sorry, Captain. We heard the sounds of fighting, and more often than not, it's early morning brawling."

"No apologies needed, Sergeant. Your timing was impeccable." Sera sheathed her blade.

"Are either of you hurt?" At their head shakes, the guardsman asked, "What can you tell me about your attackers?"

"Nothing other than there were four of them." Sera pointed to an alley on the south side of the street. "They fled down there."

"I wounded one in the foot," Ora offered.

"Great. That might slow them down. If you will excuse us, Captain." He saluted and led his squad down the alley.

"Captain, huh?" Ora asked. The events of the night and all of the magic caught up to him. His knees started to buckle, and he put a hand on her shoulder to steady himself.

She looked at him, concern in her eyes. "Let's get off the streets."

CHAPTER THIRTEEN

SERA DEMOTT

After several minutes of steady walking, they were back at the Dragon's Cup. As they entered, the aroma of fresh, baked bread greeted them. The servers were cleaning up any remnants from the previous night.

Hohan was already in their alcove busily working on a bowl of porridge; a container of cream and a bowl of shelled walnuts sat on the table.

He whistled when he saw the pair. "Look what the cat dragged in."

"Not now." Sera shook her head.

"Good morning, Hohan." Ora shook Hohan's offered hand. "I'm going to have a bath, then I'm going to need to get some food. I'll see you in a bit." Ora turned.

"We need to talk about what happened," Sera insisted.

"Later." Ora looked meaningfully at the servers, then headed off to the bathing area.

"Did you run into trouble?" Hohan asked.

"You don't know the half of it—"

The door to the Dragon's Cup slammed open. Six men entered, talking boisterously and laughing. They squinted against the dimness of the room for a moment, giving Sera time to appraise them. They appeared to be wagoneers, mostly large, bearing the fitness of men used to shifting cargo and dressed in rough, plain work clothes.

One actively looked around the common room until he spied Sera watching him, then moved with the group to a larger table on one side. None of them appeared to be carrying weapons beyond a belt knife.

They weren't the normal patrons of the inn. Most of the wagon traffic was down in the warehouse district or along the main traffic way, neither of which was in this part of town. Sera mentally shrugged. Maybe they were delivering something to this section of the city.

She leaned toward Hohan. "Where's Gverth?"

Hohan shook his head. "I think he had class or something. He was gone when I got here." He put down his spoon, and his hand reached for the war hammer at his belt. "Do you think he might be in trouble?"

Sera shook her head. "After last night, I might be paranoid. Keep an eye out for Gverth. I'm going to go change and clean up. I'll be back down soon." She glanced at the men, then headed for the stairs.

Her room was on the top floor of the four-story building. Long-term guests were on the top two floors, leaving over-night guests on the second floor. Sera had reserved a block of rooms for the band, and all but Hohan took advantage of the privilege. He normally stayed at the temple's barracks.

She paused before her door for a moment and listened for any telltale sounds of an unwanted visitor. Then she bent the fingers of her left hand into an intricate position and whispered, *"Zastitit."*

The air around her thickened for a moment. Slowly, Sera drew her dagger and put the key to her lock. She gently turned it, hearing the faint click as it released the catch. She pocketed the key and threw the door open, dagger raised before her.

The room was still. Sunlight streamed in through the single large window. Dust motes swirled through the light, stirred by her sudden motion.

It was empty. She stepped into the room and closed the door behind her. She dropped the bar into place. That wasn't standard in the rooms, but she'd added it. The owner of the Dragon's Cup objected at first until she offered to have one installed on his door too to protect him, his wife, and four daughters who all lived at the inn.

"Giants, take that man!" she said in a growl.

A soft feminine voice asked Sera, "Are you all right, sweetie?"

She turned to a dressing dummy wrapped in a dark blue gown. "I'm fine, Tess."

A light green spectral image of a woman appeared on the dressing dummy, looking as if she were wearing the gown.

"Aunt Tess," the specter corrected.

"Yes, great-great-aunt Tess." Sera unbuckled her sword and set it in a stand beside her bed.

"Oh my. You are in a mood," Tess observed.

Sera stuck her tongue out at the ghost. "I've had a rough night."

"I had man troubles too, once. How do you think I ended up like this?" She waved her hand over her translucent body.

Sera sighed as she unbuckled the straps on her bracers and set them on a stand where they could air out. She pulled off her chainmail jacket, setting it on the stand. Next was the armoring jacket. She laid it on the floor inside out so the sun could dry it. Greaves and leg armor were easy. In moments, she was standing in her underwear. She pulled a fresh set of clothing out of a drawer and set them on the dresser next to the wash basin.

"Well, are you going to tell me what he did?" Tess asked.

"Who?" Sera finished undressing and wiped herself down with a washcloth.

"Do I need to yell his name? Is he in his room?" Tess turned to the door.

"No!" Sera said in a panic. Ora's room was across the hall from hers. "Settle down. Ora and I went to the keep last night."

Tess had a satisfied smirk. She was very similar to Sera in appearance. Were she alive, she could easily have been mistaken for Sera's sister.

"Go on." Tess glided over to the padded chair and sat attentively.

Sera went through the events, the Stag and Hounds, the secret passage, the ambush.

"That is quite the adventure. Do you know why Ora cares so much about who killed the king?"

Finished washing, Sera dressed quickly. "He's related somehow to the king."

"Oh?" Tess had a contemplative pose. "Related. Is he a noble?"

Sera shrugged. "He didn't say. But if you're related to a king, don't you have to be a noble?" Sera unsheathed her rapier and began examining the blade for nicks. Fights like the one she'd just had against the dagger-wielding assassins were tough on blades. Any one of the blade-on-blade contacts could cause a nick, and a rapier with a nicked blade could snap when it bent. She found several on her examination. She reached under her bed and pulled out a pair of long, leather tubes, one marked with green paint the other with red.

Tess moved over to the bed. "It depends on his lineage. Illegitimate children are often half or quarter blood. So while they're related in the loose sense, they wouldn't be a part of the royal family."

Standing next to the bed, Sera unscrewed the pommel of her sword and set it on the edge of the bed. She removed the handle from the tang of the blade and put it next to the pommel. It took a couple of taps to get the leather holding the double-ring swept guard in place to let loose of the blade. Once she finished disassembling her sword, she opened up the green-marked tube and withdrew another blade. She glanced down the length of the Delver-forged steel. A rippling pattern ran like waves of water down the length.

"So that could explain why he didn't want to tell us. No one wants to be called a bastard." Sera wet a finger and touched the leather from the guard, getting it slightly damp. She reassembled the guard, handle, and pommel. She shook the weapon to make sure everything was tight and set it back in the sheath. She took the damaged blade and put it into the red-marked leather tube with two other blades. She sighed. "Looks like I'll need to get some more blades from Delgar."

Tess sniffed. "The price of doing mercenary work. I really wish you would take up something safer, like the family business."

"That worked so well for you." She laughed at the sour look on Tess's face.

There was a knock at the door. Tess looked interested. "Whomever could it be? You should invite him in," she said coyly.

"Begone, Auntie." Sera made for the door. She heard a small pop as Tess returned to wherever it was she went.

"Who is it?" Sera asked through the door.

"It's Ora. I'm headed downstairs." Her heart skipped a beat, and her face grew hot. Had he heard them talking?

"I'll meet you downstairs."

"Right," his reply came through the door. She couldn't tell his tone as the thick wood muffled any tone or inflection. She could hear his boots head down the hallway.

Sera hurriedly pulled on her boots, belted on her sword, and donned a jacket cut in a style similar to those of the mercenary company she had served in. However, this jacket had plates sewn in to cover her vital areas. She checked herself in the mirror, turned her head. "Not bad."

At Tess's faint, spectral laugh, Sera stomped out the door, barely remembering to make sure it latched. She tromped down the stairs, all the while fuming at being caught preening in the mirror. Entering the common room, she made her way through crowded tables back to their alcove.

Ora and Hohan were laughing about something. Hohan's laugh easily carried above the din of the room. Her irritation flared at another round of laughter. "What's so funny?"

She watched with a mix of guilt and satisfaction as the men's smiles melted off their faces. When they looked at each other before answering, her anger sparked anew. "Well?"

Both men stammered before Hohan stood up suddenly and pointed past her.

Hohan said, "Look! Gverth has returned."

Sera narrowed her eyes. She turned to where Hohan pointed to find Gverth. Sure enough, there he was, threading through the room toward them. As her anger died, she realized there were more people in the room she hadn't noticed before. A lot more than normal. Warning bells went off in her mind.

"Something's wrong." Sera scanned the crowd. Too late, she noticed one of the wagoneers from earlier had approached Gverth from behind, intercepting him midway across the room with a dagger in his hand.

Gverth's eyes went wide with shock. He spun while stepping back at the same time and went down in a tangle.

The wagoneer met her gaze for a moment before yelling, "Fire!"

Everyone jumped to their feet, sending dishes and benches everywhere. The man disappeared in the commotion.

"Hohan! See to Gverth!" Sera pushed her way forward. She tried to see the attacker, but couldn't. Frustration welled up in her, and she felt the need to crush something.

A hand grabbed her arm, and she spun with a fist swinging. Ora surprised her by simply grabbing her hand, stopping her punch. *By the Giants, he's fast.*

"Sera!" Ora yelled. "It's me."

"I need some help with Gverth," Hohan interrupted. "He's been stabbed." Sera tamped down her irrational anger and helped Ora and Hohan move Gverth into their alcove, where they set him on the table, facedown.

"What happened?" Gverth asked weakly. "Why is it so cold in here?"

Both Ora and Hohan glowed with their Life Magic as they tended to the wound.

"It isn't closing," Hohan said through gritted teeth.

Ora lifted the blood-soaked cloth, and dark red blood welled from the wound. He looked at Sera. "Get more towels."

Helpless to do anything else, Sera raced to the bar. "I need some towels."

Satya handed her a stack from the ones they kept there. Sera's heart beat loudly as she rushed back. Both men were still working on Gverth. She stepped up to press a fresh towel on the wound.

"We're missing something." Ora examined the rest of Gverth quickly. "No other wounds." He leaned close to Gverth's head. "How are you doing, Gverth?"

"I'm so sleepy," he mumbled a reply. His eyes closed.

"He was cold, now sleepy." Ora leaned close and smelled the wound. Other than the metallic smell of blood, he detected a sickly, fishy aroma. "Henbane—" he looked up "—Poison."

The two men pressed their palms together above Gverth, and white tendrils wove down into the wound.

Sera removed the towel and watched as a thick, black liquid oozed up out of the wound. She grabbed a fresh towel and mopped it up.

"That was close," Hohan said after a couple of minutes.

"Very." Ora slumped in a chair.

Gverth's eyes fluttered open.

"*Ahem.*" They looked up to see Te'zla standing over them, hands folded under his robes. "Is this a bad moment?"

CHAPTER FOURTEEN

SANKARA MURCHALA

Sankara pulled the reins, bringing his horse to a stop at the top of the ridge. A wide, lazy river split the long valley before him. A castle perched on a hill overlooked a modest town. Farms and pastures divided the valley. The early morning mist muted the vibrant yellows, oranges, and reds of changing leaves.

Lavinia joined him. "An impressive view, isn't it, my lord?"

Sankara nodded and returned to the vista. "How many troops reside in the castle? Will we need siege engines?"

Lavinia's laughter was like a cascade of light bells, delicate and engaging. He turned in the saddle to regard her. His eyes drank in her beauty and his face flushed with desire for her. He tamped down on that. *Now is not the time for that foolishness*, he told himself.

She stopped laughing.

Sankara hoped his face didn't betray his thoughts.

"Forgive me, my lord," she said. "Our scouts have been watching this barony for a month now. They have five officers and thirty soldiers that patrol, stand watch at the keep, and enforce the peace in the town." She beamed, and it thrilled him to the core.

"Thirty?" He turned back to look at the castle. "Only thirty soldiers?" In his district, they had to be on guard against border raids. A castle that size could easily house ten times that number of troops. "No outposts or garrison in the town?"

"No, my lord. Only the thirty." She shifted her horse closer to his. "Lord Houshkulu told you they have minimal forces in this land. They haven't known warfare for close to a thousand years. What military they do have has done nothing more than hunting bandits and stopping the occasional Orc raid or rampaging Troll."

Sankara snorted. "Orcs and Trolls? Surely those are children's tales?"

Lavinia shook her head. "These lands are a bit more... wild than Lathranon." Her response surprised him.

Sankara admired the view for a moment more, then turned to Rajan, his troop commander. "You may begin. Take the castle first. And intact, if possible."

"Very well." Rajan saluted smartly, then turned his horse.

Sankara watched as the orders rippled throughout the troops. Helmets were strapped on. Arrow quivers shifted to the front of saddles to be drawn while mounted.

In less than five minutes, scouts were already headed to either side of the main body of soldiers. Rajan returned to Sankara's side as the force moved past.

Sankara glanced to where Lavinia was talking with her scouts. They were a rough-looking bunch. Their leader bowed to her, and the group headed off into the forest away from the castle. He put them out of his mind as the last of his men passed him and he fell in behind with his staff.

CHAPTER FIFTEEN

ORA EARL

verth struggled to get up, eager to greet his master. Ora helped him off the table. Sera took the lead while the others cleaned up the mess.

"Master Te'zla, please join us." She indicated an empty chair at the table.

Gverth sagged into his own chair near his mentor.

Te'zla set the wrapped tome on the table, well away from the mess, took the offered seat, and studied Gverth. "Is everything all right?"

"We had a bit of excitement just before you arrived," Hohan explained.

"They attacked Gverth." Ora looked at Sera. "It was the Gorgon."

Te'zla sucked air in between his teeth.

"They're a fable." Sera snorted.

"No, they are not," Te'zla said softly.

Everyone turned and stared at him.

Te'zla shrugged. "The High King tried to eradicate them for several hundred years as they were the ones who were responsible for the princess's murder."

"The Guard never found them, and the Gorgon seemed to evaporate like so much smoke. Every Gorgon-infested outpost or stronghold found had token resistance," Ora said grimly. He took a deep breath, then let it out slowly.

"How long ago was that?" Hohan asked.

Ora felt Sera's eyes on him. "A long time ago."

Te'zla waved a hand. "That's immaterial. Why do you think it was the Gorgon who attacked young Gverth here?"

"They stabbed him with a poisoned blade."

Hohan nodded. "It took both of us to heal the wound. Knife wounds are hard enough, but this was something different."

"It made me cold and sleepy and left a strange, metallic taste in my mouth," Gverth shivered and took a drink.

Ora leaned forward. "It was Henbane."

Ora saw Te'zla's eyes widen at that. *The Reader knows the truth of it. The Gorgon are involved*, Ora thought.

"Well, I am glad your friends were able to intervene." Te'zla smiled at the young man.

Sera crossed her arms. "I find it hard to buy. The Gorgon's a fable told to children. They're not real."

"Master Reader," Ora said, not taking his eyes off Sera. "Can you tell Sera what these fables are supposed to look like?"

Te'zla turned to Sera. "They wear clothing of a red so dark it mimics hearts' blood and looks black in anything but bright daylight. And they wield a pair of long knives they call 'The Dragon's Claws' that are purported to be coated in poison."

Ora saw recognition cross Sera's face.

"The people we fought in the street." She looked to Ora for confirmation.

Ora nodded. "And the one in the passage."

The moment of silence was the catalyst for Ora to realize the Reader was there for a reason. "Have you found something, Master Te'zla? We didn't expect to hear from you so soon."

The Reader hesitated a moment to collect his thoughts. "I've been working on this since you left, trying to work through the translations. The dialect is strange, but that could be because of how old it is. This book describes a schism in the Giant clan that ruled Drakanon at the time of the Human revolt."

Hohan snorted. "The gods, clearly—"

"Not now," Sera said firmly and then looked apologetically at Te'zla. "Please keep going."

Te'zla inclined his head. "To make it brief. There were two factions within these Giants. One faction wanted business as usual. Keep collecting resources, experimenting mostly to the detriment of Humankind, and performing magic. The other faction wanted to help Humans. The author of this particular tome supported treating Humans as rightful beings, not just as slaves to gather resources or to be experimented on, and the leader of that faction allied with a Dragon."

"Mushussu," Ora said without thought. All eyes turned to him. He flushed. "I heard a legend. Please keep going."

Te'zla put both of his hands flat on the table on either side of the tome and looked Sera straight in the eyes. "Were there other items that you found with the book?"

She leaned forward, resting her elbows on the table. "Our focus was on the girl. We were lucky to find this book."

Te'zla looked at the pair for a long moment. "Tell me about where you found the tome. Perhaps that will give us some clues."

Sera took a sip of wine. "We were in a nuraghi working a contract we had been given to hunt down Burrow Goblins who'd been raiding the farms southward and who'd kidnapped a girl."

"They put up a good fight," Hohan interjected. At Sera's glare, he held up his hands.

She continued, "After the fight, we found a secret passage—"

"I found the secret door," Hohan interrupted. Another icy glare from Sera had him sipping his ale to show he wouldn't do it again.

"The door led down to a vault. Unfortunately, it was locked with a disk full of the symbols—"

"Ora was able to figure out the symbols," Hohan interrupted Sera again.

Sera slapped her hand on the table. "Would you let me tell the story?"

Te'zla glanced at Ora. "You figured out the symbols?"

Ora shook his head. "Not all of them. I knew the rune for 'open' and aligned the symbols from the different rings. It opened."

Te'zla nodded and seemed impressed. "Please continue."

Sera glared at Hohan. "Inside the vault were shelves. All of them were empty except for the tome. We were pressed for time, so we just grabbed it."

"There wasn't anything else in there?"

Sera narrowed her eyes. "What aren't you telling us, Master Reader?"

"According to what I could discern—" he patted the tome "—there was a hidden compartment in the vault that contained more items."

"You want us to go back," Gverth whispered loudly. "Don't you?"

Te'zla nodded. "Those items, if they are what I think they are, are very important."

"Important to who?" Sera scoffed. "That place was a dust pit."

Te'zla considered her for a moment. "How about valuable?"

"Just how valuable are we talking about here?"

"Depending on what is in the vault, it could be worth a life-altering amount." Te'zla looked around at the group. He had everyone's attention. "There are things left over from the War for Power that should be kept safe."

"You mean kept safe by the Readers, don't you?" Sera pointed at Te'zla. "How does that benefit us?"

Te'zla held up his hands. "We aren't trying to take all magic out of the world. We want to get the items that could inadvertently kill entire villages." He tapped the tome. "There are a number of powerful magics listed in here that are beneficial—to us and to everyone. Those we want out in the world. There are also lower-powered magic weapons that are better than anything you've ever seen. Those you can keep."

Te'zla leaned back in his seat. "Well, what do you think?"

Sera glanced at the others. At their nods, she turned back to Te'zla. "Master Te'zla, you have a contract."

CHAPTER SIXTEEN

ORA EARL

tay with the horses, Teer. If anything threatens you, ride your horse back to town," Sera said firmly. "And let me have that spear again."

"But I have the sword Ora gave me," he insisted.

"Listen to her, Teer." Ora put a hand on his shoulder. "We know you're brave, but sometimes being brave means doing what you're ordered to do."

Reluctantly, Teer handed over the spear and led the horses to a stream.

"Do you think the Goblins would have returned?" Gverth asked when they entered Fagan Nuraghi.

Ora squinted at the path between the buildings, looking for tracks. "I don't see anything here, but it rained a couple days ago. If they stayed inside, they wouldn't make tracks."

"Keep your eyes open." Sera hefted her spear.

They entered a darkened hall. There wasn't any light, and nothing stirred. They retraced their steps to the secret door to the Giant's vault. They found the catch and entered the passageway. Once they pulled the door closed, Gverth made light, and they made their way as quietly as possible until they stood in front of the vault's doors.

Ora turned the rings to align the runes, and the door opened.

Gverth held his flaming fist high in the air, and they stood for a moment without saying anything.

Hohan broke the silence. "Where were we supposed to look for the other items? Because there isn't anything in here."

"Apparently we missed something," Sera said.

"Check it for false panels?" Gverth asked.

Ora nodded and pulled out a pry bar he had brought along just in case they needed it. Starting on the top shelf, he used the pry bar and tapped each of the walls. He repeated the process for each of the shelves until he was crouched and bent in half, looking at the bottom shelf.

Hohan snorted. "I doubt a Giant would—"

Thunk! A hollow sound cut him off.

Ora looked up at everyone. "Well, how about that? The last place a Giant would look. Gverth, if you would be kind enough to use your Land Magic?" Ora shuffled out of the way so Gverth could search the space for the latch.

After a few minutes of searching and mumbling, Gverth let out a whoop. "It's here on the lip underneath the next shelf." He pointed at a spot.

Ora felt along the shelf until he found the spot. A knot of wood sticking out slightly more than the rest of the shelf. He pressed firmly on it, and there was an audible click as the catch let loose. "Can you see what opened, Gverth?"

There was a gentle scraping. "Oh, yes. There's stuff in here."

Ora crouched down to look. In the cubby rested a small basket big enough to hold a couple of apples. Next to it was a cloth-wrapped item that appeared very much to look like a sword. Resting in the center of the space, there was a coin about two inches in diameter. It looked to be made of the same metal as the seal on the door.

Ora reached in and grabbed the basket. Inside was a plum-sized orb made of a milky stone. He put that in his pack and looked at Sera. "Do you want to hold the sword?"

She shook her head.

He thrust it through a loop in his pack and then grabbed the coin.

As he touched the coin, a slight shock ran through his fingers. A distant memory from years past. He'd felt this kind of magic before.

He didn't tell the others and quickly dropped it in his pack. He cinched it up and put it back on.

Gverth bent down and checked for other hidden panels but didn't find any. "I think we've cleaned it out. Should we check the walls down here just in case?"

The group spread out and looked for anything that might indicate a door or false panel. Ora tapped with the pry bar, but they didn't find anything else.

The group headed back up to the secret door. Gverth doused the light.

Opening the door, a strange smell hit their nostrils. It was reminiscent of spoiled milk and hadn't been there when they'd come in. It seemed familiar to Ora, but he couldn't place it.

They eased into the hallway, and Hohan closed the door. Something skittered on the floor in the direction of the library where the little girl had been kept.

"Pay attention," Sera hissed.

She pointed at her ear, then at the library. She motioned for them to go back to the dining hall.

Ora nodded, and they eased back as quietly as they could. They had almost made it to the hall when, in his haste, Hohan accidentally kicked a ceramic pot like it was a kid's ball. It flew into the hall and exploded in a shower of pottery. The sudden sound in the little hall was shocking.

Screams erupted from all around them, coming from every direction and echoing through the hall.

CHAPTER SEVENTEEN

JERRON CARTER

The wagon creaked down the road. Jerron took another bite of apple and twitched the reins with his left hand.

Large oak trees on either side blotted out the sunlight. The horses whinnied, and the wagon lurched to a stop, having run into one of the draft horses that had collapsed.

"Woah!" He pulled on the reins instinctively. He dropped the apple and shielded his eyes. That was when he spotted the fletching of arrows in the horse's neck. "What in the Giant's name—"

Figures stepped out from behind the trees and up from the long grass to either side of the road, pointing bows and spears in his direction. They yelled something in a sing-song language.

"Wut?" The driver looked behind him at the other two wagons. They were also surrounded by the strange men. He turned back, heat rising in his face. "Ya kilt my horse. The baron will hear of this!" He stood up in the wagon. Several spears were leveled at him by the strange soldiers. For a moment, no one moved. Jerron's heart hammered in his chest.

They spoke Eshitan with that same sing-song cadence that Jerron could barely follow.

"You and the others climb down from the wagons and stand over there." A soldier pointed to one of the oaks beside the road. The man wore a gold sash and seemed barely old enough to put on armor. The sharp spears they carried, however, didn't look like toys.

"Do as he says," Jerron told the other drivers. "We'll see what this is all about."

In all of Jerron's time as a wagon driver, he had never seen bandits in this part of Eshita.

The men wore strange leather armor that had little metal disks riveted to it. They bore swords, spears, and conical helmets that looked nothing like that of any of the baron's men or any of the village watch in Leodbury or even Ricsigbury.

"Who are you? Wut do ya want?" Jerron asked. "The baron won't put up with this."

"We don't care what this baron wants. He'll be joining you soon enough." The young man waved as he walked away.

"Hey. I ain't done talkin' with ya."

Pain lanced into Jerron's gut as he realized he'd been stabbed with a spear. The soldier pulled the spearhead back sharply. Blood welled out of his side.

"Ah!" he clapped a hand over the wound and stared at his assailant. "Wut are ya doing?" He staggered back.

Jerron heard gurgling behind him and turned to see warriors stringing up the other drivers. He sagged to his knees in horror. "Wut..." he said weakly.

"String him up too," Jerron heard as his vision faded.

CHAPTER EIGHTEEN

ORA EARL

A spear flashed past Ora's head, causing him to jerk to the side and into a wall. Burrow Goblins followed the spear out of the passage, their shrieks earsplitting.

Ora kicked one who charged at him, stabbed a second with his Delver-forged long sword, and slashed a third with his short sword.

As he fought the creatures, a flood of Goblins surged past him to run headlong into Hohan's hammer and Sera's green, flaming spear.

Ora sidestepped a clumsy swing and skewered the Goblin he had kicked. The sour, rotted milk odor overwhelmed him for a second, almost causing him to gag.

Then he remembered the smell. "Corrupted!"

The creature erupted from a side passage. It shuffled surprisingly fast on mangled limbs. It appeared to be made up of leftover parts from a graveyard and had too many arms and three legs. It hulked over the smaller Goblins that dodged out of its path. Its head was a mash of multiple faces, and its seven eyes burned with a purple hate.

It swung a massive chair like it was so much gossamer and smashed it into Hohan.

As Hohan flew across the room he yelled, "Enki!" The power of his god manifested lightning, ripping great furrows of bright blue destruction into the Corrupted's head and torso. The detonation from the lightning was echoed by Hohan slamming into the wall.

The Corrupted staggered for the barest of moments before it locked eyes with Ora. Its smoking visage opened its maw and swiped a bloated purple tongue over blackened, broken teeth. It took a step forward—

Gverth sent a searing, white bolt of fire blasting through the Corrupted's chest, then flung a handful of azure icicles into a group of Goblins. The Corrupted deflated in a pus-filled spew of putrefaction. The stench even made the Goblins gag.

Sera stepped over the dead Goblins to face the next rank. "Ora, check Hohan. We need him back in this fight," Sera commanded. She spun in mid-air, whipping her spear in a broad arc, the leaf-bladed spearhead slicing through Goblin armor, hide, and bone.

Ora dashed to the big man where he lay in a heap, sending his Shimmershield out to probe and heal. Hohan stirred a bit and Ora sighed in relief.

"Watch out!" Gverth called.

Ora spun, thrusting with his long sword right into the chest of another Goblin.

It stood transfixed on Ora's blade, arms raised overhead. The crude axe it had been holding fell to the ground.

Sera killed another Goblin, when the air near her head thickened as an arrow shattered on her spectral shield. "Archer!" she yelled and put a column between her and her attacker.

Ora yanked his sword from the Goblin's chest and grabbed the front of its armor to hold it up. It shuddered as two arrows thwacked into it. One pierced its neck, spraying its ichor everywhere.

"Gverth, do you see it?" Ora called out. He kept holding the Goblin up and turned to look at Hohan. "Stay down!"

Another two arrows clipped the Goblin body, a third slammed into the wall next to Hohan.

"Any time now, Gverth," Sera said. She peeked around the column but had to pull back as an arrow chipped the stone near her head.

Gverth hunkered down, using a large chair for cover. "They are down the far passage, but I can't see them. Sera, use your fog power!"

"I can't while I have my spectral shield up. So do something!"

An arrow *thunked* into the chairback, tearing through the upholstery.

CHAPTER NINETEEN

RISALDAR RAJAN MARCHANDANI

Rajan rode at the head of his squad of eight soldiers and stiffened as they came around the bend. There ahead of them were three wagons on the road, with the wagoneers hung from the trees. The bodies swayed in the breeze, and blood still dripped from them. "By the Giants."

He turned to his sergeant. "Who told them to ambush the wagons and kill everyone?"

Sergeant Vijay shook his head. "They do what they want. They claim to report to the pointy-eared woman." He said it with such venom, it caused Rajan to hiss and glance around.

"Do not let anyone hear you say that," Rajan cautioned. "I don't know how the Commander puts up with her, especially with things like this going on."

Rajan guided his horse over to the soldiers. Several groups sat in the shade or picked through the wagons. Four archers stood on the slight rise away from the bodies. They watched him and his group as they approached. Rajan dismounted.

"Who's in charge here?" he demanded. A young man wearing a gold sash of a junior officer over his disheveled uniform turned from the lead wagon.

"Who are you to ask?" he responded arrogantly. The men with him laughed.

Rajan took a step toward the man and flipped his riding cloak back revealing his sash and insignia. "I am Risaldar Rajan Marchandani, Naib Subedar, and you will address me accordingly."

In the Amaranth military, a risaldar was an officer of the cavalry and commanded a hundred men including four sub-officers of naib subedar rank. In this instance, Rajan was the highest-ranking officer who reported directly to Commander Murchala.

"Apologies. I didn't see your rank... sir." He said it with just enough of a pause to fall within the bounds of courtesy.

"Who told you to attack the caravan and kill the drivers?"

"Lavinia did... sir," he said with a smirk.

Rajan stared at him for a moment. *I told the commander it was a bad idea to let her bring her own soldiers through that blasted gate.*

Sergeant Vijay stepped up next to him and bent close. "We need to tell the commander what happened here. He ordered us to keep a low profile."

Rajan nodded. "I know. Get the men ready to move on." He looked back at the young man and considered him and his fellow soldiers for a moment. Vijay was right. They couldn't afford to confront these men and the commander needed to know. "I need to continue with my orders."

The naib subedar grinned. "Have a safe ride. These woods can be dangerous." The men with him laughed darkly. That sent a shiver through Rajan. He mounted his horse, and his squad turned back onto the road and headed for the mountains. The space between his shoulder blades itched in anticipation of an arrow, but none came.

Once they were well enough away and around the bend, Vijay leaned in his saddle. "That will not go well with the locals."

"Not well at all."

CHAPTER TWENTY

GVERTH REDBURN

We can't stay here much longer, thought Gverth. The hail of arrows was breaking through their cover. He could hear more Goblins coming from the side passages, and he wasn't sure how many archers there were, but soon enough, one was going to score.

He waited until an arrow *thunked* into the frame of the chair, then gave a quick peek down the hall. He saw nothing but darkness, meaning he couldn't aim his magic.

He ducked back as an arrow whizzed past his ear.

More Goblins and another Corrupted rushed out of a side passage and engaged Ora.

Sera tried to move to help, but arrows buzzed in front of her, causing her to duck back behind the column.

"My sword can't get through this Corrupted's hide," Ora shouted.

Gverth looked just in time to see a backhand swing from Ora slam into the creature and the long sword rebound with no effect and fly from Ora's grasp.

He glanced around for something, anything. Nothing. Just the gray dirt covering everything.

He froze. Dirt. Earth.

Maybe I can manipulate it like I did the gravel for the box?

Hohan yelled in pain.

"Are you all right?" Sera called.

"Just a graze," Hohan replied as he parried another Goblin thrust with his hammer.

Gverth peeked over to see Ora pull the sword they had found. Ora's arm glowed with blue bands of energy as he fought the Corrupted.

Beyond Ora, Hohan put his back to a wall. He must have been out of sight of the archers, as the arrows fired at Gverth increased in volume forcing him to duck back down.

Gverth reached out to the dirt and dust and willed it to move.

"Whatever you are doing, Gverth, do it soon," snapped Sera.

Slowly, the earthen debris began to swirl. His heart lifted as motes rose up, gaining speed and pulling more of the dirt and dust up with it to thicken the effect.

"Here goes nothing." Gverth stood up and interposed the swirling mass between him and the passage with the archers.

As soon as he stood, he heard the twang of bowstrings. Arrows sped to the dirt cloud and flew off to either side.

"I did it!" he called out.

Suddenly, Ora cried out in pain.

Gverth looked over to see an arrow sticking from Ora's side. He realized the vortex he'd created was pushing the arrows into his companions. He panicked for a second, then took a deep breath. *Solve the problem,* he told himself.

He pushed the wall of dust forward toward the passage. As soon as it had passed Sera's position, she reared back and threw her spear. It flew across the room like a green meteor and skewered the Corrupted in the ribs.

It howled with pain and surprise.

That was just the opening Ora needed, and he clove his sword through the Corrupted's neck deep into its torso.

Hohan caved in a Goblin's head with the backswing of his hammer, sending the body hurling back and into the dust cloud. For a moment, it floated in the cloud before being thrown to the side.

Gverth threw the vortex down the hall at the hidden archers, earning high-pitched Goblin screams.

"Let's get out of here." Sera looked at the arrow sticking out of Ora. "Can you move?"

He snapped the shaft of the arrow, leaving the head in, then nodded.

Gverth let the magic of the dust storm dissipate and immediately felt weary.

"That was great! When did you learn how to do that?" Hohan asked as they rushed out of the hall.

"Just now." Gverth glowed with pride at having figured that out. "I'll have to practice with it more."

Ora glanced back at him and gave a tight, close-mouthed smile. "I'd appreciate that."

CHAPTER TWENTY-ONE

ORA EARL

O ra focused on staying in the saddle. Every step the horse took sent a shock of pain through his side. It seemed as if he had been riding along forever. He tried to pull Shimmershield to give him strength, but it wouldn't come to him. It was as if it were just out of reach.

It's the sword, he thought. *It's blocking it.*

The horse did a stutter step. Ora grimaced with pain and closed his eyes

"You need to hang on, Commander," Atticus said to him. "Just a little further and we can make camp. The Legion's healers are waiting for us there."

"You're a good aide, Atticus. Where have you been?"

"You haven't needed me before now, Commander."

"I've always needed you, my friend." He squinted at his second-in-command, leader of the first cohort.

"I died, Ora. I fell in the battle with Wrok in the campaign against the Corrupted." His voice faded. "Stay strong, Ora. It isn't your time yet."

Ora slumped in his saddle. "Atticus, don't leave me."

Hands grabbed him, and his hand went to his dagger in a flash.

Atticus spoke again as if from far away. "Let them help you, Ora."

Ora let the hands pull him from the saddle.

"Look at all the blood," a woman said. Her voice seemed familiar.

"I know you," Ora said softly.

"By the Giants, how far gone is he, Hohan?"

A deep voice answered, "Let's hope Enki is paying attention."

"Why didn't he heal himself?" a younger man asked.

"I think it was the sword. He used his magic to wield the accursed sword, and it now robs him of his Life Magic."

Pain blazed in his side as someone touched his wound.

Ora grunted, and the fog cleared a bit. Ora glanced around with just his eyes, as his head was being held in place.

"Gverth—" Ora said through gritted teeth "—use your magic to pull the arrowhead straight out. And by the Giants, don't wiggle it."

His speech and lucidity startled everyone, and they all began talking over each other.

"Stop," Ora croaked.

They fell silent.

"Gverth, do it. Hohan, try to heal the wound from the bottom up as the arrow comes out." The effort to tell them what to do took a lot out of him, and Ora sagged back.

The pain of the arrowhead coming out was blinding. Ora wanted to simultaneously scream, throw up, and cry. After what seemed like an hour of agony, a cool wave of relief replaced the pain.

"Roll him on his back," Hohan said.

Ora stared up into Sera's face. Worry lines creased her brow.

"How do you feel?" she asked.

Ora thought for a moment. "It doesn't hurt."

Her eyes narrowed in sudden anger. "You idiot! You scared me—all of us, half to death."

Ora tried to sit up, but Sera held his head in her steely grip.

She leaned down close to his face. Her anger drained away, and she whispered softly to him, "You almost left me. Please don't do that again."

His mouth went suddenly dry, and his words caught in his throat.

She released her hold on his head and stood up. "Let's set up camp here. I'm sure someone is going to need food." She patted Teer on the shoulder. "Let's go take care of the horses."

Gverth hovered over him holding a wickedly barbed arrowhead coated in Ora's blood.

"You probably didn't realize the damage this—" Hohan pointed at the arrowhead "—did to you, and you probably just started feeling sleepy as you slowly bled out." His face was grim. "The same thing happens when you hunt deer. You hit them near the heart, and they leap off, not knowing they are already dead."

Ora just stared at Hohan.

Gverth broke the moment with a slap on Hohan's upper arm. "What's the matter with you?"

Hohan looked chagrined. "I'm sorry, Ora."

Ora waved a hand. He meant for it to be a quick gesture, but his arm just flopped. "I had the strangest dream about my aide in the Legion."

Ora struggled for a moment but finally undid the buckles on his armored vest. Gverth helped him as he pulled it off, and examined the hole in his armor. Almost in a fog, he poked a finger through it.

Feeling their gaze on him, he looked up into his companions' stunned faces. "What?"

"You said you were in the Legion," Gverth whispered.

Ora's tired mind struggled to recall what he had said. "Yes. Surely, I've said that before. That's where I learned to fight." Ora was puzzled. "Why is that strange? Sera was a mercenary captain. I was in the Legion. We all started somewhere."

Hohan's eyes narrowed. "How long ago?"

"Too long, apparently." Ora held out a hand to Hohan who helped him to his feet. "It looks like Sera and Teer need some help. How about I gather some firewood?"

He wavered slightly but was able to remain upright. He smiled wanly at the two men and pointed to Sera. "Go help. I'll be fine." Ora watched as the two men reluctantly moved off. Once they were well on their way, he turned and staggered off. He leaned heavily on each trunk, moving tree-to-tree until there were several between him and the others. He slid around the trunk and slumped to the ground as his vision went dark.

Ora wasn't sure how long he had been unconscious. His head throbbed and felt as if it weighed twenty stone. He blinked until his eyes could focus and squinted up at the sky trying to discern the position of the sun. He couldn't.

He leaned back against the tree and closed his eyes. Around him the sounds of the forest continued. Squirrels chittered. Birds called. He reached for Shimmershield and… nothing.

He opened his eyes.

It had been a long while since he couldn't do magic. It felt like standing in a snowstorm without clothes. *I've been wounded before, but maybe this was worse than I thought?*

He struggled to get to his feet. He held onto the tree and waited for the nausea to pass. Overall, he felt a little better, but still weak.

Ora moved slowly and gathered twigs, sticks, and some of the smaller fallen branches. When he had an armload, he returned to where the others were setting up the tents. He dropped the wood and scraped clear a space with his boot. He began building the fire as the others finished up.

"Gverth, will you light it" Ora asked.

To almost everyone's surprise, Teer addressed Gverth. "May I light it?"

Sera cocked her head.

Gverth waved at the stack. "You may."

Teer rushed over and knelt next to the arrayed wood.

"Just like we practiced," Gverth said in an encouraging tone.

Teer reached out a trembling finger and whispered, *"Pir."* A blue-white spark popped from his fingertip and into the kindling, instantly igniting the tinder. He looked up, and Gverth beamed with pride.

"Excellent." Gverth patted Teer on the shoulder.

"He can do magic?" asked Sera.

"By the Grace of Enki, this boy has been blessed." Hohan held up his hammer with the symbol of Enki toward him.

Ora sat with his back against the trunk of a tree. "That was well done, Teer. I'm impressed."

Teer beamed. "Thank you, Master Ora!"

Sera had recovered her initial surprise. "Very impressive. Now go get the pot and the stand so we can get dinner prepared."

After the young man went for the provisions, Sera glanced at Gverth. "Training him in magic? Do his parents know he has ability?"

Gverth shook his head. "He just started showing signs on this trip. I don't know how deep that river runs yet."

Teer returned with the pot and the tripod to hang it from. Ora slowly fed more wood into the fire while everyone worked on dinner. The evening's fare was dried rabbit and vegetable stew.

As they prepared dinner, Ora attempted to touch his magic. It finally trickled to him as they finished with the stew.

Once the stew was cooking, Sera brought Ora his pack. The sword had been wrapped back up and was tied to the front of it.

Gverth scooted close. "Let's see what all we got from that place. It had better be worth it."

Ora undid the buckles on his pack. "Teer, bring me a blanket." Once the blanket was spread out, Ora placed the sword, coin, and basket onto it.

The coin had the ancient script on it and bust of a person. The details had faded over the years, but they could make out that it was male. On the back was the symbol of a dragon in profile with one wing curling in the shape of the coin.

Sera unwrapped the sword. It appeared to be made of the same metal as the coin.

Ora sat straighter, looking at the runes etched into the blade. *I've seen a sword like this before.*

He reached a hand out to touch the hilt. This time he was paying attention, and he felt it cut off his Shimmershield immediately. And just as immediately, his nausea and headache returned with a vengeance. He snatched his hand away so quickly it startled the others.

"This sword is trouble. It's made of magic metal, and if we're not careful, it can kill you over time."

Hohan cocked his head. "You mean it has Mavric iron in it?"

Ora nodded. "See for yourself."

Hohan reached the finger out and put it on the pommel, concentrating. A blue energy coalesced around where his finger touched the metal. He nodded grimly. "I *knew* it was accursed. If I wasn't attuned to Life Magic, I wouldn't be able to repair what it did to me in just that short period of time."

He looked questioningly at Ora. "I also felt a different flow of Life Magic when you touched the sword just now. I didn't notice it in the nuraghi since we were distracted with fighting. What was that?"

"I don't know."

Sera stared between Hohan and Ora. "Does this mean if we use the sword, it'll kill us? It didn't kill Ora."

"Let's ask Gverth's mentor when we return to Draco," answered Ora.

Sera pressed her lips together, then took a deep breath and nodded.

They looked in the basket. Within was a small, milky-white sphere of some unknown stone. None of them had ever seen the like.

Hohan closed his eyes and touched it. His eyes sprang open. "It's whispering to me!"

"Who is?" Sera asked.

"The stone!" Hohan exclaimed. "It's saying something. I can't make it out though. It's just a whisper right on the edge of my mind." He looked at Ora. "See if it talks to you."

Ora reached his hand out to the orb and concentrated.

"Well?" Hohan asked impatiently.

Ora withdrew his hand and shook his head. "Nothing. It didn't say anything to me."

"I wonder what that means," Sera said.

🟊 🟊 🟊

The next day, they made it to Somerville and Teer's parents. They entered the house, leaving Teer to take care of the horses. Inside, they told the parents of the fight at the nuraghi. All six of Teer's younger siblings were arrayed around their parents as they listened with wide eyes.

"We'll give a report to the constable," Sera reassured them. "There are more than Goblins up in those ruins. We took care of a lot of them, but we didn't have time to do a complete sweep through the whole place. A larger force will need to go through and make sure the place is emptied of them."

Teer's father cleared his throat. "Mistress Sera, we aren't rich folk like yerselves. And all we want is a better lot for our children than what we have."

Ora watched Sera's reaction. He'd guessed this was coming.

"Yes?" she asked.

"I was wondering if you would be amenable to taking Teer on for your student?" asked Teer's father.

Teer's mother gasped. "Gentry, no."

He patted her arm. "Miriam, we can't provide for him like he needs. And he needs more than this farm. You know he wants more." Gentry turned back to Sera. "Mistress?"

Teer walked into the house at that moment and looked at the group around the table. "What's going on? Why's Ma upset?"

Teer moved over to her. As soon as he was within arm's reach, she pulled him close and held him.

The silence continued for a long moment before Sera spoke. "Teer, your parents have asked that I take you on as a student. What do you think of that?"

Teer flushed as all eyes turned to him. "I..." He looked down at his mother, then met his father's gaze. His father nodded slightly. "I would like that very much."

He grimaced as his mother held him tighter.

"Why don't you show them what I taught you?" Gverth pointed at an unlit lamp on the table.

Understanding dawned on Teer's face, and he bubbled with excitement. "Ma, Da, lookit what I can do!"

He extracted himself from his mother's grasp and moved around the table. He hesitated for just a moment, then whispered, *"Pir."* Once again, a spark appeared and lit the wick.

Light flared across his parent's astonished faces. Teer's siblings rushed him.

"Do it again!"

"That was amazing!"

"Show me how!"

Gentry stood and clapped his hands. "Enough! We are talking." The four boys and two little girls fell silent instantly.

"Wish that worked for me," Sera said wryly, shooting a sidelong glance at Hohan and Ora.

Hohan flashed her a grin.

She turned back to Teer. "You should pack your things and say your goodbyes. In the morning we head to Draco, and that means we must make everything ready."

"Mistress," Ora inclined his head to Teer's mother. The children giggled at the formality. Ora made his way outside with Sera, Hohan, and Gverth.

Hohan spoke first. "A student?"

Sera shrugged. "Gverth already started teaching him magic. Might as well see what else he can do."

"He's a bit young, wouldn't you say?" Gverth asked.

"I started with the temple at his age. Learn how to fight now before he learns bad habits. Training will put on muscle." Hohan flexed his massive arms to emphasize his point.

Sera looked at Ora. "What do you think?"

Ora considered it for a moment. His son had been younger than Teer when Ora began sparring with him. "I think it would be good for him to be able to defend the horses if we are going to bring him with us."

"That's settled then. When we get back to Draco, I'll draw up a training schedule. We could all use a little extra time in the training hall." She poked Hohan in the ribs. "Gverth, I'll need some paper to draw up a contract."

"Of course. Would you like me to write it?" He fished in his pack for a leather tube with caps on both ends and a writing kit.

Sera shook her head. "No, it's my group, my task." She turned back toward the house.

The others waited for her to enter before talking.

"What do you *really* think, Ora?" Hohan asked.

Ora regarded the younger man. "Do you think we're making a mistake?"

Hohan shook his head. "I'm just worried with all the fighting we've found with our contracts." He gave a toothy grin. "I have my hands full, keeping you alive."

"Ha!" Ora took a playful swing at Hohan. "Seriously though, don't you wish you had teachers like us when you first started out?"

"There are things I'd do differently." He pointed at a faint scar on his upper arm. "Some lessons don't need to be quite so harsh."

The trio entered the house for the evening. All too soon, the cock crowed, giving his greeting to the rising sun.

The team saddled the horses, giving Teer a final few minutes with his family.

Sera handed a small pouch over to Gentry, who tried to protest. "It's his first month's wages," she said softly.

With that, the band headed down the road with their new member asking a thousand and one questions.

"How long will it take us to get to Dracopolis?" he asked eagerly.

"Draco," Gverth corrected him.

"What?" Teer asked.

"We just call it Draco," Gverth explained. "And it will take us the better part of three days to get there.

"Longer with every question you ask." Hohan laughed.

In the early evening, they made camp. They took turns explaining what needed to be done and the why of it. Once Teer had bedded down, exhausted from all the chores and the excitement, Sera sat next to Ora at the fire.

"Do you think I made the right call with Teer?" she asked.

"In all your time in the company, or with us, have you ever doubted one of your decisions this much?"

"No, but I've also never taken on a student before."

Ora looked at her closely for a moment. She met his gaze. He could tell she was worried, so he smiled to reassure her. "You took me on, didn't you?"

That evoked a light laugh.

"You were already housebroken."

CHAPTER TWENTY-TWO

ORA EARL

They tore down the camp and were back on the road early. Teer's questions were less frequent this time. Each of the party took some time riding with him, answering as best they could. Occasionally the questions and answers sparked laughter in the group. It was Hohan's turn to answer. They were in the process of shifting the riding order.

A heavy rope snapped taught across the road and seven men with strange armor and curved swords surrounded the party. The band pulled hard on the reigns bringing their horses to a rough, sudden stop. One of the ambushers barked something at them in a peculiar language, an angry expression on his face.

"I don't know what he just said, but I don't think it's a love poem." Hohan hefted his hammer.

The man spoke again, but it was obvious that he struggled with Eshitan. "Get down from your horses." He pointed at Hohan. "Drop the hammer, and the rest of you, keep your hands away from your weapons." His accent was thick, making the words almost unintelligible.

Ora tensed, waiting for a signal from Sera.

"Get down!" The man threatened with his sword, brown eyes darting from each of the party members.

Sera's spear blazed in green flame, and she threw it at the speaker. As the spear struck, a thick fog sprang up, obscuring everyone. Startled cries rang out, along with a yell of agony that must have been from Sera's spear throw.

Ora pulled on the reins, turning his horse to the center of the road. He fed a trickle of Shimmershield into his mount. Then he slid off the horse and slapped its rear haunch.

One cry stood out from the others. "Teer," Ora whispered, mentally chastising himself for not preparing the lad for a possible ambush.

He pressed his thumb to his right eye and fed in some Life Magic. While the magic wouldn't let him see through the swirling dense mist, it did let him make out shapes better. He pulled his swords and advanced toward his foes.

He could make out a figure ahead of him and stepped suddenly to the left as the figure crouched. A spear tip passed where he'd just been.

Ora sprang forward, long blade thrusting at his opponent. A cry of pain turned into a wet gurgle as Ora wrenched his blade free. He turned to his right, blades up to block any wild swings from the mist.

The fog muted sounds, making the others seem strangely distant.

Ora stepped forward hesitantly.

Then, just as suddenly as it had appeared, the mist was gone. Ora could see a little too clearly now. His horse had jumped on another man, crushing his conical helmet and skull. He turned. The others had dealt with their opponents.

Sera wiped her blade with a rag. Hohan muttered a prayer over the broken body at his feet. Gverth moved his horse away from the still smoking soldier nearest him.

"Anyone hurt?" Hohan asked. He wiped the spike of his hammer on a cloak taken from a fallen opponent.

"Teer?" Sera called.

Ora moved over to the young man, who was pushing himself up. "He seems fine. Just stunned." Ora glanced down the road. "I'm not sure where his horse is though."

"We have a problem," Gverth called.

Ora spun, weapons up. He relaxed when Gverth was standing over a fallen man.

"What is it?" Ora asked.

"Weren't there seven of them?" Gverth asked.

Ora had two on his side. The speaker lay on the ground with Sera's spear in his chest. One each lay by Sera, Gverth, and Hohan. Ora walked to the edge of the battle and began traversing a circuit around the group looking for tracks or some other sign of where the last man had went.

"Nothing. No sign of him." He met Sera's gaze. "What do you want to do?"

She pointed at the bodies. "Ora, Teer, gather weapons and armor and anything else that may be useful. Gverth, use some of your Land Magic and open up a shallow grave. Hohan and I will move the bodies over after Ora and Teer are done." She looked at each of them. "Any questions?" They shook their heads and started moving.

Ora said softly to Teer, "First dead body?"

Teer nodded quietly, eyeing the man.

"It's never easy. Just watch me."

The boy nodded again, swallowed, then began removing armor.

Ora pulled a pouch off the dead man and poured the coins into his hand. "These are strange."

"The coins? Maybe from a different kingdom?" Teer asked.

Ora shook his head. "I don't think so. I've seen the coins from all the kingdoms and the city-states of the Nids. This is something new." Ora put the coins back and pocketed the pouch. He held up the man's sword and dagger. "These weren't made around here and should be worth something a little more than the trash we normally find."

"How can you tell they aren't from around here?" Teer examined the weapons.

"This region favors straight blades. Curved blades are more useful when fighting on horseback or on a ship."

Ora stood up and looked around.

Teer perked up and drew the dagger. "What is it?"

Ora shook his head. "If these are riders, where are their horses?"

Sera shook her head. "They must have been picketed well off the road. That's probably where our missing bandit went. We need to finish up quickly and get out of here."

"You should put this on." Hohan held up a jerkin of their armor for Teer. Once they put the vest on Teer and buckled it, Hohan helped Teer bundle the equipment and lift it onto the pack horse.

"You all should look at this." Gverth held a cloth from the other pile of gear that might be useful. "It's a map."

"Where is it a map of?" Teer asked.

"Nowhere I've seen," said Sera. "But we can figure that out later. Let's get out of here."

Sera held a hand for Teer and pulled him up behind her. With a cluck, they started down the road.

"By sundown, we should be at Draco," Sera told Teer.

"Then what?" he asked.

"By Enki's grace, we will figure out who attacked us and why." Hohan pulled up beside her. "I will pray for guidance."

"Remember to keep your eyes open while you pray," Gverth called.

Ora listened to his friend's banter and speculation. Over the past year, he had seen a bit of the local region. Early in his reign, he traveled all over Drakanon, but he'd never encountered people like ones who had attacked them.

The only kingdom that had given the High King problems before was Chacoton. *They couldn't be the ones behind this, could they?* To his knowledge, Chacoton only wanted to take over the Nids, the islands to the southeast of Drakanon proper, but the armor of these raiders looked nothing like what he remembered from that realm.

"Is that Teer's horse?" Gverth pointed off to their right.

"Ora, can you get it without spooking it?" Sera asked.

"*I* can." Teer slid down off Sera's horse and made for the animal.

Sera made to call for Teer, but Ora stopped her. "Let him try."

The horse surprised everyone when it actually came when called.

"Enki provides," Hohan said sagely.

"Ask Enki to provide a safe trip the rest of the way to Draco." Gverth made a theatrical gesture.

"We have a hard day's ride if we are to hit the city. Let's go!" Sera coaxed her horse into a canter.

The sun was just setting when the city came into view. A wide swath of buildings nestled right up to the high wall that surrounded the inner portion of the city. The road they were on set a straight path to the gates.

Teer expressed his amazement. "How can it possibly be so big?" He didn't wait for an answer before letting loose a flash flood of questions.

CHAPTER TWENTY-THREE

SANKARA MURCHALA

isaldar Marchandani led the soldier into Sankara's tent where he was looking at maps on a table and discussing options with Lavinia.

Sankara looked up. "What have you brought me, Rajan?"

Rajan hesitated, first looking at Lavinia, then back at his commander.

Sankara motioned for him to continue. "You may proceed. She'll hear about it, regardless."

"Commander, this soldier has just returned from an ambush patrol. They've been interdicting wagons and travelers on the other side of the pass. He was the only one in his unit to escape."

Sankara's blood surged with anger causing his heart to hammer in his ears. "Who authorized that patrol?" Sankara raised a clenched fist. The soldier withered before his commander's wrath.

"I did." Lavinia's silky voice cut through Sankara like she had thrown a bucket of cold water on him. "We need to keep up the pressure on the locals in this region."

She stepped past him to address the soldier directly. He stiffened to attention under her gaze. She smiled at the soldier.

"You can relax," she said in a honeyed tone. "Tell us what happened, and please, be brief."

Even in his anger, Sankara's heart sped up a bit, and he felt a brief stab of jealousy at not being the focus of that incredible smile.

The soldier nodded. "Our patrol surprised five riders. Somehow, they got the upper hand. My jemadar was the first one struck down. Then they conjured a fog. They struck the men on either side of me down from within the mist. I was the last, and I couldn't see anything more."

He wiped the sweat from his prow with a trembling hand. "I knew I needed to report so I grabbed our string of horses and rode them here."

"You did the right thing in letting us know." Rajan patted him on the shoulder.

Lavinia just stared at the man. "They used magic?"

The soldier nodded vigorously. "I barely escaped with my life."

The anger he had suppressed flared up again. It was fueled by his frustration of having his men ordered into activities without his knowledge. It might be petty, but this felt like the perfect outlet.

"We need to hunt these dogs down and exterminate them!" Sankara spat. "Rajan, assemble your full troop, and I want you—"

Lavinia stopped him mid-sentence with a hand on his chest. "Patience, my Lord Commander." She turned the smile on Sankara, and his breath caught in his throat, and his anger evaporated like smoke on the wind. "My agents will deal with them. We need you to focus on this region. Take the barony and keep word of our doings from getting out."

She shifted her glance to the soldier, who had paled. "May I borrow him? I'd like to get a detailed description of our travelers." She met Sankara's eyes. The violet in her eyes flashed a startling blue for a moment.

Sankara took a deep breath. "Give the lady what she needs, then report back to Risaldar Marchandani."

Lavinia inclined her head. "By your leave, Commander." She took charge of the soldier and moved off down the hall.

Sankara watched her go, lust and fear battling within him. He sighed, then turned to Rajan. "We need to stop letting her commandeer our people. At the rate she burns through our troops on stupid things like this, I'm not going to have enough when we meet the actual enemy army, which will be sooner than later."

He motioned to the table. On it, a map showed the lands around their encampment. "This is our next objective. I'm going to shift Risaldar Shawkat and the Second Troop past the castle to catch any who flee." He tapped his finger on a spot on the map. "I need your unit to push through this castle and into the village past it."

"Yes, Commander. At once." Rajan saluted and left.

Sankara examined the map for a bit longer. "It's only a matter of time before someone comes looking to see what we are doing."

CHAPTER TWENTY-FOUR

ORA EARL

 set of bright lamps lit the two hundred yards of the road into Dracopolis. The ornate lamps provided an eerie, white light that was too bright to stare at for very long.

Gverth chided Teer when he tried. "They are powered by magic, my young friend. All staring at them will get you is a headache and night blinded for a bit."

Ora smiled. "I'm sure you know from experience."

Gverth flushed, telling Ora he had guessed right, but the young mage continued, "This area is called the Haunted Fair. I suspect it is because of the lamps."

Teer turned to Gverth. "Who made them? How long have they been there? What happens in the rain?"

Ora had to smile. Even after the incredibly hard day they'd had, the young man's curiosity seemed unquenched.

Gverth made his best effort to keep up with the torrent of questioning until they reached the entrance to the city. The sixty-foot tall, ironbound gates on massive hinges were propped open.

In all of Ora's time in the city, he could only recall two times they'd been closed. Neither time had been because of hostilities.

Gverth said something that caught his attention.

"...during the Giant Wars, the city had been closed up for close to a year." Gverth had his arms stretched wide, pointing at both gates.

Hohan snorted. "Myths."

"Then how do you explain the burn marks so high up the doors?"

"Lightning." Hohan sniffed then looked at Teer. "If you want to learn the genuine history, not children's fables about Giants and heroes, I'll take you to the temple."

"Or, you could just ask Ora." Gverth hooked his thumb at him. Ora's heart leapt into his throat. "He's almost thirty. He's ancient." They all laughed.

Ora gave a close-mouthed smile and inwardly breathed a sigh of relief.

As they rode through the gates, Teer craned his neck around, trying to take in everything.

"Overwhelming, isn't it?" Sera asked.

Teer nodded. "I thought the village at Mill's Corner was big." He gaped and pointed at just about everything until Sera pulled up next to him.

"I know it's exciting, but you need to calm down. You are drawing attention to us, and that isn't always a good thing." Ora could see him sag a bit in the saddle. "Don't worry, you can still look, just don't point."

"Come up beside me, lad," Hohan offered. "I'll point out the more interesting things still open at this hour."

They mounted the bridge to cross the river, and Teer squeaked.

"Are you all right?" Hohan asked, looking around for anything that might be a threat.

Teer pointed at the river before quickly snatching his hand back. "I... I've never been this high up and over a river." Everyone looked out. They'd all crossed this bridge hundreds of times and never thought of it.

"It's fine, Teer." Sera leaned back and took his reins and led the boy's horse down the center of the bridge. The rest of the band surrounded Teer as they traveled. Once they were across, Teer visibly relaxed. Sera handed his reins back to him. "See, across safe and sound."

"Thank you, Mistress." Teer looked up past Sera and almost pointed. "What's that?"

Sera turned to look at what he was talking about and then hung her head a bit. They rode closer to the building in question. It was a wide building with balconies on the second and third floors. Many bright lanterns showed off the scantily-clad women at work in the world's oldest profession.

They called out and blew kisses.

"Hohan!" one called. The others quickly picked up the scent and called out too.

Sera looked at him with an arched eyebrow.

"Oh! Are they friends of yours, Hohan?" Teer asked, evoking a laugh from the rest of the group.

"Yes, Hohan." Gverth snorted with laughter. "Are they friends?"

Hohan waved at the women. "The word of Enki must be spread."

Gverth guffawed at that.

"Keep riding." Sera sniffed at Hohan and moved on down the street.

Hohan turned to Ora. "What did I do?"

Ora shook his head and held up his hands. "I don't have a lizard in that fight."

He clucked his horse to move after Sera. In short order, they turned into the alley next to the Dragon's Cup that led to the stables in back.

The stable master came out to assist them. "It is good to see you again, lady."

"Terrik, this is Teer. He is going to be joining my company, and I want him to care for the horses in the morning. He needs the familiarity."

Terrik beamed at her. "Of course, lady. I'll make sure he does a good job and learns properly."

Sera turned to Teer. "In the morning, I expect you to report to Master Terrik—" Terrik preened at the title "—but tonight, you need a bath and food, then bed."

Sera led the way to their private alcove. The panels had been pulled closed. Sera jerked one back, and the group stepped into the area. Two people stood up, surprised at the sudden intrusion, Te'zla and a young woman who wore the attire of a Reader.

"Master Te'zla?" Gverth asked.

"Gverth! So good to see you. We've been waiting," said the Reader.

"I'm sure," said Sera with a cautionary look at Ora. Then she stepped to the threshold and caught Satya's attention. The pair talked quietly for a moment. The waitress nodded and headed off.

Sera pulled the partition closed and turned back to Te'zla. Sera dumped her bags on the side and hung her cloak on a peg set up on the wall.

She pointed at Teer. "This is my student, Teer. He will be headed for a bath—" Teer protested, but Sera's stern gaze and raised eyebrow killed any argument "—and I asked that dinner be brought. I ordered for all of us, including you and…" Sera looked meaningfully at the woman with Te'zla.

"Ah, yes." Te'zla turned to the woman. "This is my assistant, Anya." The woman was in her late twenties with dark hair and dark eyes. She was attractive, but not overly so.

Greetings were exchanged all around. There was a rapping on the partition, and it opened. Satya poked her head in.

"The bath is ready for the boy. Drinks are right behind me if you are ready?" At Sera's nod, Satya shifted out of the way and two other servers brought in drinks and a platter with meats and cheeses.

"Teer, go with Satya. Come right back here when you're clean."

He mumbled a quiet assent and followed Satya out.

The partition slid closed. All eyes turned to Te'zla and Anya.

Te'zla took a long pull on the mug that had been placed in front of him. "That's quite good." He set the mug down. "Welcome back. I hope your trip was fruitful?"

Sera nodded. "We found three items."

"Can I see them?"

Sera thought about it for a moment and then nodded.

Ora began digging in his pack.

Sera squinted at Te'zla. "You knew there would be more things in that vault. How did you know?"

"The tome described them." Te'zla's eyes were bright with interest.

Ora set them on the table. "In the vault, we found a secret compartment inside the back of the bottom shelf."

"Tall people would have issues finding it," Te'zla murmured.

"Yes," said Sera. "We found this sword and these two other items." She pointed at the bag. "A coin and an orb."

Hohan leaned forward. "Before you touch it, the sword is made of Mavric iron. I could feel it tearing my flesh. The coin is made of the same metal, but for some reason, doesn't hurt like the sword did."

Te'zla could barely express his eagerness. "May I see the weapon?"

"Certainly." Hohan unwrapped it.

Te'zla's eyes glowed as he looked at the weapon.

Ora watched him intently for any hint of recognition or indication that he might know something more about it.

Te'zla ran his hand an inch above the sword, up the full length of the blade. His hand glowed yellow when he reached the hilt.

"Interesting." He shifted his attention to the cloth bag and placed the coin and the orb on the table.

"The orb talked to me," Hohan said.

Te'zla looked at him sharply. "What did it say?"

Hohan shrugged. "I'm not sure, as I didn't recognize the language, but it seemed to want to talk to me. I've never experienced anything like that. Surely it is from Enki."

Sera rolled her eyes. "Obviously."

Te'zla pursed his lips thoughtfully. "It's possible, but I'm not sure. I will have to do some research and see if we can figure it out."

When Te'zla turned his attention to the coin. He started.

Ora noticed the reaction. "You recognize that, don't you? You've seen it before?"

Te'zla gave him a sidelong glance and then looked at the coin, gently reaching out and turning it over to look at the Dragon symbol.

"I need to check on something, but, yes, I have an idea of what this might be. Without confirmation, I don't wish to guess. I realize I'm asking you to trust me, and I know you only have my title of Master of the Readers and Gverth's experience with me to base that trust on, but I would appreciate it."

To everyone's surprise, Ora nodded. "We'll trust you, but I take it as a promise that you will tell us what this is about."

Te'zla nodded grimly. "Agreed."

Ora tapped the sword with a plain ring on his right hand, hitting it against the pommel, causing a faint metallic sound. "Tell us about this."

"I haven't studied a lot about weapons specifically, but somehow this seems familiar." Te'zla's curiosity was obviously piqued. "Weapons like this were made for the War of the Giants when Humans and other races fought against the Giants. They made weapons of power by bringing the five separate magics together to imbue items with wondrous powers and abilities."

"The Pentad," Ora said.

Everyone looked at him again with curiosity in their eyes, except Te'zla, who nodded.

"Yes exactly. The Pentad, who wove five magics together to bring forth wondrous items. So, were you able to feel the destructive aura of this blade?" Te'zla asked Ora.

Ora nodded. "Yes, though I almost paid the price with my life when I had to use the weapon. What is its purpose? The runes on the blade hint at something, but I can't make them out."

Te'zla studied the runes for a moment. "I'll need to confirm, but I believe this weapon has something to do with Dragons."

Gverth pointed at the fourth rune from the pommel. "This, what's this symbol here? Isn't this protection?"

Te'zla considered it. "I'll need to confirm, but perhaps protection of Dragons? Protection from Dragons? I'm not sure, but I'll check."

He's not telling us everything. He decided to bide his time and wait for Te'zla to reveal what he would.

Sera stood. "It's been a long and hard adventure, Master Te'zla. You have research to do. I have a destiny with a bath."

Te'zla wrapped up the tome while Anya made a charcoal rubbing of the sword's blade onto very thin paper. She rolled up the paper and stuffed it into her pouch. Te'zla handed her the tome, and they made ready to leave.

"One moment," Ora stopped them, bringing out the coin purse. "Bandits attacked us on the road back. Rare, but not unheard of. But they were carrying these."

Ora dumped the contents of the purse onto the table. He didn't take his eyes off the Readers' faces.

Te'zla picked up a couple of coins to examine. He offered them to Anya. Ora couldn't see any reaction beyond curiosity on either of their expressions.

"The people who attacked you had these?" Anya asked.

Ora nodded. "Along with strange weapons and armor."

"The one who addressed us didn't sound like he spoke normal Eshitan," Gverth said.

He looked at Sera, tilting his head to Gverth who had the map they'd found. She shook her head once.

"May we keep a couple coins? I'd like to show the other Readers." Te'zla held up two of the coins.

Sera nodded. "The faster you can get some answers, the sooner we will know what is going on."

When there was a tap on the panel, Ora scooped the other coins into the bag. Hohan pulled it back to reveal a server with a tray of bread and bowls of soup. The steam rising brought the aroma of herbs and simmered tomatoes. His stomach grumbled loudly enough the others threw him glances.

"We'll take our leave. I'll send word as soon as I have something." Te'zla gave a slight bow, then ushered Anya out of the alcove.

CHAPTER TWENTY-FIVE

TE'ZLA HARDEN

Te'zla held the door open for Anya, and both exited the Dragon's Cup. Four Readers who looked to spend more time lifting books than reading them awaited on the street outside. They arrayed themselves around the pair.

Anya leaned close to Te'zla as they walked. "You're not going to let them keep the plunnos, are you?" Her tone dripped with indignation.

Te'zla smiled. "You have very peculiar notions of my authority, girl."

Anya sputtered for a moment before Te'zla cut her off. "Let me ask you this…" He gave her a sidelong glance. "How would you have proposed we separate them from it? More specifically, from *him*."

Finally, she spoke, "We could have asked them for it."

"True, but that would have told them it had value." He grinned as she realized where he was going with it.

Anya nodded at the idea. "They will think it is a token since by itself it does nothing. Then we can get your student, Gverth, to loan it to us."

"And we don't have to argue or fight for it. They'll give it to us." Te'zla spotted a pastry shop still open. "Would you like a tart?"

CHAPTER TWENTY-SIX

ORA EARL

Teer glanced nervously at the blunt, steel practice sword in his hand and flexed his fingers around the leather-wrapped hilt.

They were in the training hall of Jon Jepsen, who'd been teaching students the art of war since he had retired from the Imperial Guard. He had a reputation as a stern yet fair instructor. He got results and charged a commensurate price.

Sera spared no expense on Teer's training, that's for sure.

His training hall held little more than a spotless, canvas-covered, wooden fighting-space and floor-to-ceiling windows that allowed the midday sun to enter.

"Get your point up," Sera called from the side where the rest of them watched Teer practice.

Teer brought his point up.

The weapons master nodded and then stepped in, swinging his practice sword at Teer's head. Jepson moved at a slow speed, allowing Teer to block and attack as best he could.

The group called out helpful comments.

"Take a step back—"

"Shift to your left—"

"Wait for his blade to come to you—"

"Don't reach for it—"

While each comment was well-intended, all they did was make Teer frustrated.

Ora turned to the others. "Give him a break. He doesn't need three mother hens clucking at him constantly."

Sera looked sheepish, but Gverth and Hohan simply exchanged coins.

Ora raised an eyebrow. "Betting on the boy already?"

They both grinned back at Ora. "Of course, what else are we going to do to amuse ourselves?" Hohan flipped a coin in the air with his thumb before catching it.

Jepson turned and pointed at the rack of various training weapons. "You could pick up blades. The mistress rented the training hall for the hour."

Gverth held up his hands. Little flames danced finger to finger before he blew them out with an exaggerated breath. "I'm fine. Thanks."

Hohan flexed his wrist a little. "I think I'm practiced out today."

Sera just sniffed at the two of them and looked at Ora. "Shall we?"

"Absolutely." Since Ora had joined the party a year ago, he and Sera had practiced several times a week.

She strode to the practice stand and selected two swords. She extended one hilt first to Ora.

Ora focused on his form and resisted the temptation to use Shimmershield as he would in actual combat.

Sera used a rapier in combat and that dominated her fighting with thrusts and lunges, a very linear style.

Ora's main weapon was his long sword. It had a double-edged blade that tapered to a point. Ora's style was more circular, flowing with the weight of the blade as he moved it to perform cuts and slashes. After a few passes, they paused to catch their breath.

The weapons master asked, "Would you care to change partners?"

Ora shrugged.

"Sure, I think it would be good." She moved over to face Teer, leaving Ora and Jon to match up.

"Are you warmed up?" the weapons master asked.

"I am." Ora raised his sword into a ready position.

"Quarter speed for calibration?"

Ora inclined his head, and the pair raised their blades. At a moderate pace, the weapons master tested Ora first with a flat snap to Ora's left side to see if Ora was paying attention.

Ora easily intercepted the blade and countered with a slash of his own toward Jon's left thigh.

Jepson smiled and took a half step back, forcing the blade to miss completely.

They both raised their tips.

After a few more passes, blades flicking and blocking, Jon asked, "Full speed?"

"Sure." Ora shook out his right arm, then made ready.

The speed of Jepson's first rush astounded Ora. For a few moments, it was all Ora could do, fighting purely defensively, to keep Jon's blade from touching him.

Soon enough, though, Jon landed a blow on Ora's left side.

The opponents stepped apart.

"Very nice," the weapons master complimented Ora. "You have some skill, though you fight in a style that is not entirely familiar to me."

"I learned a long time ago in one of the southern kingdoms." Ora stretched out his wrist.

"Which one? Drounid?"

"Yes, I was in the Legion."

"You did not learn that from the Legion." Jon raised his blade. "Go again?"

Ora stretched his neck from side to side to loosen it up, then shrugged his shoulders to get the blood moving and raised the point of his blade. "Ready."

Now that the cobwebs had been blown off, Ora was a lot more comfortable this pass. He met each blow with a quick riposte and blocked Jon's counterattack with his blade, shifting his feet to the side slightly. Called "fighting in the round," the method relied on the notion that attacks tend to be very linear, and if a fighter can move off line even just a little, it can throw their opponent's attack off target.

Their blades flashed in a whirl and dance of steel. Ora was lost in the moment, one with the blade—blocks and attacks flowing like water.

The weapons master twisted his torso in the middle of his attack and just barely got the tip of his blade onto Ora's side, a mere moment before Ora smacked his blade into Jon's ribs. Both men were panting.

"Good hit," Jon congratulated Ora.

Ora shook his head. "It was just a moment too late. You got me first."

Both men stepped to a table that held mugs and a pitcher of water where they took drinks, catching their breath.

The room was quiet. Ora suddenly noticed the stillness and glanced up to see all four of the others standing there. Both Gverth and Hohan stood, mouths agape. Teer's eyes were shining with enthusiasm.

Sera watched him with a speculative look on her face that made Ora slightly uncomfortable.

"That was amazing!" Teer came over to them, eyes bright. "I've never seen anything so fast. Did you use magic?"

Ora laughed and tousled Teer's hair. "Of course not. That wouldn't have been fair."

"He didn't need magic for that fight," Jon said. "That was most impressive, Ora. I've never seen some of those techniques that you use, other than in old training manuals. It was very... archaic in form."

Ora laughed and wiped the sweat from his brow. "Like I said, I learned long ago how to fight from people who'd been fighting for even longer."

Jon wiped his brow. "My experience with the Legion and Drounid was nothing like what you showed me. It might be time for me to take a sabbatical and learn some of those things."

Sera interjected. "Perhaps we can come to an arrangement as there will be plenty of time for learning as we train Teer. Maybe Ora can show all of us some of those techniques."

Ora caught her glance and flushed at the frank look of admiration she had. He wasn't used to getting so much direct attention.

"Can I go again?" Teer asked eagerly. "I want to try some of those moves." He waggled his sword and stamped his foot in a couple of forward steps. The others chuckled.

Sera smiled at the youth's enthusiasm. "Give it a go."

After they finished, Jon stepped to Ora and shook his hand. "I look forward to our next session."

"As do I."

Their next stop for the day was Aaron Olufsen's. He was a Delver with light hair, light eyes, and the strong, stocky build typical of his race. He made good armor, priced it fairly, and wanted to buy all they could glean during their adventures.

Sera got Aaron's attention, then turned to Teer while Aaron finished with his customer.

"I've been coming to Aaron since I first got to Draco." She put a hand on Teer's shoulder. "Treat him right and he will return the favor."

Sera turned as Aaron approached.

Hohan set a large bag next to the counter so that Aaron could get to it.

The Delver opened the bag and peeked in. "What have we here?" Aaron poked at the contents. His eyes widened, and his voice was soft with wonder. "These are very interesting. Where did you say you got this?"

Sera dropped her hand to the hilt of her rapier. "Perhaps we can discuss this in your back room?" She glanced meaningfully at the dividing curtain.

Aaron looked at her speculatively and then called over to his coworker. "Terrel, watch the store. I'll be with our friends."

He held the curtain aside and motioned for the others to precede him through. The back area had a workbench along one side of the room. Unique pieces of armor decorated racks, including jerkins and hauberks of every composition of steel and leather, cuirasses and breastplates of a variety of designs, and pauldrons, gorgets, vambraces, gauntlets, and other pieces.

The near side of the room had a wide table, and Aaron pointed at the table for Hohan to put the heavy bag on it. Hohan had already been moving towards it. This wasn't the first time they had been to Aaron's shop selling gear.

"Before you look at this, we need something for Teer here." Sera clapped a hand on Teer's shoulder. "Aaron, meet Teer, my new student."

"It is a pleasure to meet you, young squire." Aaron extended a massive hand. Teer tentatively extended his, and they shook. He eyed Teer speculatively, his hand on his chin.

Ora could almost hear gears turning in the Delver's head as he leaned his head side to side stepping around Teer. "I think I have something that would be perfect for you."

Aaron looked over at the array of armor and shifted to one covered in a cloth. He strode to it and pulled it off the peg without unwrapping it, and handed the bundle to Teer. "This was a commission from one of the merchant lords who, strangely, never came to pick it up. It's been mostly paid for, and I could offer it to you at a discount for your fledgling."

Aaron stepped back and watched as Teer eagerly unwrapped the bundle, revealing a fantastically crafted set of scale armor.

Sera sucked in her breath. "Aaron, we can't possibly afford that."

Aaron held up a hand to stop her. "Sera, it's mostly paid for, like I said."

"But what if the person who commissioned it comes back?"

Aaron shrugged. "It's been five years, and it's just collecting dust. I want it out of my shop and into someone's hands who could make good use of it."

Sera inclined her head. "Very well, let's see what the appraisal brings, and then we can negotiate a price."

Aaron nodded and then headed to the table. Hohan had pulled pieces of armor and gear out of the bag while they were getting the armor for Teer.

The Delver stopped when he saw the chest pieces and other bits of armor. "Where did you say you got this?"

"People wearing this attacked on the road from Somerville," Gverth explained.

Aaron looked at him sharply. "Elves wearing this armor attacked you?" There was heat in his voice that surprised everyone.

"Men," Ora emphasized. "Men attacked us. They spoke strangely, had strange coins, but definitely men." He narrowed his eyes at Aaron. "Why do you think we killed Elves?"

"This style of armor is Elvish in origin, and I haven't seen the like in this half of the continent."

Ora looked thoughtfully at the armor, then at Aaron. "I've met the Elves of Braizolux, but I don't remember armor like this." He looked up, catching strange looks from Sera and Hohan. Ora shrugged. "It was a long time ago, so things could have changed."

Aaron shook his head. "No, things haven't changed so much. Sets of armor like this would be family heirlooms or ceremonial. To see day-to-day armor, in this style, used for battle, is strange indeed." He spent a moment, then asked in a cautious tone, "How much do you want for this?"

Sera shrugged. "I'm not sure. What would you think it's worth?"

Aaron squinted at her, then shook his head and spent several minutes laying out the armor, matching up the pieces into sets. As he worked, he mumbled, counted on his fingers, looked at the different pieces, and marked runes on a small slat of wood with a charcoal stick.

Once he was done, he squared his shoulders and faced Sera. "I can't go any higher than three thousand Draconic crowns for this."

Sera gasped. "Are you kidding me? This is not a joke, Aaron."

A normal contract might pay twenty Draconic crowns. A week at the Dragon's Cup was a single Draconic crown. The sum Aaron had named was enough to set up a barony.

The look on his face was pure surprise. "Sera. You don't understand. I've never been able to *buy* armor like this before. I don't know that I could even make it." Aaron held up a vambrace made up of small, intricate, overlapping plates that allowed it to flex. "The techniques used in this armor are fantastic. I've met no one outside of the Elves who can make this kind of armor, and I'm a Delver."

Ora stepped between the pair. "Sera, how about we ask our friend Aaron to give us a lesser amount and throw Teer's armor kit here in on the deal?"

He then turned to Aaron, who looked confused at what was happening. "My friend, you've given us a generous offer. But, and speaking for the group, we cannot take that much from you." Aaron opened his mouth to speak, but Ora held up a hand to stop him. "Let's agree on the sum of a thousand Draconic crowns—" he heard Sera choke behind him "—and Teer's armor. Would that be fair?"

Aaron nodded emphatically. "I would be in your debt."

"No," Ora emphasized, "you would not. If you feel you are taking advantage of us, and we feel like we're taking advantage of you, then it's a good deal for everyone. Agreed?"

Aaron smiled, then suddenly strode for the far workbench. "We must seal this agreement with a drink." He reached under the workbench and brought out a steel flask of Delver make, covered with intricately carved figures and runes.

He unscrewed the top, held it up, and toasted, "By the Giant's grace," then took a big drink.

He passed the flask to Ora, who repeated the gesture and the phrase and took a sip, then Sera, who handed it to Hohan.

"Enki." Hohan took a drink and passed it on to Gverth. After he toasted and took a drink, they turned to Teer. His eyes were wide as Gverth extended it to him.

"Go on. You know what to do." Sera encouraged him.

Teer raised the flask. "By the Giant's grace." Not seeing the smirks and smiles on everybody's face, knowing what was about to happen, he took a very large drink.

Delver Fire is a thing of legend. When aged in the wooden barrels smoked in Delver forge-fire, it imparted a flavor and consistency next to molten fire going down an unaccustomed throat like Teer's.

His eyes immediately watered, and he held the flask out suddenly.

Hohan grabbed it from him, lest he spill a drop.

Teer doubled over, unable to speak or breathe.

After several tense minutes that made Ora wonder if he needed to intervene with Life Magic, Teer finally recovered enough to say in a creaky voice, "That's good."

Everyone laughed. Not at Teer, but because they'd all experienced the same thing: their first time drinking Delver Fire.

Afterwards, Ora stood with Aaron, looking down at the strange armor. "What are you going to do with it?"

"I'm going to take one set and disassemble it to see if I can make it." Aaron picked up a pauldron and turned it over. "I've got to learn the secrets of how this was put together." Aaron looked up at Ora. "If you encounter more of this…"

Ora nodded. "We'll bring it to you."

CHAPTER TWENTY-SEVEN

ORA EARL

The party was back at the Dragon's Cup, in their alcove, except for Teer, who'd been sent off for another bath. Satya had promised to bring fresh mutton and vegetables soon, much to Hohan's delight.

While they waited for dinner, Sera looked at the others. "So, what are we going to do next? We still have the open contract that Deveris wants us to do, if it's still open, and we have a couple others that we keep talking about and then getting interrupted." Sera looked pointedly at the door and waited for just a moment. When nothing happened, she smiled and turned her attention back to the group. "Well?"

Ora said, "I still want to find who killed the king."

Sera nodded slowly. "And we need to find more information about the people who attacked us."

"Which time?" Hohan asked. Sera shot him a glance. "I'm serious, Sera. You seem to attract a lot of attention, and not the good kind."

"He has a good point." Gverth shifted in his chair to rest his arms on the table.

"Let's talk this through." Sera held up a finger. "The people who attacked us after we went in the secret passage in the—"

Gverth interrupted, "You mean the people who stabbed me?"

"Yes."

Hohan asked, "Do you think there's any connection between those people and the strange men who attacked us on the road from Somerville?"

"I can't think of a connection, but that doesn't mean anything." Ora rubbed the whiskers on his chin contemplatively.

Then there was a tap at the partition, and Satya opened it and brought in platters of the mutton roast. She set the different platters in front of each of them and headed out of the alcove.

She stopped in the doorway. "Will there be anything else?"

Ora caught a flash of motion out of the corner of his eye. He shifted his chair slightly back to see what it might be. As he moved, something small whizzed past his head and Satya slumped to the floor.

Immediately, Ora pulled on Shimmershield and turned toward the door, reaching for a weapon.

A dart hit him in the neck, and he felt like a puppet with its strings cut as he slumped to the floor. The Shimmershield he'd just used might have been the only reason he didn't go unconscious, but everything around him seemed distant, like calling across a courtyard.

Three figures leapt through the door to their alcove, long knives in their hands, and yelled in a strange language. Ora had to struggle to focus on what they said.

The fog in his brain called him to slumber.

No, focus! He could barely reach his well of Life Magic, and he grabbed what he could to fight the poison.

"Who are you?" Sera asked. "What do you want?"

"Be quiet, woman," one of the men barked at her. His accent was the same as the people who had stopped them on the road from Somerville.

Another man said something in a language that Ora could not make out, and the first man hissed at the second, "We can't kill them. There are too many people here. We'll hold them in this room until people leave."

Bit by bit, Ora used Shimmershield to burn the poison away, but he didn't move. He just lay there and bided his time.

Since Ora faced away from the group where he lay, he watched the partition slide open silently. Teer peeked his head in.

Ora redoubled his efforts to turn the poison, suspecting Teer was about to give him the opening he was looking for. It felt like it took a hundred years before Ora regained the ability to move his extremities. His arms and legs felt like they'd fallen asleep, and now a thousand needles ran over every inch.

As uncomfortable as it was, Ora tried not to move too much. He didn't want to get the attention of the attackers, but he was quickly running out of time before the lad struck.

The leader said something in a harsh whisper, then addressed Sera. "Put your weapons on the table. Slowly."

"Now!" barked Sera. Teer let out a blood-curdling battle cry from behind them, streaking in through the door and swinging a pan he must've pulled from the kitchen.

The combination of surprise from Teer's sudden appearance and Sera's shout threw the attackers into disarray.

Ora struggled to his knees, and with all of his weight behind it, shoved a chair into one of the attackers. The attacker went down, and Teer beat him with the cast-iron pan.

As quick as a cat, the leader threw a blade that sunk into Teer's chest with a meaty, wet *thunk*, and Teer fell on top of the man he had been beating.

Sera manifested an ice knife in her hand and stabbed it through the leader's neck.

Gverth shouted, *"Pir!"* and the room lit up from an incandescent bolt that blew a hole through the last attacker's chest. The attacker fell face first into the table and rolled off and onto the floor. The acrid smell of burnt meat and fried blood flooded the little room.

Ora slumped back to the floor, still weak from whatever poison they had given him. Hohan rushed over to help him.

The priest glowed with a blue radiance as he touched his hammer to Ora's chest. Whatever magic Hohan had used on him, it was not Life Magic.

Ora tried to speak, but nothing would come out. A healing wave washed through him, and he regained his voice. He pointed at Teer and croaked, "Help him."

Sera checked on Satya. Her face and neck had swollen, and dead eyes stared at the ceiling. Sera shook her head. "She's dead."

At that moment Malkiel, the innkeeper, rushed into their alcove, meat cleaver in one hand and a large pewter mug in the other. The carnage stunned him, then he spotted Satya. He knelt next to her, his eyes welling.

Sera stood. "Hohan, how's Teer?"

The large man hunched over the young man, eyes closed and hands out.

Gverth shook his head. "He's still working. Teer lost a lot of blood."

Sera moved over to Ora. "Ora?" she whispered.

"I was poisoned." He held up a dart. "It was powerful. I'm still working through it."

"Can you sit up?" she asked.

"With your help." He held out an arm for her to assist him into a chair.

Sera looked at the bodies of the three attackers and frowned. They were dressed in the same red-black robes as the four who had ambushed them on the street several days ago. "It's a shame we killed them all."

The innkeeper turned at that. "You didn't." He pointed at the open panel. "The lad brained one out there. Gerald is sitting on him."

The large mastiff who normally slept in front of the fire lay across another one of the attackers. Whenever the man stirred, Gerald put his massive jaws around the back of the man's neck and growled. The man instantly stilled.

"Good boy, Gerald." Sera smiled grimly. The dog's tail thumped loudly against the bar at hearing his name. "Oh, I have plans for you, my little friend."

The tone made Ora shudder.

"Sera!" Hohan called. "I need help."

Everyone's heads snapped around to Hohan and Teer, who was convulsing on the floor, blood welling out of his mouth.

Ora slumped onto the floor next to Teer on the other side of Hohan.

Hohan peered closely at Ora. "You don't have the strength for this." He glanced down at Teer, where he writhed on the floor. He sighed. "I don't have the strength for this."

"There *is* a way," Ora said softly. "We pull the strength of the others."

"I don't know how to do that."

Ora smiled grimly. "I learned in the Legion." Ora raised his head up and addressed the group. "If you're willing, Teer needs your help."

"What do we need to do?" Sera stepped forward.

"I need some of your energy. Put your hand on my shoulder." He looked at each of them. "All of you."

Gverth, Sera, and Malkiel each put a hand on Ora.

"This will feel... odd," Ora said.

He reached his hands over Teer and pulled on his Life Magic. He wove a small flow to loop through each of the people. "Are you ready?" Not hearing any objections, he began. Ora raised up both hands, palms to the sky, and in a deep voice almost not his own, he uttered, *"Ghendo donam."* He pushed the healing energy down into Teer. He heard gasps from the trio behind him, but didn't stop. Ora concentrated on the gravest part of the wound, Teer's pierced heart.

He felt the heart stop.

Ora snarled, "No!" He yanked all the healing force he could reach, and in a flash, the heart started, beating as strong as ever.

Gverth leaned over to the side and retched into a bucket meant for dirty dishes. Sera sat down heavily on the closest chair. Ora looked up at Malkiel, who had a dazed look on his face.

"That was a hell of a thing." The innkeeper shook himself, then turned to Satya's body and called to one of the other servers, "Bring me a tablecloth."

Teer coughed, then faded into unconsciousness.

Hohan looked him over. "I don't think he'll be wrestling any pigs soon." He looked at Ora. "What about you? What was that you said? What language was that?"

Ora made it over to a chair where he sat heavily. "The channeling of power like that is an ancient rite. I spoke in Old Akkermenian, and it means 'I accept your gift.'"

The door to the Dragon's Cup slammed open, startling everyone. Four Wlewoi stalked into the center room.

"The Blood," someone hissed.

They scanned the crowd with their feline eyes.

The leader pointed at the man under the dog. "Seize him." One of the Blood moved toward him. The dog growled at the Wlewoi.

"Gerald, heel," Malkiel commanded. The dog obediently came and sat at his master's side while watching the Blood closely.

"That's our prisoner," Sera said, stepping to the threshold of the alcove.

The leader of the Blood took two quick strides to stand before her. "Do you challenge our authority here?" He took in the other bodies in the room, then stared down into Sera's face. "Maybe you need to come with us as well."

They stared at each other for a long moment until Sera dropped her gaze.

He sniffed at Sera, then looked at each of the others. "Do you wish to say something?" No one held eye contact.

He turned to look at the center room. "Does anyone dispute our authority here?"

People purposefully avoided his gaze, paying attention to their drinks.

He turned back to Sera. "We are watching you." Then he stepped close to her and leaned in to say something quietly.

Ora enhanced his hearing.

The Blood said quietly to Sera, "You don't want to end up like your father."

Sera stiffened, shock painted her face.

The Blood smiled and stepped away from her. He made it a couple of steps into the room before he stopped. His head tilted, and he sniffed the air, almost like he was scenting prey. The room watched him for a moment. The Blood shook his head.

One of the Blood by the door, with gray markings in his fur, shoved a man. "Be careful you don't end up like the king."

The sound of screeching chairs and hiss of drawn weapons accompanied the sudden movement of everyone in the bar standing up at once. The feline ears on the Blood went flat, and they bared their fangs at the palpable tension in the room.

The innkeeper's flat voice cut through the room. "You'd better leave while you still can." The leader cocked an ear at Malkiel and nodded for the others to move out. One of the Blood held the prisoner with a clawed hand around the back of his neck, and in moments the Blood and prisoner were gone.

As soon as the door swung shut, the Dragon's Cup erupted with cheers. "To the king!" and "To the Lightbringer!"

The hostility the group had shown at the insult to the old king, combined with their cheers, brought tears to Ora's eyes. He didn't expect that.

Ora looked over at Sera. He wanted to ask her about what he had heard, but she was focused on Teer.

The enthusiasm in the room ebbed, and Malkiel came with several others to collect up Satya.

Sera addressed Malkiel. "I'm sorry for your loss. She was always friendly and took care of us. I'd like to help with the funeral expenses…"

"What do you want me to do with them?" Malkiel pointed at the other bodies.

Sera snapped a finger to get his attention. "Gverth, search them for anything useful. As to this trash, do you have someone with a cart to dump them in the river?"

"It will cost a bit of coin," Malkiel said.

"Get Tamaroa to get rid of them?" Ora suggested.

"Even better. He wanted to buy us a drink. He might as well earn something as well." Sera nodded. "Malkiel, can you send a messenger?"

"Make that two messengers." Everyone looked at Gverth. "I found another map and more of those strange coins. I know we agreed to hold the map back, but two of them is too much. Master Te'zla needs to see this."

Sera glanced at the others. "Any disagreement? No?" She turned to the innkeeper. "Can you please send a messenger to the Reader house?"

Malkiel nodded. "Two messengers."

"Thank you." Sera handed him several coins from her pouch.

"I'll have the bodies taken out back."

"I'll get Teer taken care of." Hohan carried the young man up to his room.

While he was gone, the servers and housekeepers quickly removed all traces that there was ever a fight. They brought fresh platters of food and cold drink.

Despite his fatigue, Ora devoured the mutton and vegetables. Working magic came at a cost.

When Sera pushed her untouched plate away, Ora pushed it back. "You gave to the healing magic, and you need to eat."

She shrugged and grimly took a bite of mutton.

❦   ❦   ❦

When Hohan returned, Master Te'zla came in with him. Gverth leapt to his feet, knocking his chair over. The sound pulled Ora out of his stupor.

"Please be seated," Te'zla said with a smile that betrayed his amusement at his pupil and took an empty chair. "It looks like you've had quite the adventure. What happened?"

Gverth relayed the attack, the saving of Teer, and the encounter with the Blood.

When he was done, Te'zla sat back in his chair. "You should steer clear of the Blood."

"We intend to." Sera looked at Gverth. "Show him what you found on the attackers."

"Oh!" Gverth reached under the table and set out the map, the coins, daggers, a black leather case, and a foot-long bone tube.

Te'zla picked up each item. When he opened the black leather case, his eyes narrowed. He looked up at the group. "Were any of you struck by one of these darts?"

Gverth pointed at Ora. "Ora and Satya, the serving girl who died, both were."

Te'zla turned his intense gaze on Ora. "Describe the effects."

Ora shrugged. "It was some kind of poison. It came on like a charging bull, and if I didn't have Shimmershield already primed, it probably would have killed me like it did Satya."

"Was it burning, or did it make you cold and sleepy?" Te'zla asked.

Ora thought for a moment. "Cold and sleepy. I'm still feeling lethargic."

Te'zla nodded. "It is Somnul. The Nox use it, and it is very difficult and expensive to acquire anything from them. It brings on an instant and deep sleep, but it shouldn't have killed someone." He looked pensively off in the distance. "I didn't know they had dealings on Drakanon."

Ora wasn't sure he meant to say that out loud.

Hohan leaned in so others outside the room might not hear. "I thought the Nox were a myth? More stories to frighten children."

Te'zla shook himself. "Oh, they're quite real."

Ora blinked the sleep from his eyes. "Why did it kill Satya if it was just a tranquilizer?"

Te'zla shook his head. "Hard to say. It is very powerful. Maybe they used a different poison on her?"

Gverth tapped the map suddenly. "Sera, isn't this where that contract Deveris wanted us to take is located?" They all leaned in.

Sera pulled out the paper map the factor had given them and compared it with the cloth one. "The features look similar."

With each hand, Te'zla pointed at a spot on both maps. "This is the same location.

"Coincidence? Or are we being set up?" Gverth asked.

"I don't know. But if we know it is a trap, I want to know why we are being targeted." Sera folded the paper.

The conversation was interesting, but Ora was struggling to stay awake. "Regardless," Ora stood up, "I need to sleep. Bar your doors tonight. They know where we are now."

Ora made his way up the stairs.

He wasn't afraid of another attack right away, at least not so soon, but he made his way deliberately, checking each shadow.

He closed his room's door behind him and dropped the bar into place across it. In the dark, by feel, he located the box on the table holding the punk, a lit charcoal stick that barely smoldered when the box was closed. It brightened when he opened the lid. He blew on it to bring it to life enough to ignite the wick of the lamp on the table. He returned the punk to the box and closed the lid.

That was when he heard a sound behind him.

He whirled, drawing his sword in a single smooth motion, pulled on Shimmershield to bolster his flagging strength and froze.

A female Wlewoi wearing the harness of an Esroi of the king's true guard stood across the room from him. She dropped to one knee, pressed the knuckles of her right hand into the floor, and bowed her head.

"Your Majesty."

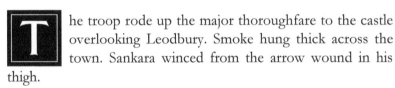

CHAPTER TWENTY-EIGHT

SANKARA MURCHALA

The troop rode up the major thoroughfare to the castle overlooking Leodbury. Smoke hung thick across the town. Sankara winced from the arrow wound in his thigh.

His aide pulled up next to him. "Are you all right, Commander?"

Sankara waved his hand. "I'll make it, Rajan."

As they approached the castle, they observed two figures, a woman and a soldier, moving on the wall above the moat, one right behind the other. A sudden motion, and the second figure pushed the first off the wall. They heard a woman's shriek that abruptly cut off.

An icy shiver ran down Sankara's spine. He set his face in a grimace and put his spurs to his horse.

They rode through the open gates, and the thick odor of death almost made him gag. There were bodies everywhere. Only half looked to be soldiers. The rest were women and children. The troop rode to the keep.

Several soldiers stood near the steps.

Rajan quickly dismounted and pointed to the nearest soldier. "You! Go fetch a healer." He turned and helped Sankara off his horse. With the help of another of the riders, they got the commander to the stairs.

Sankara surveyed the destruction in the courtyard. More servants than enemy soldiers lay in heaps around the space. His soldiers had laid the bodies of three companions from Kinderkesh out on an ornate tablecloth. Sankara could only guess it was from the baron's table. The more he looked, the less he liked what he saw.

The regiment's zokurios, practitioner of Life Magic, came hustling out of the keep. Lavinia strutted after him, followed by two of her henchmen. She gave the troop a once-over before turning her attention to Sankara.

The healer quickly began work on Sankara. He pulled a small, clear bottle filled with a green liquid from his satchel. "For the pain."

Sankara downed the draught in one pull then turned to Lavinia. "What's the meaning of this?" He waved at the courtyard.

"We took the castle while you dealt with the troops." She said the term derisively.

He sighed in exasperation. "Did you leave anyone alive? Servants? The baron?"

"The servants killed one of my... your men. That emboldened the other locals who killed our other two soldiers before we could dispatch them." She leveled a cold smile at him. "Would you have me leave your soldiers unavenged?"

"No more wholesale slaughter, Lavinia. If I'm going to rule this land, there need to be people here to rule. Unless you want me to get Houshkulu to task you with milking cows and collecting eggs?"

The zokurios murmured, "This will hurt, Lord Commander."

Sankara winced at the healer's ministrations, but his work closed the wound. "Thank you, my friend."

"Of course, my lord."

He refocused on Lavinia and gave her a grim look.

Her eyes narrowed.

"Well?" he asked.

She shook her head.

"Good. Now clean up your mess."

Lavinia hesitated for the barest of moments and flashed him a more winsome smile. The cruelty still in her eyes dampened the ardor he felt.

Rajan watched her go. "Be careful with that one. She is an adder waiting to bite."

Sankara nodded. "It is only a matter of time until we see if I am a rabbit or a mongoose."

CHAPTER TWENTY-NINE

ORA EARL

O ra funneled some of his Shimmershield into enhancing his vision, making the faint light from the lamp illuminate the room as bright as noonday. He took in every detail of the Wlewoi. He saw the dark brown markings in her light fur that denoted her clan. It was a clan he knew, the Blade Stalkers. They were predominantly around the big delta in the kingdom of Reosha.

The harness she wore looked very new, the detailing on the leather still crisp and the colors in the ornamentation vivid and unfaded.

"You haven't been an Esroi long, have you?" He sheathed his sword and unbuckled his belts, hanging them on the post by his bed.

He paused, surprised she was still in the same kneeling position. He sighed. "You may rise."

She stood with a feline grace, whiskers twitching. "I am newly selected by the Council."

Ora motioned her to the chair while he removed his armor and other gear. "What Council?"

She tilted her head, eyes glowing in the reflected light. "The Pentad. But you knew that, didn't you, Your Majesty?"

"You need to drop the 'Your Majesty' right now." He gave a meaningful glance at the door. "People don't know about my *past*."

Once she nodded, he removed the heavy rings he wore on both hands, setting all eight of the bands in a row on the side of the washing table. The City Watch frowned upon a weapon like brass knuckles, but who would begrudge a man some ornamentation?

"What's your name?" Ora sat on the stool by the washbasin.

"Mayomi, Your... um..." She shrugged, hands spread out.

"Ora. Call me Ora."

"Very well, Ora. I am Mayomi of the Blade Stalkers. I have answered the call of the Council and have pledged my life in service to you." Her eyes were bright.

"But I'm not the king. He's been murdered."

"We didn't pledge to that king. They pledged us to the Lightbringer." Her gaze was firm. "To you."

"I don't mean to go in circles, but I abdicated the throne eight hundred years ago. The Esroi protect my line."

"No, the Esroi were bound by the Pentad to you. You hardly left the keep for centuries. It made it easier to seem like they protected the king."

Ora was skeptical, and it must have shown on his face.

She tapped her head with a finger, then pointed at him. "You can feel our bond, even now, can't you?"

Ora grunted and closed his eyes. He turned his head and knew he could point straight at her no matter where she was in the room. He opened his eyes. "And you can feel me?"

Mayomi nodded.

"But this differs from the other Esroi that had been with me, doesn't it?"

"Yes. The Council decided they needed a different approach. That was why they selected me for the trials." Mayomi took off her cloak and laid it across the back of the chair. "That was why they sent a female."

Ora considered that. "Why now? I've been out of the keep for over a year."

"The Council didn't know anything was amiss until someone killed one of the other Esroi. There must always be five. It took time to select the candidates and hold the trials. I underwent the ritual three days ago." She sat with her back straight, and only the tip of her tail moved. "Now I watch and wait."

"What about the other Esroi? Have you heard from them?"

"No. Nothing. Because of the Pentad, I have certain abilities. I can locate you, but I can't sense them."

Ora frowned. "Could they be dead?"

"No, the Council would have known, and there would be five of us here now."

I should have paid more attention to my protectors.

In the early days of becoming the High King, he'd taken them for granted. They were a reminder of home. Of growing up in Drounid around Wlewoi. Then they reminded him of his Wlewoi guard when he took the Legion against the Demon. They were comforting. He'd participated in the first ceremony, but it wasn't until now he understood the true enormity of their sacrifice.

Ora looked at the young woman, now sworn to protect him. He stood and bowed to her, his hand over his heart.

She shot to her feet, tail twitching. "What was that for!"

"I honor the sacrifice you have made for me." Ora held the bow until she returned it, then straightened and offered her his hand. "Please sit. Do you need anything? Food? Drink? I can send down to the kitchen?"

Mayomi waved his offer away. "I've eaten recently enough." Her stiff posture shouted to Ora that there was something else.

"You still seem upset. What is it?"

She stilled, ears flat on her head, tail stiff. Ora watched her eyes dilate, then settle back to normal, and she relaxed a fraction. "How do you know…"

He spoke to her in the guttural, hissing language of the Wlewoi. "Your body talks to me. Remember, I grew up in the care of the Shadow Hunters."

She slowly rose and bowed. "Please forgive this kitten her ignorance. I didn't realize you knew our tongue. No one recorded it."

Ora laughed softly. "Kitten indeed. Remember, Mayomi, I was born a thousand years ago. They lost the details of my early life to legend." Ora rubbed his chin. "Sometimes they are even lost to me."

He sighed at the memories, then focused on her. "We have a problem here in Draco. There are other Wlewoi here, and I don't know who they are allied with. It is almost certain they have something to do with the king's death."

Ora spent the next hour going over his encounters with the Blood at the king's viewing, in the secret passage, and the assassins, especially focusing on the following encounter with the Blood.

Mayomi nodded. "I thought I smelled something as I waited. Do you know what clan they're from?"

"No. I didn't recognize their clan markings at all."

Mayomi bared her fangs in a feline grin. "I'm looking forward to asking them."

Ora wanted to make sure he wasn't anywhere near that discussion.

"Earlier, you mentioned the Council wanted a different approach. What does that mean?"

She settled back in the chair. "I know you grew up around the Wlewoi, but do you understand why our females aren't in the military or haven't been a part of your guard before?"

Ora thought for a moment, then shook his head. "I could make guesses, but no, I don't know the reason."

"Wlewoi men are pretty things. They play at fighting and make a good show of it. *We* do the killing." She tilted her head, both of her ears focused on him. "Do you understand the difference?"

Ora's mind raced. In all this time, he'd had it wrong. He assumed because the Wlewoi men he had fought beside were big and strong, that was why there were no females. She nodded as she watched him work through it.

He whispered, "It's because the females are ruthless."

"It's more complicated than that, and exactly that." She moved from the chair and paced the room. "Never send a boy to do a woman's job."

"Does the Council think it's really that bad? To need you here?" Ora reeled as he tried to fit all the pieces together. Dead king, dead Esroi, missing Esroi, strange soldiers attacking them, stranger assassins coming after them in the inn. Now a female Esroi.

"From what you have told me, yes." She sat back down and folded her hands on her knee. "But enough of that for now. You need sleep."

Ora blinked at the sudden shift from Wlewoi-incarnation-of-death to mom in a single second. He glanced at the bed.

"Ah, you can take the bed," he quickly offered.

Her laugh surprised him, a delightful blend of a Human laugh and a chuff.

"I will stand watch—" she held up a hand when he protested "—and will wake you to take your watch. Fair?"

Ora begrudgingly nodded. He pulled his boots off and sat on the bed.

"You aren't going to sleep in your clothes, are you? And you haven't washed."

Ora's ears burned. "See, this is why there haven't been female guards. I don't need a mother."

Mayomi's amused gaze made his face grow warm.

"Yes, Mother." He got stripped down to his undergarment and stepped to the washbasin.

"You are very well-muscled," she observed. "I'm sure the females appreciate it."

"By the Giants, are you always like this?" His tone brought another amused laugh. Ora did a quick wipe down with the cloth dipped into the cold water. Finished, he climbed into the bed and pulled the blanket over himself. "Wake me in four hours."

"Of course, my king," she breathed. Ora watched her settle in to watch over him. She kept one ear cocked to the door, as he closed his eyes.

● ● ●

A warm hand rubbed his shoulder and called his name.

"Ora, time to get up."

He murmured softly, then consciousness flooded back into him, and he shot into a sitting position.

The cinnamon and cream of Mayomi's fur glowed in the morning light that streamed in through the window. She had pulled the curtains open, letting in the early rays of sunlight.

"You didn't wake me."

She had changed her outfit during the night. Now, she wore simple leather armor over a dark purple shirt and pants. Unadorned leather vambraces protected her forearms, and matching greaves covered her legs. A pair of swords were her only visible weapons. She looked like any traveler on the street. A female Wlewoi wasn't that rare as a traveler.

But how am I going to explain this to Sera and the others?

CHAPTER THIRTY

ORA EARL

ra led Mayomi to their alcove. He slid the panel open and stepped through first. Hohan, Gverth, and Sera were already in the room.

Sera looked up, concern plain on her face. "Ora. How are you doing?"

"I'm well." He looked at each of them. "There's something I need to tell you."

Mayomi stepped from behind him and pulled the hood of her cloak back.

Sera hissed and shot to her feet, manifesting an ice dagger in her hand and sending her chair over backward. Both Hohan and Gverth held out their respective hands to use magic.

Ora stepped forward. "Stop!" he barked in his best Legion command voice. Even Mayomi stilled instantly. "This is Mayomi. She is a friend."

Sera's eyes were venomous. She spat, "Why should we trust one of the Blood?"

Ora pulled the panel closed. He pulled out a chair for Mayomi and took a seat in another, putting his hands flat on the table.

"To answer your question, you shouldn't trust one of the Blood, but Mayomi isn't one of them. Not every Wlewoi is Blood."

Sera looked skeptically from Ora to Mayomi.

"Let me ask you this: have you ever met a female Wlewoi under arms?" Ora asked. Sera shook her head. "No, you haven't and there's a reason for it."

He leaned back in his chair and folded his arms across his chest. "I can't get into it now, but with the assassination attempt yesterday and the Blood threatening you, it all adds up to us needing to get out of the city."

Sera's face paled, and her eyes went wide.

He added, "Yes, I heard what that Blood said to you."

"We could go to the temple," Hohan offered. "Enki will protect us."

Ora shook his head. "That curate has no love for us. Is the head of your order back?"

"Not yet."

"Then I don't trust her, and we need to get Teer someplace he can recover. Out of Draco."

Sera let the ice dagger dissipate and righted her chair. "We can take the Gnoll contract."

Gverth sucked in air through his teeth. "I thought we determined that's a trap. Especially with the map we took off the dead assassin."

"They wouldn't expect us to head there."

"What if we confuse them?" Ora said thoughtfully. "They know they hurt Teer. Let's make like we're going back to Somerville, then under cover of darkness and some of your fog magic, we slip away to the Gnoll camp."

"I think it might work, but only if we can get out of the city without being followed." Sera tapped the table. "And it might mean they attack Teer and his parents."

"What about Tamaroa? He could arrange things, I'm sure."

"He's supposed to buy us a drink, isn't he?" Hohan added.

"We sent word asking him to come to us, so he should be here soon." Sera looked at Mayomi. Her expression had not softened at all. "I don't trust her."

"You don't need to trust her right now," Ora said. "You need to trust me."

"She doesn't look like much. I could take her."

Ora put a hand on Sera's arm and looked her in the eyes. "No, you can't."

Sera looked at him for a long moment, searching for an answer in his eyes. She nodded slowly. "Okay. I'll trust you."

Sera looked at Mayomi. "If you cross us, I'll end you, regardless of whatever secret you are keeping."

"I swear on my oath to His—to Ora, I will not betray you." Mayomi stood, and with her right hand on her heart, she bowed.

Sera stared at her for a moment, then glanced sideways at Ora. "You had a busy night?"

Mayomi sat. "No, he spent it asleep."

Sera turned to Ora, eyebrows raised.

"She protected me while I slept." Ora spread his hands. "She's my bodyguard, after a fashion."

"When did you have time to get a bodyguard," Sera said with a frosty tone.

"Her employers gifted the contract to me." Ora really wanted to talk about anything else. He looked at Gverth for help.

Mayomi sat forward suddenly. "Is she your mate?"

Hohan spit his drink on the table.

"Your what?" Sera's voice rose an octave.

At that moment, the panel slid open, and Tamaroa stepped into the room. He paused. He must have felt the tension as he glanced from person to person.

"Thank the Giants." Ora stood abruptly and extended a hand to Tamaroa and shook his tentacle-hand enthusiastically. "Thank you for coming, Master Tamaroa. You know my companions. This is Mayomi. She just recently joined our merry band. Please have a seat. Can I get you a refreshment?"

Tamaroa let out a laugh and took the offered chair between Sera and Mayomi. He didn't sit down so much as his tentacle-legs enveloped the chair. "I believe I am the one to provide refreshments."

"You can get the next round." Ora stepped out of the room to order. Malkiel met him with a tray of beverages.

"He ordered for everyone." Malkiel handed him the tray.

"Thanks." Ora sighed, then stepped back in the room, studiously avoiding Sera's burning gaze.

Once everyone had their drink, Tamaroa lifted his mug. "May the Giants bring you fortune."

Everyone echoed the toast and took a drink.

"Now we talk business. What will it take for you to come work for me?" Tamaroa's eyes gleamed with excitement.

"Actually, we have a predicament and need your help." Sera laid out all the events over the last couple of days. Tamaroa listened attentively and stopped her occasionally to ask a clarifying question. When they got to the part about the drug, he became very excited. "Can I see it?"

Gverth pulled the leather kit they'd recovered from the assassins and handed it to him.

Gingerly, Tamaroa opened the case to reveal the darts and vial of Somnul. He fairly shook in exuberance. His head-tentacles writhed sinuously. "This is very rare indeed." Tamaroa gingerly picked up a dart by its fletching to avoid any contact with the poison.

"You've heard about the Nox?" Sera asked.

Tamaroa replaced the dart and closed up the case. "I have indeed. I am a purveyor of rare items, and this, my friends, is a handsome find." He looked at Sera with great interest. "How may I assist you?"

"We need to get out of town." Ora pointed at the case. "They attacked us here, in this very room. One of our band took a grave injury, and we need to get him to a place he can recover without being tracked."

"You will need a wagon to carry your man," Tamaroa said.

Hohan set his empty mug on the table. "And some men to go with Teer to protect him and his family."

"And supplies for the trip." Gverth moved his mug away from Hohan.

Mayomi set her untouched mug on the table close to Hohan. "May Enki bless you, child." Hohan beamed at her and claimed the mug.

"How fast do you think you can arrange it, Tamaroa?" Sera asked.

Tamaroa looked at them. He was counting things on one of his tentacle-hands. "What you ask—and the timeframe..." He caressed the leather case. "Would you be willing to part with this?"

Sera was about to respond, but Ora coughed loudly into his hand.

"May I have a moment to confer with my colleague?" Sera shifted over to the corner with Ora.

"What?" she whispered.

Ora leaned into her, putting his mouth next to her ear. "This is too easy. If that stuff is half as hard to get as Te'zla mentioned, then he should pay us."

She nodded and moved back to her seat.

"My dearest Tamaroa." Sera took his hand in hers and gave it the gentlest of squeezes. "Knowing what we need and the time we need to have it in—" she let go and put her hand on the case "—the real question for you is how much you are willing to pay for the Somnul."

Tamaroa laughed. "You are fantastic! You must come work for me." He picked up the case. "The wagon, the men, the supplies, and arranged to be here by sunset. I will provide that and a hundred Draconic crowns."

Sera didn't hesitate. "Four hundred crowns."

"I might be able to pull together one hundred and ten." Tamaroa waved a tentacle arm.

"Three hundred eighty." Sera crossed her arms across her chest and leaned back.

They went back and forth for twenty minutes. Tamaroa complained about Sera taking food from his children. Sera countered with the need to feed hers. It went on like that, each claim getting more outrageous until Tamaroa shouted, "Done!" They shook hands.

"You drive a hard bargain, Master Tamaroa." Sera drained her mug.

"Do you want the money today too?" Tamaroa asked.

Sera shook her head. "I want you to hold on to it. If anything happens to us, keep half and get the other half to Teer in Somerville."

"Done and done." Tamaroa stood to leave.

"This needs to be done quietly, discreetly."

Tamaroa laughed. "I'm Ohtovid." He stepped to the wall and immediately disappeared from sight.

Everyone but Ora and Mayomi gasped in surprise. They looked all around the room before Mayomi pointed to a spot next to the door.

Tamaroa dropped his camouflage for a moment and grinned. "They'll never see me." He winked at Mayomi and faded away again.

⬟ ⬟ ⬟

"The wagon's here." Gverth grabbed Teer's pack and headed to the front of the Dragon's Cup.

Ora and Hohan picked Teer up and followed.

Teer protested weakly but was in no position to walk on his own.

The late afternoon crowd was arriving at the inn, and the servers were bustling. They dodged one group carrying platters of mutton. The aroma of spiced meat made Ora's mouth water.

Outside, Gverth dumped the pack into the wagon and climbed into the back to help with Teer. Together, they hefted Teer up and into Gverth's waiting arms.

"Gverth, stay with him. I'll bring your horse." Ora sized up the men that Tamaroa had hired. All of them looked like they knew what they were doing. They watched the street and crowd, barely glancing at Ora and the others.

Ora nodded in approval and headed back inside, Hohan in tow.

They passed Sera and Malkiel at the end of the bar.

"We'll be gone for a few days getting Teer back to his family. If anyone asks where we went and they can't wait for us to return, tell them Somerville." Sera pressed a small coin purse into Malkiel's hands, then motioned for Ora and Hohan to head out back.

It only took a few minutes to gather the horses, as they'd already been saddled and loaded. They led them down the alley that opened onto the street right behind the wagon.

Sera called to the wagon. "Let's move out." She mounted her horse.

Mayomi stepped to Ora from where she had been leaning against the front wall of the inn. "You're being watched."

She looked down the street and up. Then she stepped away and moved the opposite direction to pass the wagon and continue down the street.

Ora lifted his chin to Sera and held two fingers of his right hand to his eyes.

Sera nodded slightly and guided her horse ahead of the wagon. Hohan tied the reins of the other horses to a ring set at the back of the wagon and mounted up. They followed the wagon. Around them, four men on sturdy mounts formed up. Gverth sat with Teer in the back while the driver and a crossbowman drove the wagon.

Ora glanced at Hohan. "We'll be hard to miss."

"Even a blind man could see this group leaving." He laughed at Ora's puzzled expression. "They can smell us leaving." He pointed at the wagon and Ora understood. At some point in the wagon's recent history, it had been used to haul fish and had a pungent aroma.

Glad that's not me back there.

CHAPTER THIRTY-ONE

TARTOK OF EHOTA

Tartok watched the wagon and riders leave the Dragon's Cup. The window he watched from gave him an excellent view down the street. He dipped a hand inside his vest and pulled out a small, round ball. He looked into it and spoke a command word. *"Tloqai."*

The ball flashed as if filled with purple swirling smoke. It pulsed brighter when a female voice came from it. "Report."

He watched the wagon get smaller as it moved down the street. "They appear to be leaving the city. They have an armed escort. Six mercenaries of some sort and all five of their group. The boy and one other are in the wagon. The others are riding."

The orb pulsed again. "Follow them."

"Yes, Mistress." The orb went still. He glanced at the darkening sky. He had a couple hours until sunset.

He pulled the window closed and arranged the curtains. He glanced over at the now-still bodies of the old couple who'd lived here. A purple steam rose from them. Their lives had been used to power the sphere. He contemplated them for a brief moment, then left.

CHAPTER THIRTY-TWO

ORA EARL

They'd been traveling for three hours before Sera called a halt. Mayomi had joined with them on the road. The group gathered at the front of the wagon while the horses rested for a bit. The leader of the guard, Nathan, joined them.

"You know what to do?" Sera asked him.

Nathan nodded. "We'll take the boy to his house in Somerville. We have supplies in the wagon for a month. If we don't hear from you or Tamaroa in that time, we head back to Draco."

Sera shook hands with him.

She turned to Ora and Hohan. "Can you help the horses?" They both nodded and infused them with Life Magic to give them the equivalent of a day's rest.

"May Enki protect you and keep you safe." Hohan held up his hammer, and it glowed briefly in the dark.

Ora applied his Shimmershield-enhanced night vision and waited.

Nathan waved, and the wagon and riders started moving.

Sera concentrated, and a light fog rose around them. This fog wasn't as dense as what she'd used during the ambush, but it obscured anything beyond twenty yards. "Gverth, Mayomi, do what you can to cover our tracks. Let's go."

She clucked, and the horses moved off. Ora heard Gverth murmuring. Between Gverth's Land Magic and Mayomi dragging a branch behind them and Sera laying down a fog, no one should have seen them leaving the group.

They stopped after a mile and dismounted.

Mayomi ranged off to see if their ruse had worked while the others watched.

Around them, the night creatures resumed their evening discussion.

After twenty minutes, Mayomi returned. "No one's following us."

"Are you sure?" Sera asked. Her voice sounded more tense than usual.

"I am Wlewoi."

CHAPTER THIRTY-THREE

SERA DEMOTT

S era walked her horse along the creek. Mayomi ranged far ahead of the group. Gverth and Hohan walked side by side, talking softly. The pair of them had been with Sera from the beginning.

She smiled, remembering when they'd applied for her job posting, thinking she was recruiting for one of the big mercenary companies. She had set up a table at the recruiting hall when the annual event happened.

Gverth had worn his best clothes and stammered through his introduction. It took him three tries to light a candle because his hand shook so much.

Back then, Hohan was just a novice at the temple, who didn't have a strong magic background. Sera had anyone applying to be a healer cut themselves. Hohan didn't hesitate, he pulled out a dagger, sliced his forearm, and healed it after a single drop of blood had fallen.

Ora came up from behind. "The trail behind us is clear. Are you feeling fine? You look tired."

She smiled. "There might have been a bit going on the last few days, but the resort up ahead will have baths and a massage, I'm sure."

He laughed. "Let me know if you need anything or if your night sight begins to fade." He moved on ahead to talk with Gverth and Hohan.

"So that's him? He's delicious."

Sera jumped. "Tess!" she whispered harshly. "What are you doing?"

"Oh, don't fret. They can't hear us. Besides, they're wrapped up in whatever men like to prattle on about."

Tess glided along the ground. Thankfully, she didn't have her full glow on. If it weren't for the Life Magic-enhanced vision, she wouldn't be able to make the ghost out at all in the darkness.

"So… have you told him?" Tess had a mischievous grin.

"By the Giants, do you have no sense of propriety?" Sera shot Ora a panicked glance. He was still talking with Hohan.

Tess laughed. "My daddy used to say, if the fish aren't biting, change the lure."

"Are you lonely, or did you just come to torment me?"

Tess flashed out of sight as Gverth dropped back to the packhorse in front of her. He fished some food out and headed back up to Hohan and Ora. Tess popped back next to Sera and took her free hand in hers.

"Dearest niece, I worry about you." Tess smiled and acted like they were out for a stroll.

Sera shook their hands gently and gave her aunt's hand a squeeze. "You've never explained how you can touch me, but nothing else." Her spectral hand felt like wood wrapped in wool, since she wasn't actually tangible.

Tess frowned. "It has to do with our bond. It's the same conduit that allows you to use the spectral abilities. I can't really explain it beyond saying, you are what tethers me to this world."

That surprised Sera. "You mean I've somehow trapped you here?"

Tess laughed again. "No, sweetie. It means I want to help you like I did your mother."

Sera stopped suddenly. "What do you mean, you helped my mother? What did you help Mother with, specifically?"

Tess glanced at the retreating group. "Your friends are leaving."

"I can catch up. Spit it out. What did you and Mother do, and how did you help her?"

"At least keep walking so they don't get suspicious."

Sera started walking but didn't let go of Tess's hand.

"When your mother was young, before she met your father, she decided to hop on one of your grandfather's merchant ships bound for the island of Ebraipia. Along the way, pirates attacked them."

"Hold on, you're telling me my mother left Grules and pirates attacked them?" Sera's mind was awhirl. "My mother? The one who wouldn't step out of the house with a hair out of place?"

"Yes. While they held her, I showed her the basics of the spectral abilities. I was afraid of what the pirates might try to do to her." Tess had a fierce expression. "I showed her the ice knife."

She glanced at Sera and there was sadness in that look. "They came for her that night. Two of the pirates. One stood watch at the door while the other tried to get your mother's dress off. I made myself visible and screamed. It's one of the things I can do. I can use the Scream of the Damned. It stunned both men long enough for your mother to conjure the ice knife and cut both of their throats."

Sera walked in silence for a bit. It was a lot to take in. While stern, her mother had always been caring and, to her knowledge, had never killed so much as a mouse.

Hoarsely, Sera asked, "Then what happened?"

"My scream awakened the entire ship. The other pirates burst into the room and saw what was happening." Tess smiled grimly. "While pirates, these ones had a code about women and children."

She patted Sera's hand. "They set your mother ashore at the next port and left with all the wool she'd brought to sell." Tess giggled. "Your mother had to work as a serving girl at the local inn to make enough money for the voyage back to Grules."

"She did what?"

Tess popped out of sight.

"Is everything all right?" asked Hohan, coming back to her with Ora and Gverth.

Giants take that ghost, I must have said that last part too loudly.

She spent a couple minutes reassuring the group that she was, in fact, fine and just talking with herself, working on the plan for the contract.

"Go on back to leading the group." She smiled at the trio and really appreciated their concern for her.

As soon as they were back and leading the other horses, Tess reappeared.

"So how long have you been…" Sera waved her hand.

"Helping the members of my family?" Tess asked. "That really is a story for another time."

Sera heard a sound behind her and turned to see what it was. Mayomi walked up the trail behind them and must have kicked a stone. She drew even with Sera and Tess.

"Sera." Mayomi slightly bowed her head. Then she looked right at the spectral figure. "Tess." And inclined her head again.

To Sera's surprise, Tess returned the gesture and greeting. "Mayomi."

Mayomi sped up and returned to the front of the small caravan.

Wide-eyed, Sera looked at Tess.

Tess just shrugged. "We've talked."

CHAPTER THIRTY-FOUR

ORA EARL

As the sun rose behind him, Ora shifted in the rocks opposite the camp. He looked for a better vantage point of the Gnoll camp where it sat at the base of a hundred-foot tall bluff. It was comprised of a tower and three smaller buildings, all constructed of rough logs and looked as if they had been built in a hurry or by someone who didn't care about permanence.

With his enhanced vision he could make out a sentry in the tower—who appeared to be sleeping—and three Gnolls by the fire. They sat on stools made from sections of a larger log. Crude and practical at the same time. They were turning some small game on a spit over the fire.

Their language carried on the wind. It was a series of yips and yowls and sounded like puppies playing.

Ora looked to where Sera and Gverth were positioned off to his right. Sera watched him. He held up four fingers. Then he held up three and made a motion of eating. Then he held up one finger, pointed upwards, and held his hands like he was sleeping.

Sera nodded.

She pointed at Ora and made the motion of eating. She pointed at Gverth, then pointed up.

Ora nodded and whispered to Hohan, "We're going after the three eating. Gverth will take the tower."

"This will be a good day." Hohan prayed, "Enki, give me strength to make it through this day."

Sera waved, and they moved out from behind the boulder they had been using for concealment.

"Let's go." Ora stepped out and trotted to the camp. He didn't want to move too fast lest his armor jingle and give him away. He also didn't want to move too slowly and risk getting caught in the open.

A yip sounded from the tower.

The guard had been faking!

Four Gnoll archers rose on the bluff and pulled back on their bowstrings.

"Ambush! Get to the buildings," Sera yelled.

The tower exploded in a wreath of fire. "Got it!" Gverth yelled as he sped to the buildings.

They all poured on the speed. Ora fed energy into his legs and sprinted ahead of the group. Their rush to the buildings threw off the aim of the archers, and the first volley of arrows fell well behind them.

The Gnolls pulled arrows back for another shot. They were so focused on Ora they didn't notice the figure emerge from the brush behind them. The first sign that they had a problem came when Mayomi front kicked one Gnoll off the bluff. His scream caught all of them off guard.

Ora brought his attention to the Gnolls at the fire who pulled out weapons and charged the party. Hohan and Sera engaged two.

The Gnoll who came at Ora wore dark leather armor and wielded a sword and shield of surprising quality.

Ora shifted to the Gnoll's left, forcing him to fight over his own shield.

Ora had a blade in each hand, his longer blade in his right. Most people, regardless of race, fight with their left foot forward. This presents the defensive object, sword or shield, foremost to their opponents.

The Gnoll swiped with his long sword.

Ora parried with his short sword and stepped again to the Gnoll's left. This meant the Gnoll again had to step forward with his right leg. One more exchange and Ora stepped again to the Gnoll's left. The Gnoll made to swing again, this time pulling his shield back a bit to get a better angle on Ora.

That was the opening Ora had been looking for. He faked stepping right again but instead stepped into the swing. His sword rode the edge of the shield directly into the Gnoll's exposed thigh. The Gnoll howled. Ora pulled back with his right hip, creating a whipping motion as he pulled the long sword up and across the Gnoll's throat.

Sera had her Gnoll down. Hohan spun in a tight arc and brought his hammer up into the Gnoll he was fighting. That Gnoll tried to interpose his shield, but Hohan struck him solidly, sending the Gnoll flying backward to land on the blazing fire. The foul smell of burnt meat and singed hair inundated the camp.

The Gnoll howled and rolled off the fire, only to meet the sharp point of Sera's rapier.

Another scream from the cliff as another Gnoll dropped. Ora looked up in time to see Mayomi wielding her two blades as she fended off the last two opponents.

"Should we go help her?" Hohan asked.

"No. We won't get there in time." Ora watched as she blocked and moved back so they couldn't get on either side of her.

One Gnoll swiped with a sword. Mayomi just leaned back out of his reach and followed the weapon back in with a blade of her own. The third Gnoll went down.

She squared off against the last Gnoll just as an incandescent bolt from below took him square in the chest. That stunned him long enough for Mayomi to deliver a quick flurry of blows ending the fight. She waved a big, full-arm wave, then turned and ran into the brush.

"Is that all of them?" Sera looked around.

Gverth pointed to the building against the cliff face. "I thought I saw one go in there."

Hohan readied his hammer and yanked the door open. The building concealed the entrance to a tunnel. They all stepped into the building and looked down the passage. After a bit, their eyes adjusted to the dimness, and they could make out faint light on the tunnel's ceiling.

"What do you think is down there?" Hohan whispered.

"Only one way to find out." Sera looked at Ora. "Do we wait for Mayomi?"

Ora shook his head. "She can catch up. Besides, I don't want to give whatever's down there too much time to prepare." He looked at the others. "Are you ready?" Nods all around.

He headed into the tunnel. Someone yanked him off his feet and pressed him into the wall of the tunnel as a spear went past him and into the front wall of the building.

The Wlewoi held him pinned to the dirt wall with her forearm, her head turned, peering down the tunnel.

"Well, we definitely don't have to wait for Mayomi." Gverth laughed.

Mayomi met his gaze for a split second. "Your... um, Ora." She pulled a thin blade that was just smaller than a large nail from her vambrace and threw it into the tunnel. A yelp and the sound of feet retreated down the tunnel. "Shall we?"

With a last look at the spear still vibrating in the back wall, Ora stepped into the tunnel with a bit more caution. The tunnel headed straight and level into the bluff for about thirty yards, then turned to the left and sloped downward.

They peeked around the corner, but they could see nothing in the dimness. Ora cursed and pulled on his Shimmershield, putting a thumb on each of his eyelids. The tunnel brightened immediately. He looked at Mayomi.

"I can see just fine in here." Her pupils were round saucers of black.

"Ora," Sera whispered. He reached over and touched each of her eyelids. She smiled at him. "Thank you."

Now that he could see, there was an oddness in the rough-hewn wall just before the passage turned to the left. He quietly signed to the others to watch that spot and moved toward it.

Sera readied her spear about diaphragm height.

He stepped past the odd section.

A Gnoll leapt out at them with a sword in each hand. He yowled as he impaled himself on Sera's spear.

A quick sword thrust silenced him.

"I'm glad I spotted that." Ora wiped his blade on the Gnoll's hide armor.

Mayomi moved past Ora and Sera. "Let me scout ahead." She padded silently forward. When they caught up to her, she pointed down. "Trip cord."

If Ora didn't have enhanced vision, he wouldn't have been able to make it out. Even now, with Mayomi pointing directly at the line, he could barely see it. They each stepped gingerly over it. Ahead, the tunnel opened into a large space.

Mayomi crept forward along the left wall. Just before the threshold, she stopped and looked around. She held out a hand with all five fingers extended and waved for them to come up.

Gverth hissed, "When I yell 'apple,' close your eyes for a two-count and go."

They all murmured assent.

Ora readied himself for the charge.

"Apple!"

Even with his eyes squeezed shut, Ora could see a bright light passing the party and headed into the room. The flash burst even brighter, and a roar of flames preceded a hot rush of air. It was as if the door to a blast furnace had been opened, then it vanished.

"Go!" snapped Sera.

They charged into the room. The howls and screams of burning Gnolls filled the air. Ora moved toward a Gnoll that looked singed but otherwise still willing to fight. It bore the same sort of high-quality sword and shield.

The Gnoll blocked Ora's first two attacks but didn't expect a fast wrist-twist that brought the back edge of his long sword slicing across the top of the Gnoll's chest. It split the hide armor and bit deep into its chest, sending out a spray of blood.

The Gnoll snarled and tried to swing its sword, but the wound prevented an effective attack.

Ora easily blocked the attack with his short sword. Frustrated, the Gnoll pressed his shield into Ora and stretched his neck out to bite Ora's upper arm. A fang left a nasty gash where the armor didn't quite cover his bicep.

In response, Ora stabbed the Gnoll in the side of the neck with his short sword. It easily slid into the flesh. Ora stepped back and pulled down. The motion opened the Gnoll's throat in a fountain of blood. Ora looked for the next opponent.

Hohan's hammer flashed in the cavern light, a blue hue surrounding it as he struck the Gnoll he was fighting. A minor pop accompanied the crunch of bone, and the Gnoll fell to the ground.

Ora moved toward Sera, who was fighting the largest Gnoll he had ever seen. Her spear blazed with green, spectral flame, and she thrust it neatly past the he Gnoll's guard into its chest. The spearhead erupted, pouring green flame into his chest, causing the Gnoll to howl.

In a flash, it struck out with its glaive, but Sera sidestepped the strike.

Ora stepped up, and the Gnoll surprised him when it swung the glaive at him, not Sera. Fortunately, he'd had his blades up and managed to block the strike.

Sera twisted her spear deeper through the Gnoll's hide.

"Pir," sounded behind them, and a bright bolt of flame intersected with the Gnoll's head, flash-frying its eyeballs, causing both of them to pop, spraying super-heated fluid into the air. It screamed hideously, lungs crisping from the fire, and slumped to the ground, dead.

Sera looked for another opponent, but all the Gnolls were dead. She noticed blood trickling from the wound on Ora's arm. "You're wounded?"

Ora looked down at his arm. "Can you believe one of them actually bit me?"

"Hey, there's some cells over here," Hohan called from the far corner. He held a blanket aside that revealed another passageway. The group moved over, and Sera followed Hohan into the passage.

The Gnolls had bolted iron bars to the rock across a narrow section of the tunnel, held closed by a chain with a crude lock. Inside were two figures.

"Are there keys somewhere?" Sera asked, looking back at the bodies. A sharp, metallic crunch caused her to whip her head back to the passage.

Hohan grinned and shook his hammer. "I have a key right here."

CHAPTER THIRTY-FIVE

SANKARA MURCHALA

Sankara and Rajan mounted the stone steps of the keep to the main hall where Lavinia had set up her operations. She'd removed the once-lavish decor and replaced it with functional furniture and a large, sturdy table from the servant's hall.

That surprised Sankara.

I would have figured a woman like her would be in love with the comforts of life, he thought. He shook his head. *I wonder what she wants from me today.*

Since he had chastised her, she had not wanted to be in his presence much. She was meeting with some of the unorthodox soldiers that reported to her as he approached. He overheard their conversation.

Sankara and Rajan reached her door, and he overheard her talking with one of the soldiers who reported to her.

"The ambush failed, and we lost communications with the prison," one man reported.

Sankara entered just in time to see Lavinia stab a dagger into her table. It stood there, quivering from the force.

The man looked at it, then back at her.

"What is this about a prison?" asked Sankara.

Lavinia looked over at him like he had just spilled a drink on her favorite carpet. "Lord Houshkulu's dealings aren't your concern." She handed him a piece of paper. "You need to concern yourself with the mounted patrol that is headed to the castle where your staff are encamped." She waited a moment. "You can leave."

Sankara raised an eyebrow at her tone and deliberately took his time looking over what she had given him. It was a rough sketch of the roads between Ricsigbury and the surrounding villages. Someone had marked the map with several squares, and an arrow pointed to the castle. Notes in the margin gave a rough timetable of advance.

Sankara smiled at her. "Thank you for the information."

He handed the paper to Rajan and left the table. When they were midway down the stairs, he turned to Rajan. "We need to be careful. Every time I talk to her, I trust them less and less."

CHAPTER THIRTY-SIX

SERA DEMOTT

The two prisoners were a swarthy Human man and a Delver. They looked like they hadn't eaten for days, and blood and dirt covered them.

While Ora and Hohan tended to the wounds of the freed prisoners, Sera handed out bread, cheese, and sausage. "Eat slowly," she cautioned.

Gverth set up a pot over the fire to make a broth. He put in a packet of herbs and mushrooms. While it heated, he retrieved cups from the packs.

Once everyone settled and they had posted the watch, Sera pointed at the Human man with dark hair and skin. He had the weathered look of a man who lived and worked outdoors. "Who are you?"

"My name is Staveros." His accent was thick. "I am from Nuradasar on the Amaranth coast."

The party looked at each other in confusion.

"And where is Amaranth?" asked Sera.

Staveros's eyes narrowed. "You've never heard of it?" He sighed. "I must be very far from home indeed."

"It's all right." Gverth handed him a cup of the broth. "Drakanon is a big place."

"Drakanon?" Staveros blinked. "Are we in the Empire?"

Sera looked at the others, then back at Staveros. "Please tell us your story."

"My business partners and I bring goods from all over." He sipped his drink. "We market in rare goods, supplies, wine, weapons, and... other items."

"Other items?"

"It was the other items that put me in this predicament. Simi, my right-hand man, brought me a contract to get some items from a nuraghi in a remote area of the Kolyvan Mountains. There wasn't anything unusual about that request. We sent expeditions and buying parties all over the place, including challenging places like that."

He shrugged. "This request was problematic. It was in an area few can get to and took someone of my particular skills."

"What happened?"

"That bitch—" He looked up quickly. "I mean no offense to yourself."

Sera waved a hand. "I've heard worse. And I promise you, you will know if you offend me. Please, continue."

"Ah, right. So this woman gave us the specific details and the location for what we needed to retrieve. Seemed pretty reasonable. Go to a spot, get the items, bring them back." He held up a finger. "Where I got suspicious was in how hard Simi pushed for us to take the contract."

Gverth leaned forward. "You think Simi was setting you up?"

"I did. And later I found out he was, but that was after I had obtained the items they wanted." He glanced nervously at Mayomi as she patrolled the perimeter. "Does she have to keep moving?"

Sera glanced from Staveros to Mayomi and back. "She's one of the people who helped free you. What's your issue with her?"

"Where I come from, cats like that eat people."

Mayomi stopped for a moment. "Here too." She gave him a toothy grin, then kept moving and watching for any threats.

The exchange amused Ora, but he wanted to nip any prejudice in the bud. "Friend Staveros, here, the Wlewoi—" he pointed at Mayomi "—are an honorable people. They have a great capacity for violence that is only eclipsed by their compassion for other beings."

Staveros shook his head and turned to address Mayomi. "I apologize if I've offended."

"I took no offense." She chuffed. "This time."

"I have to admit that I wouldn't be here if a Human hadn't betrayed me." Staveros looked deep into his cup before taking another drink. "And that is the story you want to hear. When I got back from the expedition, I hid the items before I met with that bi—strange woman. There was something about her I didn't trust."

"What was strange about her?"

"She had weird eyes, and I've never seen anyone with ears so pointed."

"Pointed?" Ora looked at Sera, then back. "An Elf?"

"A what?"

"You don't have Elves where you come from?"

"Never heard of them." He shrugged. "All I know is that during the meeting, they poisoned me with a dart to my neck."

Ora touched the spot where the dart had struck him on the neck. He met Sera's eyes for a moment before focusing on Staveros again.

"I woke up tied to a chair," said Staveros. "The... Elf was there, as was Simi. She killed him when he failed to hand over the items. Serves the barnacle right." He spat into the fire. "The Elf tried to get the location of the items out of me, but couldn't. So she had me crippled with symmajea."

He pointed to his right eyelid. They all leaned in close and could see a spiderweb thin pattern inked onto the tender flesh there.

Gverth gasped. "They used Line Magic on you against your will? What does it do?"

"It drains my magic." Staveros's shoulders slumped, defeated.

"Can it be removed?" Sera asked.

"I don't know how."

"What about Shimmershield?" Sera looked to Ora.

"I can try." Ora moved over to Staveros. "Close your eyes. I need to touch you."

Staveros obeyed.

Ora touched his fingertip to the lid and let the Life Magic flow into it. He pulled his hand away quickly. Staveros opened his eyes.

Ora sat back. "It sucks magic. It sucked all the Life Magic I used for the probe and pulled more out of me. If there is a way to remove it, I don't know it."

Staveros nodded and looked at his hands.

"That doesn't mean it can't be done. It just means we don't know how."

"Maybe Master Te'zla would know?" Gverth asked. "We can ask when we get to Draco."

Hohan poured more broth for Staveros. "Drink. So what happened next in your tale?"

"They tattooed me and told me as soon as I gave the items to them, they would remove the magic and restore my abilities." He crossed his arms across his chest. "I told them they could jump into the ocean."

"Good man," said the priest.

Staveros shrugged. "The Elf didn't like that and beat me. For a little thing, she was very strong. They beat me until they got bored, then they said they'd send me someplace for me to think through my options and come to the right conclusion. I woke up here." He waved his hand. "Wherever here is."

"The Kingdom of Eshita," said Gverth.

"Wherever *that* is."

Ora glanced at Sera, then she asked Staveros, "How long ago was that?"

"I don't know."

The Delver they rescued spoke up. His voice was rich and deep. "They brought him in three months ago."

"Three months," Staveros breathed. "They had me for a month before here."

Ora put a hand on the man's shoulder in sympathy. "What about the items? What did they send you to get?"

Staveros shrugged. "A box, a rod, and a coin. They were hidden in a secret chamber in the nuraghi."

The four members of the band exchanged glances.

Gverth asked, "What kind of coin?"

Staveros held his thumb and forefinger two inches apart. "It was about this big and made of a strange metal. One side had two runes I've never seen surrounded by a laurel wreath. The other showed a sapphire scroll."

Sera shifted on the ground. "And this Elf wanted it?"

"She said her master wanted it. She never mentioned who that was."

Sera turned to the Delver and refilled his broth. "How about you? What's your name and where are you from?"

"My name is Konungr. I am the leader of the Dragon's Reach Delvers." He pointed at Ora's sword. "My people made that sword. I can tell from the hilt." He glanced at Sera's rapier. "And probably that. May I see the blade?"

Sera pulled her sword part way out of the scabbard.

Konungr nodded. "Very nice work, but not one of mine."

"No, I have a guy in Draco. He's from Stuitor." Sera returned the blade to the scabbard. "Why were you locked in that cage, Master Konungr?"

"Please, just Konungr among my friends." He smiled at her and raised his mug. "It isn't Fire but, thank you for rescuing me."

Hohan laughed and clapped the Delver on the shoulder. "I have some, if you want to make a proper toast." He brought out an ornate flask. Sera raised her eyebrows. Hohan shrugged. "Aaron had one he was willing to part with."

Konungr stood abruptly. "Aaron Olufsen? My height with light hair and blue eyes like mine?"

"Yes, that's him." Hohan extended the flask to Konungr, who grasped it. "Do you know him?"

Konungr scrutinized it. When he looked up, his eyes were moist. "He's my brother." Konungr uncapped the flask and held it up. "You honor me. By the Giants' grace."

They quickly passed it to each person, who toasted in response.

"Aaron and I have the same father," said Konungr. "I haven't seen him in a long time. He was going to head east to meet Elves."

"He handles our equipment needs," Sera explained. She told him about the armor and goods shop Aaron ran in Draco.

"Good for him." Konungr nodded and examined the party. He smiled. "I can see his handiwork in some of your armor. It also explains how Ora possesses one of our blades. I assume you got it from him?"

Ora shifted uncomfortably. "It's a lot older than that." He unclipped the scabbard from his belt and handed it to Konungr.

Konungr pulled the blade to examine the maker's mark. When he saw it, his eyes widened. "How did you come by a blade made by Eldor Jorvarsson? I've only seen two in my lifetime. He was a master bladesmith in the time of the Demon War."

"It was a gift," Ora said.

Konungr admired the blade for a minute longer, then handed it back to Ora. "That was a princely gift. As talented as my people are, they don't make blades like Eldor Jorvarsson did." He sighed. "Not anymore."

"Konungr, how did you end up in that prison?" Sera asked again.

Konungr took a long pull of the broth in preparation to tell his story. "We'd just finished celebrating my wife's life day. In our culture, we celebrate the day you turn into an adult. The tables were being cleared, and the deep watch was changing out. My wife had already headed to bed, so I stopped to talk with the watch captain. The next thing I know, I'm waking up in prison. I'm not sure what happened or how I got there."

Ora leaned forward. "Your people didn't help?"

"For over two thousand years, my people have populated Dragon's Reach. To the outside world, it appears to be nothing more than a keep against the side of the mountain. It is a carved community through the mountain to the other side of the range. In the past, Dragon's Reach was home to thousands of Delvers. Unfortunately, my people had to abandon the far side because of dragons."

He looked over at Hohan. "Could I have another nip of Fire?"

Hohan passed the flask.

"So, in thinking about how they took me, the intruders had to have come from the other side of the mountain. My people would not have let them inside." He returned the flask to Hohan. "Thank you."

"How far is it from here to Dragon's Reach?" Gverth asked.

"I'm not exactly sure where *here* is."

"Ah, right." Gverth flushed in embarrassment and fished in his pocket for the cloth map. He crouched down next to Konungr and spread the map out. He touched a point on the map. "We're here."

Konungr looked at the map, reoriented it, and rubbed his chin with one hand. "I think Dragon's Reach is three days north of here." He traced a line along the map toward the mountains. He looked up at the group. "It's been a long time since I've been home, and I'm sure my wife must be worried, as well as my family. I'd be grateful if you could help me get there."

Sera looked at the group. "Well, we wanted to get out of Draco for a while. Who wants to go see a magnificent Delvers' hall?"

Nods all around.

"That's settled then." She glanced at Ora and Hohan. "What did you two get out of the caves? Anything these two can use?"

When they had laid out everything, Konungr picked up one of the nicer blades. "I don't recognize this maker's mark." He sniffed the blade. Then he tasted it with his tongue. A sour look crossed his face. "I don't know where they got the metal for this, but it wasn't anywhere on this half of the continent."

"How can you tell?" Gverth asked.

"The metallurgy is all wrong. Iron from our mountains will have different minerals in it than, say, iron from Stuitor or even up in Gardshom." He flexed the blade. It bent pretty far and returned to straight after. "They made it well, though."

"Well, pick one. It isn't safe, well... anywhere." Sera pointed at the selection.

Staveros picked one up and a couple of daggers that looked to be from the same maker.

"What is that?" Sera pointed at a small, gray orb.

"Not sure. It was with the Gnoll leader." Hohan picked it up and handed it to her.

She looked it over and handed it to Gverth. He closed his eyes, then quickly dropped it.

He had a disgusted look on his face. "It is some kind of magic that uses life to power it."

"Is it dangerous?" Sera looked at the sphere where it lay on the blanket.

"I don't know, but I sure don't want to use it."

"How about you hold on to it, and we can ask Te'zla in Draco."

He sighed and picked it up. "Very well, but I have a bad feeling about it."

CHAPTER THIRTY-SEVEN

SANKARA MURCHALA

T he scout rode down the road and pulled up in front of Sankara. "They are approaching, Commander."

They stood at the edge of the forest, the early morning sun at their back. It was cool now, but the humidity in the air promised it would be very warm in the afternoon.

Several hundred yards down the road, the Eshitan troops advanced along the road. He could make out a square of armored foot soldiers, each carrying a spear and shield with strange ornamentation on it.

"How many of them are there?" Sankara squinted trying to count them.

"Fifty-foot, two mounted, Commander," the scout replied. "We didn't see any cavalry."

Sankara swatted at a horsefly. "No cavalry? Strange indeed." He turned to his artillerist. He was responsible for both normal and magical ranged attacks. "Manoj, tell the archers to engage them as they come into the clearing."

It impressed Sankara with how accurate Lavinia's information was. He was able to time the enemy's movements almost perfectly. Like shooting sheep in an enclosure. The launch of arrows resembled the sound of a swarm of angry bees, only this sting was more potent. From his vantage point, Sankara could tell that this Eshitan patrol was heavier than anything that they had encountered before.

A translucent barrier went up in front of the advancing troops. Sankara cursed. *Kurioi.* He knew he would eventually run into magic. He turned in his saddle. "Rajan, please kill their magicians."

"Yes, Commander. We will release the iratta vattukal."

Rajan turned his horse and shouted orders. Wooden crates were brought forward and set on the ground in front of Sankara's forces. The soldiers opened the end of the crate facing the enemy troops. Small, birdlike creatures darted forward toward the enemy. Sankara thanked the Giants that only two of the iratta vattukal, the blood ducks, turned toward his troops. The rest could smell the magic being used by the Eshitans down the road. The handlers quickly caught the two strays before they could reach either of the two kurioi in his troop. While a single iratta vattukal's venom wasn't lethal, two could kill a grown man.

The rest of the little creatures waddled forward, then took flight. These were stealth predators and thus didn't fly straight at their prey. The blood ducks were very useful on raids. Sankara waited patiently in the shade. The amount of magic the enemy was using would be like a cool, shaded pool to a man walking through the desert.

Sankara's troops kept shooting arrows at the Eshitan shield. It didn't take long before one of the blood ducks must have taken down a kurioi and the first shield collapsed. An arrow hit one of their soldiers.

There were commotions in the Eshitan ranks, and the rest of the shields fell. The pace of Kinderkesh arrows increased now that they were being effective, and Eshitan troops died.

"Excellent, send in the cavalry." Sankara wondered how the Eshitan would hold up against his raiders. His were experienced mountain troops used to fighting ground forces. Horse archers and lancers.

Sankara watched as the enemy brought pikemen forward to meet his cavalry. He admired their tactics, but they had never fought troops like his. Still, too many Kinderkesh soldiers didn't survive the charge. Those were his men that would never come back. Holes opened in the Eshita lines as the Kinderkesh shredded the opposing troops. A blast of fire erupted into the Kinderkesh raiders from one of the Eshitan kurioi. Several horses scattered, the riders trailing smoke.

Sankara sighed. "Commit the reserves." He hoped the iratta vattukal found that kurios before they could do too much damage.

* * *

It took another hour before the fight was over. Sankara walked the field hospital, checking on his wounded soldiers. This one skirmish took more of his soldiers' lives than everything they had done so far in this land.

Rajan rode up and dismounted. "Commander, we have captured several of their soldiers, but the two on horses got away."

Sankara knew it was only a matter of time before news of their invasion would spread. He looked out over the wounded. His kurioi tended as best they could, but they could not heal all wounds.

"Rajan, I need you to move the prisoners to our west staging area. I don't want Lavinia or her troops to get their hands on them." Sankara knew the men's lives would be forfeit if she got them.

CHAPTER THIRTY-EIGHT

ORA EARL

They made good time heading away from the Gnoll prison. They made camp and took care of the horses. It was Ora's turn to cook, and he handed them bowls of steaming meat. The aroma of herbs and a light spice drifted up from the spits and the bowls. Sera sat next to Staveros as they ate some of the wild game Mayomi had caught.

"I never asked you what you wanted to do, Staveros." Sera took a long drink of water.

He shrugged. "Find the bitch who did this to me and kill her?" He shrugged again. "Yeah, I'm not sure how to make that happen either." Bitterness edged his voice. "I don't really have many options right now. I'm far from home and not in the position to make demands. Especially from the people who released me." He frowned. "As long as you think I'm useful, I'm happy our paths go in the same direction."

He looked down at his uneaten stew for a moment. When he looked up, Ora could see a fire in his eyes. "If you can help me get revenge, I'd be in your debt."

Ora spoke up, "If it's in our power to help you get home, we will."

Sera looked serious. "Revenge, however, will cost you."

Staveros gazed into her eyes for a long moment, then nodded. "Fair enough. We can talk price when we get there."

The other members of the group sat down next to the pair and passed out bread. Ora handed each of them a bowl.

"Konungr was telling us about the mead they make at Dragon's Reach." Gverth seemed excited about the drink.

"They make it from different things," Hohan explained.

Konungr took a seat opposite of Sera. "We have barrels of mead, and beer, and casks of Fire." His eyes stared off into the distance with the memories.

"Master Konungr, I mean no offense, but I have to know." Gverth's eyes were bright. Ora knew that whenever Gverth started off with "no offense," he was about to insult the person, argue with them, or do both. Konungr waved for him to continue. "Delvers are renowned for making the strongest steel and mightiest weapons."

"They are." Konungr nodded.

"Then why haven't you killed the dragons that drove you from your home?" Gverth looked at him eagerly.

Konungr sat still for a long moment. Ora wondered how grave the insult was. It surprised everyone when Konungr tipped his head back and roared with laughter. When Konungr recovered enough to look at the man and saw the look of confusion, it set off fresh peals of laughter. Konungr held his sides. When he settled down enough—though still chuckling—he wiped away a laugh-tear. It took several moments for him to catch his breath.

"Forgive me, Master Konungr. I don't understand your mirth." Gverth seemed almost hurt by the exchange.

Ora shook his head at the pair in wonder.

Konungr took a deep breath before speaking. "You can have the sharpest sword made from the finest steel. If you don't have the tallest arm, you won't reach the top shelf." He giggled. They all stared at him blankly. He looked around and their expressions sobered him. "You've never heard that, eh?" He scratched his chin. "How about this: if you don't have the ability to kill a dragon, the best weapons won't make a difference. Is that better?"

"I think I understand." Hohan shifted on the log they were using as a bench. "You can't kill the dragons, so why go die trying?"

"Something very close to that." Konungr wiped another tear away. "Oh, I haven't laughed like that in a long time." He took a drink from his mug. "One dragon is hard to kill."

"Oh I know," Ora muttered. Too late, he realized he said it loud enough to be heard as the others just stared at him with a mix of expressions from admiration to raw curiosity. His face grew hot. "Please continue."

"Konungr, what have you tried to do to get rid of them?" Hohan asked.

"We tried to fight them. That was fruitless. They are huge, we are not. We tried to poison them. Instead, *we* got sick. We tried to smoke them out, but the wind was not in our favor." Konungr scratched his beard. "We tried to get one of the erkurios to use Love Magic to make them afraid of the space." He frowned. "They ate her." He shrugged. "We stay on our side. They can't really come down the main passage since it's too narrow, and we try to be outside during mating season." He made a face. "The noise is hideous."

"But you think the people who took you came from that side?" Ora asked.

"It seems to be the only explanation. Any other could only happen with a Delver's help. No one in my clan would betray me like that." Konungr put his hands on his knees and glared at everyone, daring them to disagree with him.

"You said the passage goes through the mountain range?" Gverth asked. "What is on the other side? Is that Eshita?"

Konungr nodded. "Excellent. You know your maps. We used to have a thriving trade with the barons on that side. But that has been gone for a while now."

"How long?" Sera asked.

Konungr squinted. Ora could tell he was trying to calculate how long ago it was. "It was during the previous High King's reign. So what? Forty years?"

Gverth scoffed. "That would have been two High Kings ago."

Konungr looked abashed. "Ah sorry, after three hundred years, all the kings are about the same to me. Not one has been to visit our hall since Ora the Lightbringer himself came and they had the big celebration and presented him with gifts..." he fell silent, thinking, then shot Ora a sidelong glance.

Ora's heart hammered in his chest. It was at that celebration that Eldor Jorvarsson had given Ora his sword. *I knew I shouldn't have taken my old sword with me,* Ora thought.

Ora relaxed when Konungr shook his head and looked back at the assembled group.

"I would love to show you around my home. The people are so vibrant and full of life. They will throw us a feast and there will be singing and dancing." Konungr smiled as he conjured up the fantasy of his homecoming.

CHAPTER THIRTY-NINE

SANKARA MURCHALA

Sankara mounted the stone stairs to Lavinia's room. "Lavinia, I need to speak with Lord Houshkulu."

She glanced at him in annoyance. He could see the emotions ripple across her face like a kaleidoscope.

"Fine," she said.

Her acquiescence surprised him. Sankara had come prepared for an argument.

She snapped her finger at a servant along the wall. "Bring me…" She glanced at Sankara. "… a goat."

The servant left at a trot. He returned shortly leading a decently sized male goat.

She reached into a pouch and withdrew a gray sphere made of something Sankara didn't recognize. She put her hand on the goat's head and spoke. *"Tloqai."*

Houshkulu's voice reverberated in the room, and the sphere pulsed with a purple light. "Lavinia, how may I be of service?"

"Lord Houshkulu, Sankara would like to speak with you."

"Commander, how are you liking your new lands?" Houshkulu asked in a warm and friendly tone.

Sankara glanced at Lavinia. She gestured to the stone. He leaned forward. "We have conquered a number of the baronies. As you said, they weren't much of a fight. However, today was different. The troops we encountered today were surprisingly capable, and a group got away. I need more troops as this is going to get more complicated. I need to speak with my uncle. He can get me what I need without involving my father, the prince."

There was a pause before Houshkulu spoke. "I'll get you back to Amaranth. Meet me in Wyrmhome. Lavinia, I need to see you too. Please escort our commander to the thuros."

"Yes, my lord."

The stone she held went still. Sankara glanced at the body of the goat. It looked as if it had shriveled like a raisin, and purple steam rose off it.

CHAPTER FORTY

ORA EARL

I t's just over the next rise!" Konungr kicked his heels into the horse's sides to urge it to a faster pace. The last three days on the road had been fairly uneventful.

Ora pushed his horse up next to Sera's. "I'll be glad when we reach Dragon's Reach. I have this growing—"

"Sense we are going to get jumped?" Sera finished the thought. Ora regarded her in surprise. She winked at him. "We all feel it."

"Just remember that Dragon's Reach isn't safe."

It was Sera's turn for surprise. "What do you mean?"

"They took Konungr, leader of his people, out of there against his will." Ora shifted in the saddle to see where the others were. "It wouldn't surprise me if it was the Gorgon."

"That again?" Sera scoffed.

They crested the ridge and found the rest of the group stopped. Before them was a grand view of the valley that spread before Dragon's Reach. Immense twin towers rose on either side of a massive gate.

Konungr pointed proudly. "My friends, this is my home. I welcome you."

The group rode down into the valley. As they rode closer to the fortress, they could see dragons riding the currents. Ora thought they must be far away until one dropped and landed on the crenellation of the upper wall.

"Konungr, are those baby dragons?" Ora asked, pointing.

Konungr squinted at the sky. "Ah, no. Those are draconettes. They don't get bigger than the average house cat or small dog."

Almost as if they heard the party talking about them, a few of them flew over to check them out. The creatures looked very much like miniature dragons and sported many colors of scale: blues, browns, and reds. They swooped down to circle the party.

"They are curious. But be careful they—" one landed on Ora's right shoulder "—hate people."

Konungr gaped in disbelief.

Ora immediately raised his arm like you would for a falcon. The draconette scrambled to his elbow and perched there, wings folded in.

It examined each of them with large, curious eyes. Its scales were a vibrant red that scintillated in the sunlight as it moved. The scales over its belly were cream, almost white.

Ora reached his left hand out, and the draconette rubbed its snout against his hand. It looked at Ora and chirped.

"I have never seen the like," Konungr said softly.

The draconette climbed back up to Ora's shoulder. He was thankful he had his armor on when he felt the creature dig its claws in to steady itself. He almost jumped when the draconette laid its head on top of his.

"What's it doing?" he asked.

Konungr shook his head. "I do not know."

"It's so cute." Sera smiled. "I think it's claimed you."

Another draconette flew past, giving a screech like a hawk as it went by. The draconette on Ora's shoulder chirped. Ora jumped a bit, and it leapt from his shoulder and took flight.

"Are you all right?" Sera moved her horse closer.

"Yeah, it licked my ear." Ora shuddered. "That was weird."

"Truly amazing." Konungr shook his head. "In my three centuries, I've never seen them come to a person." He looked wistfully at the draconettes riding the air currents.

"What are you going to name it?" Sera teased.

"Chirp," Ora declared. Everyone chuckled.

As they approached the gates, Ora could see the Delver soldiers moving and forming up ranks. Clearly, they hadn't been expecting any visitors.

Konungr moved his horse ahead of the group.

The gate guard shouted, "Hold where you are!" The assembled troop leveled crossbows at the group.

Konungr cocked his head, eyes narrowed. "It's me. Konungr. I have returned."

The guards looked at each other. One yelled back, "Konungr's dead."

Konungr dismounted, held his arms out, and slowly approached the guards. Everyone kept their crossbows leveled at the party.

Sera hissed to the group, "Keep your hands away from your weapons. I don't know what's going on here, but let Konungr figure it out."

One guard yelled, "Stop right there. Or, we *will* fire."

Konungr stopped. "Sven, it's me. We grew up together. You know me."

Another guard yelled, "It's a trick! Has to be. He's using magic."

Ora dismounted, holding his hands out to show he had no weapon, and slowly advanced forward. Once he got even with Konungr, he yelled to the gate guards, "If you think he's not Konungr, then ask him a question only Konungr would know."

Konungr nodded and said quietly, "That's a good one. Ask your question."

Sven stepped up. "If you're Konungr, then what's my sister's name?"

Konungr straightened his shoulders and yelled back, "How is Esmeralda? Has she forgiven me yet?"

Sven threw his head back and roared with laughter. "No, she has not." Everyone relaxed.

Ora sighed with some relief. "What did you do to his sister?"

Konungr gave Ora a wry grin. "I married someone else."

Ora laughed. "Fair enough."

Sven bounded down the stairs and caught Konungr in a big hug. "Where have you been?"

"Sven, that is a very long story, but the short version is that someone kidnapped me." Konungr turned to the party. "These are my friends. They have returned me home. Please welcome them."

Sven turned to the party and bowed slightly. "Thank you for bringing him back. And welcome to the hospitality of Dragon's Reach. Such that it is these days."

Ora could tell that statement troubled Konungr. He followed the Delvers as they went up the stairs to enter the grand hall.

The roof extended at least eighty feet up, and it ran hundreds of paces long, so far they couldn't see its end. Ornately carved stone columns ran along each side. Quartz and amethyst within those columns reflected brilliant lightstones embedded in the ceiling.

The party stopped in wonder.

"By Enki," whispered Hohan.

"By the Giants!" added Gverth.

Inside, groomsmen came to take the horses, leading them off to stables along the right of the hall. Most of the guards resumed their posts.

Sven walked next to Konungr. "I have to tell you, things aren't the same these days. Ejvind took over while you were gone."

Konungr looked at him sharply. "Ejvind? What about my wife? Why didn't she take over?"

Sven looked uneasy. "I have to leave that tale for Ejvind."

Konungr's mouth set in an unamused, thin line. "Yes. Let's go find Ejvind. I want to know what's going on."

On the road to Dragon's Reach, Konungr had told them stories of frivolity, music, and a joyous life under the mountain. As the party looked around the hall, they saw none of that. The people that they saw moved quickly, eyes downcast, with barely a glance towards the strangers. Going out of their way to avoid any contact.

Hohan edged up next to Ora. "These people look defeated."

Ora nodded. "I was thinking something along those lines myself. I don't know what's going on, but I'm afraid we won't like it when we find out."

Hohan nodded and dropped back to walk next to Staveros.

They came to a smaller, thick double-door set into the wall at the far end of the great hall. The doors stood open, and the guards on either side quickly moved out of the way as they approached. Beyond was a passage into a series of smaller halls and passageways leading off deeper into the mountain.

They wound their way to the receiving hall. Massive tables ran down both sides of a fire pit running the length of the hall. Multicolored flame danced in the pit. Despite the flame, the logs still appeared freshly cut, as if the flame didn't touch the wood.

"A Delver's Hearth," Gverth whispered breathlessly. He glanced at Ora with shining eyes. "The flames provide latent heat, but don't consume the logs."

"You're right, lad," Konungr said with a smile.

Gverth murmured, "I wonder how it works." He took a step forward, and Ora hastily grabbed his shoulder, pulling him back.

"You can look at it later. Let's figure out what's going on here."

That seemed to bring Gverth back to himself and he glanced around the room. "Where are all the people?" The hall had seating for four hundred people easily, yet there were less than twenty people in the hall.

At the far end of the hall was the head table. Several Delvers set around it with the occasional servant coming to refill drinks or bring another tray of food. As the group trooped toward that table, a Delver stood up and rushed toward them, meeting them partway in the hall.

"Konungr, is that you? I can't believe it."

Konungr didn't bother with pleasantries. "Where's my family, Ejvind? Where's Katja, your sister, my wife?"

"They took them." Anguish painted Ejvind's face.

"What do you mean, they took them?" Konungr asked. "Taken by whom? Taken where?"

Ejvind turned away with his shoulders hunched. "Why did you leave us here? Just… We looked and couldn't find you. We searched and searched."

He turned to Konungr, eyes burning with intensity. "They came."

"What are you talking about? Who are *they*?" Konungr clenched and unclenched his fists.

"The Wergoi. They made a raid through the catacombs and into the hall. They killed several people and grabbed women and fled back into the depths."

Konungr rocked back in shock. "There haven't been Wergoi here in over a thousand years. Did you go after them?"

"We tried, but a force led by a strange blonde woman stopped us."

Staveros interjected. "Was she—what did you call her? An Elf? Tall, wearing black leathers, wielding a serpentine dagger?"

Ejvind's eyes widened in surprise. "How did you know about her?"

Everyone started talking over each other.

Ora got frustrated and raised his hands. He enhanced his voice and snapped, "Hold on, by the Giants! Stop talking."

The yelling stopped.

"You're right," said Konungr.

"Let's start with your family," said Ora.

Ejvind had a haunted look and wouldn't meet Konungr's eyes. "When you left…" He struggled to get the words out. "They told me… they would bring Katja to you. That you two would be together… that you were safe in another place."

"What do you mean? Who told you I left?" He took a step forward.

Ejvind started backing away.

"What have you done, Ejvind?" Konungr took a step forward and shouted, "What have you done?"

Ejvind turned and ran for a passage on the near side of the hall. "Guards!" he yelled.

Instantly, warriors in dark armor streamed out of the passage.

Ejvind pointed at the party. "Deal with them!" He ran into the passage.

The guards pulled weapons and gathered themselves for a charge.

Gverth stepped forward, raised his hand before anyone could say otherwise, and said, *"Pir."*

A ball of flame shot from his hand directly out into the massed guards and detonated with an earsplitting peal of thunder. Flames swirled around the guards, and to Gverth's astonishment, faded away.

Once the smoke and flames died away, the guards appeared to be untouched.

Ora snapped, "Gverth, they're mostly immune to magic. Mostly."

The guards tightened their line and advanced.

Konungr pulled a sword and hammer from his belt and looked at Sven. "Are you with me, or are you with them?"

Sven bowed his head. "Lord Konungr, I'm always with you."

Gverth snapped, "They may be immune to direct magic, but are they immune to this?" He pointed up at the ceiling and tightened his fist. Loud pops and sounds of shearing. He pulled his hand down sharply as if he were yanking something.

The ceiling above the guards exploded, and rocks fell onto the massed guards. Some leapt out of the way of the falling rocks, but at least half took hits and went down. Those who remained yelled and charged the group.

Hohan held up his hammer. "Enki, give me strength!" He stepped forward and met one guard with a hammer blow.

Ora gave himself strength, sidestepped a charging Delver, grabbed the back of the guard's armor, and yanked straight down, bouncing his head off the stone floor.

Sera pulled her rapier and lit it with spectral flame. She slashed at a guard, who ducked back and stumbled out of the way.

Konungr leapt onto a table and shouted, "I am your chieftain! Yield to me!"

Their only response was to swing a hammer at him. He quickly stepped aside as the hammer smashed into the table.

Ora caught the blade of another guard on his short sword. He slashed the guard's arm with his Delver-forged blade, neatly severing his arm at the bicep. The warrior shrieked, and Ora kicked him back into the guard behind him.

Sera beat aside an attack and skewered the guard in the neck. A violent green flash and a burning hole was all that was left of her opponent's throat.

Gverth stabbed fingers at the fallen stones and clenched his fist as if pulling. The stones flew into the back of the attacking guards. While not at a velocity to kill or incapacitate, the stones surprised the guards, giving Ora and the others the advantage.

Ora stepped in, pushed speed into his attacks, and slipped his long sword over the shield of one of the warriors just as Hohan backhanded his war hammer into the helmet of another.

Staveros made a spinning leap over another guard and brought his blade into the neck of the attacker behind him.

The guard he'd just leapt over turned to strike at Staveros, but Ora severed his arm at the elbow with a vicious chop of his short sword. The attacker's cry of pain was cut short when Staveros turned and stabbed him through the heart.

Breathing heavy, Ora looked for the next attacker, but they had all been overcome.

Konungr snapped, "Sven, what's going on?"

"Things haven't been the same since you left Konungr."

"By the Giants! I did *not* leave," Konungr huffed. "They took me. How many times do I have to say that?"

Sven surveyed the carnage with sadness. "But you weren't here. Once you were gone, Ejvind, the power-hungry, opportunistic weasel that he is, took control."

Konungr sighed. "I can see that."

"Yes. He'd always been jealous of your popularity. The stonemasons from the North Quarry all followed him. Without you here, they bullied the others into line to support Ejvind."

Gverth started picking through the bodies.

Sven pulled a bench out and sat down. "At first, everything Ejvind suggested was reasonable, but as time went on and his thugs showed up and you did not return, they became less reasonable."

"And now how are things?"

"There was a group still loyal to you who opposed Ejvind openly, but Ejvind's folk caught Bjarmi alone and killed him. His faction barricaded themselves into the emerald mines to get away from Ejvind. Others of us stayed to minimize the damage that Ejvind did. Please forgive me. I could not do more."

"How could you have known it would come to this?" Konungr grimly surveyed the aftermath of the fight. "You couldn't have expected that Ejvind would go this far and attack his own brother-in-law."

Sven hung his head.

Konungr put his hand on Sven's shoulder. "None of that, old friend. We have work to do."

"Ora." Gverth pulled aside a cloak from one of the dead Delver. "Look at their armor."

Ora leaned down to the body at his feet. They wore the same intricate armor they'd sold to Aaron. "Interesting."

"What?" asked Konungr. He and Sven came over.

Sven kicked the bodies of those they'd just slain. "I don't know where these Delvers came from. No clan markings. And this Elf-styled armor. Do you recognize any of these folk?"

Konungr looked at them. "No."

Gverth pulled a medallion off one body and held it up. "What is this?"

"Wergoi!" snapped Konungr. "And they followed Ejvind's commands."

"By the Giants!" Sven was shocked. "Wergoi in league with Ejvind?"

"Who are these Wergoi you're talking about?" Sera looked at the body. She couldn't see a difference between Sven and Konungr or the dead Delver.

In a low voice, Konungr spoke, "We were once one people in service to the Giants. Long ago there was a schism when the Wergoi—" he spat on the dead body "—murdered our Human friends and demanded obeisance. We became Delvers that day, Wergoi no longer."

Sven kicked one of the bodies. "We vowed to kill Wergoi and fight the Giants until our last breath. For Ejvind to bring them into our home is unthinkable."

Konungr turned to Sven. He handed him the medallion. "Go to Bjarmi's folk at the emerald mines. If any oppose, you show them the medallion as a sign of Ejvind's treachery. We'll give chase and get Ejvind. I don't know where he thinks he's going, but he cannot escape." He sighed heavily then looked at Sven. "Go! Send aid as you marshal it."

Sven nodded and ran off.

Ora stepped to Konungr. "You have our assistance."

The others nodded, even Staveros.

Konungr clasped Ora's forearm. "My thanks and those of my people." He looked at Ora and the others. "He fled down this passage. It leads to our central warren."

He picked up one of the dead Wergoi's spears and trotted to the tunnel. The others followed.

Lanterns filled with Delver's Flame, like that in the hearth, lit the passages. They gave off light and heat to offset the coolness radiating from the surrounding stone.

Ora looked up at the ceiling and thought he could feel the weight of the mountain on top of him.

After several minutes, they made it into the main part of the Delver community. Stairs carved into the rock went up and down from the level they were on, and tiers of passageways and alcoves, lit by lanterns, were visible across the open central area.

"There." Konungr pointed across the chasm.

On the opposite side, Ejvind stood panting at another passage. When he saw Konungr and the others, he turned to run.

"Gverth, can you hit him?" Sera asked.

"Pir." A bolt bright as day blossomed from his hand and lanced into Ejvind. The Delver staggered, lost his footing, and went down hard, skidding on the stone floor. "Gotcha."

"He's getting up." Hohan pointed.

"I told you, most magic won't hurt him," said Ora, who ran after him.

"He's headed to the Old Hall," said Konungr. "It used to be the market and meeting place when we occupied both halves of Dragon's Reach, but we haven't used it in centuries. I don't know why he would go there."

"Maybe he's hoping to get out the other side?" Sera asked.

Konungr frowned and picked up the pace. They rounded the corner, and a squad of Delvers trotted around the far corner, heading toward them.

Both groups raised their weapons and approached each other warily.

Ora enhanced his vision. "They're wearing armor like Sven and the other guards, not what those Wergoi wore."

Konungr nodded. "Even so, let's not be foolish."

Once they were in shouting range, one of them yelled, "Konungr, it's Dyri. We heard you were back."

"Dyri! It's good to see you, but right now, we have to catch Ejvind. He runs to the Old Hall."

"And we shall help." Dyri and his warriors followed Konungr and the others.

The passageway turned left and right. They rounded a corner and saw Ejvind pushing one half of an enormous set of ironbound doors closed.

"No!" Konungr yelled and sprinted to the door.

Ejvind closed it before Konungr could get there, followed by a heavy click as locks engaged.

Konungr pounded on the door with a fist. He turned to Dyri. "Break it down."

Dyri looked at the door dubiously. "But…"

"Wait!" Gverth commanded. Everyone turned to look at him. He flushed. "I have a simpler method." He rubbed his thumb across his fingertips and stepped to the door.

"What are you—"

"Let him be," said Sera.

A loud *thunk*. Gverth smirked and pushed on one of the doors. It swung open. "After you, my lord."

"Well done, lad," Konungr said as he led Dyri's Delvers through the door.

The party followed. On the other side was a large room with passages leading off either side.

"This is a reserve barracks in case we were ever invaded. In the old days, we had plans. If the Reach fell, we would fall back to the Old Hall," Konungr explained as they ran through.

A passage led them deeper into the mountain, and they saw the barest glimpse of a fleeing Delver rounding the next corner. That encouraged the others to pour on the speed to catch their prey.

They rounded the next corner as fast as they could and ran headlong into another group of Wergoi.

"Giants take you!" snarled Konungr.

"Giants take all traitors," snarled one of the Wergoi in return.

Dyri's Delvers charged into the line, but many Wergoi eluded their charge and attacked the party.

The engagement was a furious bout of fighting. The advantage that Sera, Hohan, Gverth, and Ora had over the Wergoi was a year's worth of Sera's small-unit tactics, and that was the decisive edge.

Each member defended against the opponent directly in front while watching for openings in the line to either side. Gverth fought from behind the line. Supporting with magic where it could help and a sword when it couldn't. Staveros worked into the line. While not as versed in small-unit fighting, he was a skilled swordsman.

Ora sent a thrust at the Wergoi in front of him, then slashed another to protect Hohan's flank. Sera's rapier, flashing spectral flame, flicked at the opponents to either side, creating openings for Hohan to pound his hammer into helmets and shields again and again.

A hammer blow knocked a foe out of the way, giving Sera a chance to strike.

Other Wergoi filled in, but not before Ora stabbed his short sword into one's gut, unleashing the putrid stench of punctured bowels. The next one charged in at Ora, but Mayomi caught him with her twin blades. The first, deflected the Wergoi's blade; the second, neatly glided into the base of his neck, nearly separating his head from his shoulders.

Sera stabbed a foot, then a different Wergoi's eye.

Staveros leveraged his bigger size and reach to slap aside blades and sever wrists. The Delver fighting next to him shouted and finished the Wergoi Staveros incapacitated.

Hohan's hammer kept crashing down like a smith at the forge. The Wergoi lifted their shields to block, but many Wergoi died at Hohan's feet from the blades of his companions.

The pile of dead slowed the rush, and then it was over.

"Anyone hurt?" Hohan gasped for breath.

A few of the Delver had been wounded, and he turned to help.

Then they heard boots coming down the hall from the way they'd come. They turned, weapons at the ready.

Mayomi sniffed the air. "They are friendly."

A moment later, a group of Delver guards rounded the corner.

"Hold!" Ora yelled.

The leader of the unit of Delver snapped a salute to Konungr. "I'm Bergmar.

"Well met." Konungr raised his bloody sword in a grisly salute. "Ejvind escapes. Leave a squad to assist the wounded and let's keep going."

They rushed past the littered bodies of Wergoi down the hall. The passage ended in a large hall.

A line of Wergoi blocked the way.

Konungr roared a mighty battle cry and charged. This time, the Delvers outnumbered the Wergoi and pushed them back into the hall. The party followed, looking for an opening.

Mayomi pulled on Ora's arm. He looked at where she was pointing. Well off to the side were several women and children watching, eyes wide. They sat on bare pallets with a makeshift wall around them. Wergoi guards around the wall hefted weapons.

Ora smelled the stink of full chamber pots.

"Sera, Hohan, Staveros look right. The hostages." He gave himself speed and ran at the Wergoi guarding the prisoners.

When he was two paces away, he shifted his magic from speed to strengthening his attacks and hit the Wergoi with a fast double-sword strike. The first blow batted the Wergoi's weapon aside, and the second sank his short sword through the eye-slot of the Wergoi's helmet.

His sword caught in the Wergoi's skull, ripping it out of his hand as his foe fell, but Ora picked up the fallen Wergoi's sword.

He just managed to block a thrust from another guard, but another blow slammed into Ora knocking him flat on his back, stunning him.

The guard stepped forward, sword raised. A bright bolt of flame blasted into the face slot of the helmet. He blinked away the bright light, but not before Hohan smashed in the side of his helmet with his hammer.

"Are you hurt?" Gverth asked, looking for another target.

"Excellent shot." Ora groaned and took Hohan's proffered hand. His ribs felt tender but probably not broken. "I think I'll make it."

He turned to the hostages. They huddled together and stared at the band with wide eyes. "We are friends of Konungr."

One woman stood up and grabbed a sword from one of the fallen. "I'm Katja, his wife. Come. We must help him."

Sera said, "He's winning that fight. I need you to help me get these folk back to your halls."

Ora looked at Mayomi. "Can you escort them to the double doors?" She nodded. "Then come right back."

"What about my brother? Ejvind?" Katja asked.

"He's over on the other side of the hall. With those Wergoi," Sera said.

Katja's expression shifted from surprise to sadness to anger. In an almost emotionless voice, she said, "Very well, I'll take them back. Please tell my husband I am safe... and to kill my brother."

🌸 🌸 🌸

The Delvers had pushed the Wergoi to the middle of the enormous cavern. The Wergoi were falling back slowly, moving in lockstep, attacking, retreating, attacking, retreating. The Delver were trying to make the most of their greater numbers, but the careful retreat blunted their blows.

Konungr stood behind the line of Delvers, shouting orders and occasionally jumping in to cover a breach.

Sera stepped next to him. "How can we help?"

"Push the defenses on a flank. Pick a direction and roll their line," Konungr replied.

Sera picked up a shield from the fallen, then turned to her band. "Push left."

She led her group around, and they charged into the flank.

The Wergoi on the end turned to meet the charge, giving the Delver in front of him a chance to strike him down from the side.

The next one yelled something in a strange language, and a small group of Wergoi in reserve pushed into Sera and the crew.

While their charge hadn't rolled up the line like Konungr had wanted, it had forced the Wergoi line to retreat faster, and now with every step back, another fell. When they had pushed the enemy to about ten yards from the mouth of the far passage, Ora saw Ejvind standing there, watching.

The last of the Wergoi actively opposing them fell.

Konungr yelled, "Ejvind you traitorous snake!"

Ejvind pressed himself against the side of the passage.

He's getting out of the way! thought Ora.

In his best battlefield command voice, he yelled, "Shields up! Archers!" A flurry of arrows and spears came out of the mouth of the passage. A stream of Human soldiers followed, armed and armored like the ones that had attacked them on the road.

A bolt of incandescent flame speared one of the foreign soldiers as he raised his bow. "Magic works on these!" Gverth whooped.

Sera faced their leader. He was a man of medium height, but his bearing and armor were a cut above the others. He fought with a horned buckler in his left hand and a saber in his right.

One of his lieutenants jumped in front of her, engaging her with a series of high-line attacks that drove her backward.

Ora shifted to the right and engaged the leader. Using his Shimmershield, he slashed a complicated combination of attacks that had never failed at some point to penetrate the defenses of any foe Ora had ever faced.

The man blocked each, despite the speed Ora sent into his strikes with skill and magic.

The leader then took the initiative. A slash to Ora's right, then one to his left nicking his forearm. Then he slid his tip past Ora's block to slice across his cheek.

Ora sliced at what he thought was an open arm, but the man's response suggested the opening had been feigned, and the leader's blade slid along Ora's thigh. The small cuts were adding up. While none were deep, they were painful and sapped his strength.

The man slashed low, pulling Ora out of position and whipped his saber over to get Ora in the middle of his left pectoral muscle. His left arm went numb.

Sensing an advantage, his opponent feinted to the right, then whipped around in a jumping kick that Ora had never seen before. The kick slammed into Ora's upper shoulder where it met his neck, sending him to the ground, stunned.

The man stepped forward, saber raised. The blade flashed down—

Mayomi flew in between Ora and the man, taking the coup de grâce meant for Ora. She went limp immediately. The man yanked his sword free and raised it into guard position.

Suddenly, one of the strange soldiers yelled something in their melodic language. The leader paused for a moment, staring at Ora, and then barked a command. They fell back as a group. As Ora got back up to his feet, the enemy moved fluidly step-by-step toward the passageway.

The battered party and wounded Delvers could not overwhelm the enemy force, but doggedly, they regrouped to give it their best effort. Gverth sent a weak bolt of flame after them, but it splashed impotently on one of their shields.

Ora looked down at a prone Mayomi and anger welled within him. He pulled on his Shimmershield and took a step forward toward the retreating enemy.

"Ejvind!" Konungr yelled as the last of the enemy men passed where the traitor stood. Ejvind raised his hand in a rude gesture and pulled a concealed lever before fleeing up the passage. A loud rumble permeated the cavern, and in an instant, the passageway had collapsed, filled with rock.

A cloud of dust billowed into the Old Hall. It took a few moments for the group to gather themselves. Bloodied cuts were everywhere.

"Konungr." Sera got his attention. "Where's another passage that heads that way?"

Konungr shook his head sadly. "There isn't one, by design. There is only one passage from each side into this space. What Ejvind set off was an ancient defense designed to collapse the tunnel against an enemy."

Sera turned to Gverth. "Can your magic get through that? Open it up? Shore it up?"

Gverth stepped to the mouth of the passage and extended a trembling hand towards the rubble, eyes closed. He spent a couple minutes like that before he opened his eyes and turned to the group, wearily shaking his head. "The damage is too extensive." He slid to the floor, exhaustion plain on his face.

"Thank you for trying." Sera looked at Konungr. "I guess that's that."

"There is another way." Konungr's expression was grim. "But it's very dangerous."

CHAPTER FORTY-ONE

ORA EARL

O ra knelt next to Mayomi. He heard hissing from her wound as she breathed out. It gurgled when she tried to breathe in. He closed his eyes, and reached out with his Life Magic to probe the gaping wound in her chest.

"How is she?" Sera asked.

"It's bad. Her lung's been pierced." He dug deep into his inner well of magic and stopped the bleeding in her lung, then closed the surface wound.

Mayomi coughed up blood, but her breathing eased.

Ora sighed heavily, a mix of relief and exhaustion. He looked to see if Hohan could help, but the priest was on his knees next to one of the Delvers. The Delver's throat looked to have been cut during the fight.

Sera knelt next to Ora. "Can you take energy from me like you did for Teer?"

Ora shook his head. "We're too badly hurt and too exhausted. If I were to take energy from you, really any of us, it could kill us, and I can't risk that. I've stopped the bleeding. For now. Let's get her back to the Main Hall."

Konungr surveyed the carnage. "So much life lost for the arrogance of Ejvind." He looked down at Mayomi. "How is she?"

"She won't die if I can help it." Ora staggered to his feet. "We need to get the wounded back to the Main Hall. They need rest and food at some point. We're all pretty beat up." Ora examined the wounds on Konungr with a practiced eye. "You look like you've taken a few hits yourself."

"It's nothing."

Ora's eyes narrowed, and he leaned closer to Konungr's face, which was a shade of gray. "How are you feeling?"

"I'm fine." Just then, they heard boots coming from the far end of the hall. Sven led a unit of Delvers out of the far passage. They quickly trotted into the hall and spread out into a formation.

"Sven!" Konungr held up a fist.

Sven barked an order, and the formation trotted over.

"Konungr, we heard the crash. We weren't sure…" Sven trailed off as his eyes found the debris choking the other passage. He looked back at Konungr. "Ejvind?"

Konungr gestured at the passage angrily, then prodded the body of one of the Human enemy soldiers with the toe of his boot. "He had help, Sven. More than the Wergoi. These strange Humans."

Sven's eyes widened. "Humans wearing *that* armor? It's Elvish."

"Yes." Konungr surveyed the hall. "I need you to get the wounded and get everyone back to the Main Hall. We need to rest and heal as many of our folk as possible. I don't think Ejvind's done, and we don't know when they're coming at us."

Sera moved up next to them. "You said something about another way to the other side. Can we go out and around?"

Sven shook his head. "We can cross the mountain or travel down to one of the passes to get over the range, but it takes several days, if not a week. And even if we get around that side, we run into a big problem. We had to abandon that side of Dragon's Reach because of the dragons."

Konungr cleared his throat. "What about the Lost Caves of Kishar?"

Sven hissed. "That's forbidden!"

"No, it was never forbidden. We just abandoned it after she died."

Ora shifted closer. "What are these caves?"

Konungr took a deep breath, then blew it out slowly. "What I tell you is history that must never leave this hall."

"We promise not to say a word of this." Ora held his hand, palm over his heart, and Sera nodded agreement.

Konungr took another deep breath. "In the First Age on Drakanon, by Delver reckoning, the Great Dragon progenitors, Mushussu, the father, and Tiamat, the mother, had children. Their first daughter was Kishar. They had twelve children in all and are known as the Great Dragons. From their children came all the other dragons on Drakanon, including the lesser dragons who live on the other side of Dragon's Reach today."

"Go on," Gverth encouraged him.

He spread his arms wide. "This was Kishar's hall and the center of her influence. Hence Dragon's Reach. The Delvers here worked for her. Then, in the Second Age, the Great Dragons had various internal conflicts that sometimes turned to warfare between the different factions. Initially, it was family members squabbling over favorites and resources. Later, the conflict focused around the surface folk and the Delvers fighting the Wergoi."

"Before the War of the Giants," said Ora.

Konungr eyed him, then nodded. "Mushussu and his faction supported us and the surface folk. Tiamat and her alliance felt that resistance to their rule should be crushed, mercilessly."

Sven spoke up, "Kishar, our patron and protector, perished in that conflict."

Both Delvers bowed their heads for a moment of reverence.

Konungr looked up. "Her halls are above this structure, up there in the mountain's womb. The ways up were sealed—"

Sven cut in. "It is her tomb. Since we sealed it, no Delver has set foot in her domain. We will not disturb her rest."

"Yet we wait here for her call." Konungr shrugged. "It is said that the restless spirit of Kishar roams the halls in the mountain above."

The others stood silent for a moment.

Ora noticed the guards loading Mayomi onto a litter. She was still unconscious as they took her away.

Konungr said, "We have excellent healers for her, Ora. They will tend to Mayomi."

Ora gripped Konungr's shoulder in appreciation. "Are you proposing that we travel through those caves?"

"Yes. But there is risk. We have abandoned them for a very long time. The Giants only know what creatures might be in there."

Sven shrugged. "Or, the mountain shifted, and the caves and structures up there could be unstable or buried. No one has been up there in... I don't know, eight generations." At their confused look, he sighed. "Seventeen hundred years or more."

Sera chuckled ruefully. "That sounds fun. And our other option is to travel outside, around the mountain, where we have to deal with the terrain, the weather, and dragons." She pointed at the ceiling. "Dragons are up there too, yes?"

The pair of Delvers nodded.

Ora rubbed the stubble on his chin. "Which way is faster?"

"The caves."

Sera asked, "Which path is more dangerous?"

"We don't know," Konungr said. "We don't know what the caves will bring. My ancestors sealed them, but creatures have a way of finding places to live. Especially ones that live in the mountain."

"Or things drawn to power," Sven said gravely. He turned to Konungr. "I have concerns of disturbing Kishar's resting place."

Ora glanced at Sera then spoke to the Delvers. "I respect that this is a sacred place for your people. I feel we can be respectful, but I think we need to take the path through the caves. It's faster, and if we have any hope of catching Ejvind on the other side, I think we need to risk whatever we may find."

Sera tilted her head. "I want to get this river leech too, but is it worth the risk? And we've used much magic today. We'll need rest."

Sven seemed doubtful.

Konungr clenched his fist. "He brought Wergoi into our homes, Sven. He would have transgressed less if he'd killed my children and eaten them."

"Let's get cleaned up, get food, rest a bit, and then get started," Ora suggested.

"In that case, we should return to our hall," said Konungr. "Much as I yearn to chase him, you are right. We would be fools to rush off unprepared into the halls of Kishar."

"Right." Sera gestured to the others. "We're going to rest as much as we can, but as soon as we're able, we're chasing Ejvind."

"Good," growled Hohan, who hefted his hammer. "I can't wait to explain certain aspects of Enki's teachings to him."

Ora paused at the threshold of the passage and surveyed the cavern. The ancient market and meeting place had turned into a slaughterhouse. Blood and bodies lay as testament to the ferocity and violence of the fighting.

He turned and saw Sera waiting. He motioned her to go ahead. With a last glance at the Old Hall, he sighed and started walking.

Ora kept replaying the fight in his head. Ora had always been a good fighter. He had never really encountered anyone or anything he couldn't overcome. *Until today. My arrogance almost got Mayomi killed.* A wave of sorrow hit him, clenching like a fist around his heart. *She took the blow meant for me.*

Ora shook himself. He had spent too much time wallowing in self-pity. *My wife died of a broken heart. Rella died because of me. The Gorgon struck Teer down as he tried to help me. And now, Mayomi almost died because of me.*

"Where has the commander that defeated a Demon gone?" a familiar voice asked. "That man was bold, out in the world. Willing to take charge and lead the way into a ravening horde of

Corrupted." During his eight hundred years of isolation in Draco tower, Atticus was a frequent thought companion.

"Atticus, I wish I knew. I'm putting my friends in jeopardy."

"Perhaps the world is dangerous, and your friends live because of you, Ora. What about that?"

He lagged further behind the group as he had his discussion with Atticus. They argued back and forth over the half hour it took to navigate the passages.

"If it were only that simple, old friend."

"It could be, Commander. If you'd let it."

Ora turned in the corridor to look behind him. The lanterns flickered, but nothing else stirred.

"Maybe you're right, Atticus. Just maybe," Ora murmured to an empty hall.

He hustled to catch up with the others. As he approached, Sera turned with a worried look on her face, and some of the doubt crept back in. *I can't lose her like I lost the others,* he thought.

CHAPTER FORTY-TWO

SANKARA MURCHALA

ankara walked with Rajan down the long corridor towards Wyrmhome. The recent battle was fresh in his mind. Ahead of him, Ejvind walked with some of the Wergoi.

Rajan spoke Amaranthine so the others wouldn't understand. "Commander. What did we just take part in?"

The leader gave a side glance to Rajan and responded in the same language. "I think this Delver was Houshkulu's agent. The person who they were using to hold the magic portal to Kinderkesh open for us."

"*This* person was their agent here? Things must be going poorly, indeed, if he's the best that they can find."

"I agree. Keep your eyes open." He looked back at his troops and addressed them in the same language. "Keep your wits about you. We don't know where this is going."

"Yes, Commander," they responded.

It took the better part of half an hour, but they finally made it into the room adjacent to the portal. The smell of an unwashed kennel threatened to overwhelm them. Along with his men, Sankara gazed at the wealth just lying everywhere in the room beyond.

He shuddered at the memory of what had happened when they'd first arrived. One of his men tried to help himself to the treasures. He'd found out the hard way that toxic dragon saliva coated everything.

Lavinia looked up from where she sat in a canvas folding chair next to a little campaign table. She got up when they approached. "What kind of mess have you brought us, Ejvind? We gave you everything: money for bribes, troops to enforce your will, equipment, even elixir. And you have squandered it all."

Ejvind looked nervous. "They knew about you. What was I supposed to do?"

"How did they know about me, Ejvind?" Lavinia stalked around the Delver. "I've never been on the Delver side of the Reach."

From the way Ejvind glanced around, Sankara knew he was looking for a way out. Lavinia must've seen it too.

"What did you tell them, Ejvind?" She ran a finger across his chest.

His eyes were wide with fear. "Lavinia, I would never tell them anything. I... I am loyal to you and to Lord Houshkulu. You know I would never—"

She slapped him. "Don't lie to me Ejvind, I'm your only friend here." She leaned in with a vicious leer. "You're going to tell me everything."

"I didn't tell them anything. I swear it's just that when Konungr came back, I didn't know what to do, and he pressured me."

"And just for that, you had the Wergoi attack them?"

"Yes."

Lavinia looked at him with a cold, calculating expression. "And were they able to kill him?"

Ejvind flushed. "No. Which is why I ran."

Sankara snapped, "You're lucky I only lost one person, Ejvind. Who were the Humans?"

"I... I don't know who they are. Konungr confronted me. He beat me before I could find out," Ejvind said quickly. "And the Humans must've been whoever set him free."

Lavinia eyed Ejvind speculatively. "That must be why I haven't heard from the prison. Describe the people who were there."

Sankara said, "I fought an extremely skilled warrior who somehow used magic to aid his fighting. It took all my prowess to defeat him. He was tall, sandy-haired, and wore banded leather. Then there was the cat-person who sacrificed herself for him. What was that?"

Ejvind answered eagerly, "That was a Wlewoi, they're from the south. And there was a very tall Human, must be from the north. He had dark skin and was big like the Northmen. There was a slender Human male who looked bookish. Perhaps the Land Magician? There was a... a female soldier. She was blonde. She has to be from the east." His face scrunched up trying to recall details. "There was a swarthy man—"

Lavinia held up a hand. "Stop. Describe the swarthy man in very clear detail."

Sankara's eyes narrowed at her interest.

"Oh, sure. The man was wearing black leather armor over dark clothes. He had a Delver-made sword and shield like the ones you... um, that was in the package that had been given to me to give to your friends down south." Ejvind paused and his eyes widened.

Sankara watched Lavinia's expression change. *There must be something specific about this person.*

Lavinia stepped forward a half step. "What about his face? His features? Anything unusual?"

Ejvind thought hard. "He had long, dark hair pulled back. He looked like he worked in the sun a lot. Fisherman, maybe a farmer? Except he looked like he knew how to carry a sword."

"Anything specific or peculiar?" Lavinia encouraged.

Ejvind snapped his fingers. "He had coloration on his eyes, maybe makeup? Eyeshadow? Something like that."

Ejvind watched Lavinia like a puppy eager to please. It disgusted Sankara, who had little time for boot-lickers.

"Could it have been a tattoo?" Lavinia asked.

Ejvind clapped like a little boy. "Yes, that's it! It was a tattoo. A tattoo on his eyes." He got a puzzled look. "Why would anyone want to tattoo their eyelids?"

Sankara shook his head, looked to Rajan, and in Amaranthine he said quietly, "This is the worst interrogation I've ever seen."

Rajan nodded in agreement.

Lavinia seemed to consider Ejvind's answer.

Sankara spoke up, "Who is this person, Lavinia? Of what import is he? And why was he in that prison you speak of?"

She turned sharply to Sankara with her eyes narrowed. "I warned you not to interfere in Lord Houshkulu's affairs."

Anger flashed through him, and Sankara took one step toward her. "When I have to rescue your puppet, it becomes my affair. When they killed my soldier as he is defending your idiot, it definitely is my affair."

Lavinia laughed so unexpectedly it took Sankara by surprise.

She waved her hand as if brushing away a fly. "It doesn't matter now. They can't get to us, and Lord Houshkulu will be here in the next day. With the passageway collapsed, I doubt they're going to take a month-long journey to walk all the way around the mountain to come in the front door on this side. Would anyone like some tea?"

CHAPTER FORTY-THREE

ORA EARL

O ra looked sadly at the sleeping form of the Wlewoi. "Get better, my protector." Before Atticus could chastise him again, he said, "You've done all your clan mothers could expect and more."

He glanced around the little room they had her in. It was clean and peaceful. *Just what she needs to heal up.*

He sighed, then returned to the others. When he arrived, Hohan handed him his pack. Ora checked it over once and made sure the Dragon sword was accessible.

The party, including Staveros, formed up. A platoon of Delvers had joined Sven and Konungr.

"Are you sure, my lord?" asked Sven.

"Yes." Konungr looked at the other Delvers. "If you haven't yet heard, we go through the Lost Caves of Kishar. If you do not wish to disturb her rest, you may stay."

The platoon said nothing.

"Then we go."

The group trekked back to the central hall where the fight had been the day before. About halfway across, Konungr headed toward a wide, blank stone wall that dominated that side of the hall. He walked right to the center of it and paused.

Ora stepped up next to him and asked, "Are you sure you want to do this?"

Konungr nodded grimly. "Time is of the essence, and this is the fastest path. Besides, if we were not meant to ever go back to the Halls, why did they teach each leader the ritual of opening?"

The Delver stepped to a specific location in front of the wall. He touched the palm of his hand to a distinct spot and said something in the ancient Delver language. The outline of a door appeared and slowly slid open, revealing stairs that headed up.

A platform stood at the top of the stairs. Opposite the stairs, a set of double doors with an ornate seal across them blocked their path.

He turned to address the group. "There is no telling what we're going to find on the other side of the seal. Be careful. But most importantly, be respectful."

The Delvers all said a word Ora didn't understand.

Konungr turned back to the seal and put both his hands on it. He repeated the phrase in the Delver tongue he'd used at the outer wall. The seal split down the middle, and the doors slowly opened.

A damp, musty smell came with the air that blew out the door. Dust, an inch thick, coated the floor on the other side. Evidence that no one had tread upon these halls in a very long time.

It has to have been sealed much longer than even I've been alive, Ora thought. *Especially since I've never heard of Kishar.*

Konungr spoke to two Delvers, "You'll scout ahead and lead the way. Watch out for traps. There are no written records of what they did here. But knowing our ancestors, they would not have made it easy for someone to come in and plunder Kishar's ultimate resting place."

From the back, Staveros spoke up, "Plunder? As in treasure?"

Sven turned around, eyes grim and sword raised.

Sera, standing next to him, grabbed Staveros's arm. "Don't even think about it."

Staveros nodded quickly. "Uh, sorry."

"Just remember," growled Sven. "That which is here is hers."

The corridor before them was of polished, black stone walls reaching up to an arched ceiling easily twenty feet high. At the end of the hallway was another set of stairs heading up and back the way they had just come. These stairs, unlike the previous, were slightly taller, sized for much longer legs, and took more effort to go up.

They climbed several hundred feet of stairs. At the top, they encountered another set of double doors. The scouts checked the doors, and they were locked.

One of the Delver ran his hand over the unbroken surface of the door. "Is there a key?"

Konungr shook his head. "If there is one, I am not aware of it."

Gverth stepped forward. "Please, allow me."

Sven growled, "Watch yourself, Human.'

"Let him pass, Sven," said Konungr. "I've seen his magic before."

The Delvers made way.

Gverth put his hand on the door and closed his eyes, concentrating.

"What's he doing?" a Delver asked.

With his eyes closed, Gverth answered, "I'm using my magic to manipulate the lock." Beads of sweat dotted the wizard's brow, but finally there was an audible click, and he gently pushed the door open. He staggered back, gasping for breath.

"Well done, lad," said Konungr.

The scouts led the way. Beyond was a long passage through basalt, lit by ever-burning lanterns that threw out a weak light, made even more so by the black stone.

Along the passage, alcoves stood to either side, and archways on both sides of the passage opened into larger rooms. The architecture in here was severe. Hard columns with ridges of black stone leading into sweeping archways.

The builders of Draco Keep copied this place. Ora looked at the precise stonework. *Poorly.*

As they passed each, they went through the rooms. Odd, overly large furniture filled some. They navigated through oversized chairs and armoires, couches and divans. Ora felt more and more like a child walking through an adult-sized house.

The further they went, the nature of the rooms changed from lounging areas or meeting rooms to what looked like workshops and laboratories. They poked their heads into each as they passed. In several of the rooms, holes could be seen in the walls and ceiling.

The Delvers in front of Ora had just passed one laboratory when a blur of motion seized a Delver and darted into the next room.

"What in all the Giants was that?" Sera exclaimed.

"Form up!" Konungr ordered. The Delvers arrayed themselves into a tight knot, spears and swords at the ready. The party hung back behind them as the platoon marched into the room where their compatriot had been taken. Staveros and Hohan kept an eye out behind them.

When they entered the room, there was nothing in there. Someone or something had piled the furniture up against one wall, consisting of tables, benches, and cabinets.

"Look up top. There's another hole in the ceiling." Gverth shone a Delver lantern held high, illuminating a rough-carved hole in the wall up near the ceiling.

"Do you think whatever that was took him up there?" someone asked nervously.

Konungr looked around the room. "Where else could they be? There are no other exits, and we know it dragged Marel in here."

"What do we do?" Sven asked hoarsely.

A horrible scream flew out of the hole and echoed behind the group, then was suddenly cut short.

"How could it come from behind us?" Bergmar asked in a strangled voice.

"The hole in the ceiling." Gverth pointed out. "It could have made any of those holes we passed."

Konungr had a grim expression on his face. "There's nothing we can do. Marel Sigarsson, may the Giants bless your passing into the next life. We press on."

"Should we block the hole?" Bergmar asked.

"We'd have to block all of the holes," Gverth pointed out.

"We don't have time. We'll set a rear guard and move on," Konungr said. "Keep an eye out and hope it's had its fill for the moment."

The group reluctantly kept an eye on the hole as they formed up and moved back down the hall. Spears and blades were pointed to each archway and passage they passed. Three of the Delvers kept watch behind them.

At the end of the hall was another set of doors. These were not locked, so one of the scouts opened them. It led into a sizable room that had been split across the middle by a chasm a dozen feet across. A purple glow rose from where the center had given way.

The group edged their way to the lip to look. Far below them was a seething mass of purple liquid.

"What is that?" Gverth asked.

Konungr shook his head. "No idea. This is not of Delver make. If Kishar put it in here, we've never heard of it."

Gverth studied the chasm. "Wouldn't that be about where your hall is?"

"About that, yes."

"And you've never seen this purple stuff before?"

"No."

"How? It would get into your hall, wouldn't it?"

Konungr stared at the mage. "You are assuming that this hall wasn't created by supreme magical beings."

Gverth chuckled. "That's a good point."

"And irrelevant right now," said Ora. "All that matters is that we need to get across."

Konungr looked up at the ceiling and then studied the chasm, wall to wall. "Do you think if we get a running start, we could make it across?"

"With armor on? I don't know how fast you guys can run, but a twelve-foot jump?" Ora shook his head. "What if we go back and check some of those rooms and see if there is a bench or a table or something long enough that we might stretch to the other side?"

Sven turned to his platoon. "You four, go back and find something."

After a few minutes, the four of them came back carrying a long table made of a dark wood. They had broken the legs off it. They held the table up on one end on the near side. Two Delver held the near end of the table where it touched the tile to keep it from moving. Two of the others lowered the other end as gently as possible until it barely stretched the gap.

"What do you think?" Ora asked.

Konungr shrugged and looked at Gverth. "Lightest to heaviest. Mage, go across."

"Me?" Gverth put a hand to his chest.

"Yes, off you go."

Gverth gingerly placed a foot on the makeshift bridge. It didn't move, didn't creak. He put all of his weight on the wood.

"Come on and get a move on. There's a bunch of us that need to get across," goaded one of the Delvers.

"All right, all right." Gverth tiptoed his way across. Nothing happened. No sound and no movement from the makeshift bridge. Gverth grinned with relief.

One at a time, the party members crossed, until they were all over except Hohan. Two of the Delvers on the far side anchored the table so it wouldn't move.

"All right, Hohan, it's your turn," Sera called.

Hohan stepped onto the makeshift bridge. At his second step, the wood creaked. Hohan watched the table with his every step. It groaned, as if protesting his weight on it.

At the halfway point, they heard an earsplitting crack.

Ora yelled, "Come on, Hohan. Move!"

Hohan ran toward the others. One step from the end, the table split in half and collapsed in the middle.

Without thinking, Ora used Shimmershield and grabbed Hohan's flailing arm.

The pieces of the table fell into the chasm.

Ora twisted and fell back, pulling Hohan over the lip. Sera and the Delvers rushed to pull him up.

Hohan glanced down at the purple, roiling mass. "By Enki, that was something."

"That was amazing. I've never seen you lift something so heavy." Sera grinned at Ora.

Ora shook his head in wonder. "I can't explain it. Somehow, something about this place. When I pulled on my magic, it was far more powerful than I ever expected."

Konungr clapped Ora on the back. "You're handy to have around."

"Thank you." Ora held a hand out to Hohan. "Are you all right?"

"Yeah, just a little shaken." He took the proffered hand and hugged Ora suddenly. "By Enki!"

Ora patted Hohan awkwardly on the back. When they separated, Ora thought he saw movement out of the corner of his eye. He spun his head. It was a blank wall. Nothing was there, no broken holes something could have scurried into. He shrugged. "Let's keep going."

They came to several intersections. Konungr chose their route with confidence. They passed more rooms and a moderately-sized feasting hall with its own kitchen. They wound their way through the hall at a steady pace.

Finally, Sera asked, "How do you know we're going the right way?"

Konungr laughed. "I was born under the mountains. I can feel which direction we are going."

"It's hard to take your word for it. It feels like we're completely turned around."

"You tell us how to get around in the overworld, Human, and we'll be even," said one of the Delvers. The others laughed.

When they entered the next room, a long, low table rested along one edge. Several chairs faced an empty fireplace. Ora felt a strange cold spot in the room as he moved across in front of the table toward the fireplace. He shivered.

"You all right?" Sera asked him.

"Do you feel anything here? A breeze? A chill?"

She shook her head.

Ora called over to Hohan. When he came over, Ora explained what he felt.

Hohan also shook his head. "No, I felt nothing. You think maybe the weight of the mountains is getting to you?"

Ora shrugged. "Could be. And it could all be in my head. I don't know." He glanced around the room. Something was off, but the party moved on out of the room.

They went down another passage, and Ora smelled moisture in the air.

The head of the group called back, "There's a cave up ahead. Be careful."

They entered the next room. It was a hundred feet wide, easily sixty feet tall, and ran hundreds of feet straight ahead. An archway opened into another passage on the far side of the room.

Water dripped down the walls, and the cavern boasted an array of stalactites and stalagmites. The pathway forward wound among the formations to where the party could only walk two abreast.

Halfway across, one of the Delver accidentally caved in the side of a stalagmite with his steel-toed boot.

A buzzing, clicking sound preceded a swarm of giant cave roaches. They came pouring out of the hole and swarmed over the yelling Delver, gnawing at him. He slapped furiously at the four-inch insects. "Get 'em off me!"

The Delvers closest to the flailing warrior frantically swatted at the roaches with the flats of their blades, wounding some. But their efforts were not very effective at clearing them from their compatriot. His yelling gave way to screams, as the rock-burrowing creatures made their way around and under his armor. He toppled to the cave floor, clawing at his armor.

As the warrior flagellated and rolled on the floor, the others danced back from the thrashing Delver while futilely trying to get the roaches off him.

"Be careful of the other stalagmites, lest you bring more of them out," Sven yelled.

Everyone froze.

Gareth pushed his way to the front. The Delver writhed on the ground, his screams getting weaker. Gverth held a hand out over the thrashing warrior, whose face had already been chewed to the bone. His screams faded as the insects tore into his chest

"*Pir!*" Gverth's hand erupted with flame, ending, mercifully, the tormented Delver's life and roasting all the carnivorous cave roaches in an instant. The smell of burnt flesh and fried, roasted bug permeated the cavern, forcing everyone to gag at the stench.

Konungr stood over the Delver with sad eyes. "Adel Haroldsson was a good man, and he gave his life in a good cause. May the Giants bless your passing into the next life."

Everyone moved carefully past the rock formations and bowed their head in respect as they moved on.

CHAPTER FORTY-FOUR

MAYOMI

Mayomi opened her eyes. A stone hearth on the wall opposite her held a line of Delver's Flame. Neatly trimmed birch branches were arrayed in a crisscross pattern along the narrow mantle. She stared at the various hues and tones of the flame, enraptured by the flick and flutter of the different tendrils of fire.

She lay contented, and then everything came rushing back to her. The fight, Ora, the sword blade. She reached her hand down to her side, where it felt tender and puffy. "I'm *alive*."

"I see you're awake," a soft voice said.

Mayomi turned her head to see Katja sitting on a stool, knitting. The Wlewoi tried to speak again, but her mouth was parched.

Katja set down her knitting and handed her a cup of water.

Mayomi took a long drink and then croaked out a question, "Where is everyone?"

With curiosity in her eyes, Katja asked, "How do you know they're gone?"

Mayomi smiled. "I am Ora's protector. I am bound to him. His scent, and those of his friends, are at least several hours old."

"They have entered the Lost Caves of Kishar. They left you here with me to rest and heal."

"I must follow them." When Mayomi tried to sit up, excruciating pain lanced through her side.

Katja put a pillow behind her and pushed Mayomi to lie back down on the bed. "You need to rest and heal." She reached over to the table next to the bed and picked up a blue-glazed ceramic cup. "Here, drink this tea. The herbs will help you mend."

Mayomi sniffed at it. It smelled earthy and floral. She sipped the tea and almost spit it out, but out of respect for her host, she swallowed the most vile-tasting concoction she'd ever tasted.

Katja laughed. "No, it doesn't taste very good, does it? But it will help you."

Mayomi dutifully drained the cup.

To her dismay, Katja produced a teapot and refilled it.

"Do you not have healing magic?"

Katja shook her head. "Delvers only use forge magic, the strengthening of metals, and that is a long, slow process. One of the blessings the Giants gave us was immunity to Mavric iron. That immunity, by extension, makes us immune to most magic, good and bad. The result is that no Delver has the ability to do magical healing." She shrugged. "At least not that I'm aware of."

Mayomi grunted and glanced around the room. The light coming from the lanterns complimented the Delver's Flame in the hearth. She sniffed at the air. Must and stone dominated, and she wrinkled her nose.

Katja sat back on the stool. "You don't like it underground, do you?"

"No. I'm from the savanna. We have wide open grasslands, marsh, wildlife everywhere. Fantastic sunsets, bright and vibrant. The smell of vegetation. Flowers on the wind." She looked at Katja. "Quite different from…" Mayomi couldn't find the word.

"Living in a hole?" Katja smiled.

Mayomi protested, but Katja held up her hand. "It's all right. Not everything that we do underground is drab and dreary. In fact, how are you feeling?" Katja peered at her.

Mayomi thought about it for a minute. Her side didn't hurt as much, and she felt a little more energetic. "I actually do feel better."

Katja smiled. "Good. Do you think you might be up for a little walk?"

Mayomi nodded and tried to hand back the vile tea, but Katja pushed the cup back to her. "Drink it all, and then will go for a walk."

Mayomi complied and downed the tea in one long swallow.

Katja took the cup back and set it on the table. She moved over to the side of the bed. "Shift your feet off the bed, and I'll help you to sit up."

With Katja's help, Mayomi stood up. She was a little unsteady at first, but soon, strength returned to her legs, and she could shuffle along.

"Where are we going?"

Katja smiled at her. "There's something I want to show you in our drab, underground, dreary life."

Mayomi's ears twitched. "I'm sorry. I shouldn't have said that."

Katja just laughed. "It's all right. Compared to the wonders of savanna sunsets, I'm sure that this does seem quite cold."

They moved at a sedate pace. They turned into a long corridor which held a bright light at the end.

Mayomi had to shield her eyes as she got closer, but when they reached the end of the passage, her mouth gaped in wonder at what she saw.

"This is amazing," she whispered.

The cavern stretched for hundreds of feet. Crystals of all sizes dominated the space. They were tall and round with blue and purple light that pulsed through them. Ahead of them, great pillars of crystals, larger than tree trunks, rose from the floor to the ceiling. Fingers of crystal as tall as any Wlewoi sprang up from the floor and down from the ceiling. She was stunned speechless and stared in wonder.

"This is amazing. I didn't know anything like this could exist."

Katja smiled. "This is our Cave of Wonder."

"Where does the light come from?"

"Somewhere up above, there must be a crystal exposed to sunlight, and it travels down and illuminates the rest."

They stood there for several more minutes, taking in the beauty of the crystals and the peacefulness of the cavern. It was hard for Mayomi to tear herself away.

Katja held her hand out to Mayomi. "Do you think you're up for seeing something else?"

Mayomi took her hand. "I think I'll have enough energy for that. I'm feeling good right now. The tea is really helping."

They walked through several passages. Mayomi smelled damp soil. They turned down another long corridor which opened at the end. Mushrooms of all different colors and sizes and shapes filled the cave. Not the little forest mushrooms that Mayomi was used to either. These were easily as tall as the Delvers themselves.

Katja pointed to two Delvers by a mushroom. One Delver cut sections out of the cap with a long-bladed knife. He handed his cuttings to the other Delver, who laid it gently in a cart.

"I've honestly never seen mushrooms that big. I did not know they could grow so well."

Katja laughed again. "We have a farm outside with animals. Their manure grows excellent mushrooms. In fact, if you're up for it, we can go look at them."

"I would like to see the sky."

Katja smiled and led Mayomi back to the front entrance. The Wlewoi stopped in the sunshine and closed her eyes, face turned up to the sun. She felt the breeze ripple through her fur. She turned back to Katja. "Thank you."

Katja pointed up the mountain. "Up there is where we have our farms, and you can see up on the right where the animals graze."

Mayomi took a step out from the building to get a better angle and could see cattle and a few sheep from her vantage point.

"We lose the occasional cow or sheep to the dragons, but mostly, they go after elk, since they're better sport." Mayomi gave her a sharp look and Katja nodded. "The dragons prefer game that try to get away. Cows don't run very far or very fast."

The enormity of everything overwhelmed Mayomi, and her head swam. There was a lot more to the Delvers than she realized. "Can we head back inside? I'm getting fatigued."

"Of course." Katja guided her back to the little room and helped Mayomi back into bed. "Is there anything that you need?"

Mayomi shook her head. "No, just a little time alone to recover."

Katja fussed over her. "There's tea in the pot. There's water in the pitcher, and I'll be back at dinnertime."

"Thank you, Katja. I really appreciate it."

As soon as Katja left. Mayomi pulled back the covers and crossed her legs into a meditative position. She closed her eyes and reached into the power that the Pentad had given her to start a healing ritual.

CHAPTER FORTY-FIVE

GVERTH REDBURN

ne of the Delver scouts came back. "The passageway's collapsed up ahead, but there's something you need to see."

He led the group to where rock had fallen down, narrowing the passage. He pointed at a man-sized tunnel to the upper right of the blockage.

Konungr peered up at the hole. "Has anyone gone into it?"

Gverth stepped up next to him. "How can you tell it isn't blocked?"

Konungr shrugged. "Air is moving through it. If it were blocked, it would feel dead."

"Someone's going to need to go check that out. Someone slim of stature." The scout glanced sideways at Gverth.

Gverth sighed. He handed all of his gear to Hohan.

He moved to the hole and put his hand on the rocks. After a moment of concentration, he said, "It seems stable."

He started crawling on his hands and knees, finding it wasn't as tight as expected. He came to a bend and probed with his magic again. He called back, "I'm going down into the bend."

Here it mattered that he was the slimmest member of the group. The bend twisted around and came to a long, gentle slope upward. At the top, it opened up into a room. Nothing moved. He called back into the passageway, explaining what he saw.

Sera asked, "Can you use your magic to shore it up?"

"I can try, but I don't know that the hole will get any bigger. You're all going to have to take your armor off to get through." Gverth did what he could to cement the rocks together.

He could hear the grumbling of the Delvers through the tunnel. With all of the guff the Delver warriors gave him for being thin, Gverth smiled, amused at their efforts as, one by one, each of the group, pushing their gear up ahead of themselves, made it through the passage.

Again, Hohan was last. At the bend, he called out, "Can I get some help with this?"

Gverth quickly dipped back into the passage to get his gear and Hohan's. He shifted it out for the others to take hold of the gear and pull it out of the tunnel.

"Enki bless me." Nervousness tinged Hohan's voice as he pushed into the bend.

They froze at the sound of rocks grinding on each other.

Gverth put his hand on the rocks and concentrated. He pushed waves of Land Magic, trying to stabilize and solidify the tunnel.

The stones seemed to push back against his magic.

Gverth's heart hammered in his ears as fear gnawed at him. "Something is *making* them shift, Hohan," he snapped. "Get a move on!"

"I'm trying!" The big man scrambled faster.

Gverth pushed harder, grunting with the effort, fighting against whatever it was that hindered him.

When Hohan popped out of the hole, Gverth felt the pressure against his efforts disappear.

Hohan donned his armor again, as the Delvers had already done. Across the hall, Konungr stood looking at two branches in the tunnel, his hands on his hips. One traveled to the left, and the other headed off to the right.

Konungr motioned to the scouts. "I want each of you to go down a branch about thirty yards and then report back."

The one to the left returned slightly before the other. "Mine goes for about thirty paces past where I went and leads to a single door."

The second nodded as he came up. "As does the one to the right."

Konungr turned to the group. "I don't know which way we need to go."

Gverth pointed at the right branch. "I feel something in that direction."

Sera moved over next to him. "What do you feel, Gverth?"

He slowly shook his head. "I can't describe it. I just know that's the direction we need to go."

Konungr looked at the rest of the group. "Does anybody have any differing opinion? No? Very well, right it is. Let's go."

When they reached the door at the end of the passage, Konungr said, "I don't like this." He waved at the scouts. "Check it out."

After a moment, one said, "I don't see any traps."

"Neither do I."

Konungr nodded, and they opened the door. The room was about thirty feet square. In the center was a pit running the width of the room about twenty feet across. A series of poles, each about a handspan wide, rose up to floor level.

Ora looked over the lip of the pit. "It's lined with glass spikes. How fun."

On the other side of the pit was an ornate door.

"Over here, my lord," said one Delver. He stood by two ten-foot-long boards.

Everybody looked at the boards, then looked at the poles.

"It's a puzzle," Gverth said. "We have to use the boards on the poles, and that's how we get across it."

"It can't be that simple." Hohan hefted a board.

Gverth shrugged. "If we don't try, we can't succeed."

"He has a point," Sera said.

Konungr looked at the poles for a minute. "Let's do it."

Two Delvers grabbed the boards and arrayed the first on the poles. One mounted the first board to the center pole, and it seemed sturdy enough. The board was ironwood, about a foot wide and very dense with no flex at all.

One of the Delvers picked up the second board and started across to the center pole. He held the board out toward the lip and shouted over his shoulder, "It won't reach."

"We need another board," one of the Delver said.

"We only have the two."

Gverth had his hands on his forehead, eyes closed, hands moving them like boards as he tried to envision how to get across.

After a minute, he clapped his hands together. "All right. I got it. What we have to do is we have to place the first board. Then walk across and place the second board. The people from the first board move over to the second board. One of them lifts the first board and hand it to someone at the other end of the second board so they can place it in such a way we can get across."

It took quite a while, but all of them made it across. They stood in front of the exquisitely decorated door. It was unlike anything they had seen in the complex. Panels contained scenes of animals, battles, and people. Dragons flew above in each scene.

Gverth said reverently, "That feeling I had that this was the way we needed to come. It's this. Whatever this is."

Konungr stepped up to the door and put his palm on it then recited the phrase of opening. It hummed loudly and popped open. He looked back at the group, then grabbed the edge of the door and pulled it open. Dust swirled out as he swung the door wide.

Blue and purple crystals lit the area inside the door. Each crystal glowed brighter as the party approached.

A basalt ramp stood before them, leading up and curving back around to the right. The group was subdued as they mounted the ramp, weapons ready.

Black marble columns shot with streaks of metal framed the landing above. Beyond rested a dais made of the same stone. On it was a massive sarcophagus, ornately carved with script and birds and inlaid with gems of every color. Surrounding the sarcophagus were heaps of items, strange objects, vases filled with coins and gems.

Ora pointed. "There's an inscription around the dais."

Gverth brought his lantern over, and they peered at the script. It was in the same language that was in the tome from Fagan Nuraghi.

Konungr leaned down to get a better look. "That's Old Akkermenian. I don't know it."

Ora squinted at it. "I've studied it a bit."

Sven and the other Delvers blinked and glanced at each other when he said that.

Ora read the inscription, stepping carefully around the dais, making sure not to disturb anything. "It appears this is the final resting place of Kishar."

There was a sharp inhalation of breath, then one by one all the Delvers knelt.

Ora stepped back while the Delvers paid their respects. Gverth tugged on Sera's sleeve and pointed to the side. Arrayed up against the side of the sarcophagus were several tomes very similar in size and shape to the one that they'd found in Fagan Nuraghi.

He leaned close to Sera. "We should look at those."

Sera whispered back, "That would be disrespectful to our new friends." She glanced meaningfully at the Delvers.

Gverth looked at Ora, who shook his head no. Gverth sighed and nodded in agreement.

Ora didn't realize he'd been holding his breath and let it out, hoping that they had just averted another disaster. He looked at the dais and again thought he saw movement out of the corner of his eye. He turned quickly toward it. But again there was nothing to see.

CHAPTER FORTY-SIX

MAYOMI

ayomi had buckled on her armor, arranged her sword sheaths, and picked up her pack when Katja came into the room with a fresh pot of tea.

Her eyes widened. "What are you doing? You need to rest. To heal."

"I've done that. While your race is immune to magic, I'm not." Mayomi stretched large to show she had no limitations in moving. "I'm as good as new. Well—" she touched where the hole was in her armor "—almost as good as new. But I need to catch up with Ora and the others."

Katja crossed her arms over her chest. "Catch up with Ora and the others? You'll never catch them. You won't even know how to find them."

Mayomi closed her eyes and pointed upward into the corner of the room. "They are there. I can feel them. I have a bond that will let me track where they are. They've already found a way through the caves. Between the bond and my tracking ability, I'll find them."

Katja stood for a moment, weighing her choices. "You're going to leave no matter what I say, aren't you?"

Mayomi nodded. "But out of respect, I was waiting for you to decide to help me."

Katja chuckled ruefully. "Am I that transparent?"

"I would rather say you're that caring."

"Very well. I'll show you where the entrance is, but after that, I can't help you." Katja frowned and held up the pot of tea. "Except, I can send this tea with you."

Mayomi made a face. "I accept that."

Katja went to a cupboard and got a large ceramic flask. She filled it with the tea and handed it to Mayomi. "Promise me you will drink this."

Mayomi nodded.

The pair headed off towards the Main Hall at a reasonably quick pace.

As they traversed the Main Hall and the warrens, women and children who the party had rescued came up to Mayomi for a quick greeting.

Once they had reached the Old Hall, Mayomi sniffed at the door to the Lost Caves of Kishar.

There are terrible things in there. All the more reason to hurry.

She turned and embraced Katja. "I appreciate you showing me around your lovely hole and taking care of me."

Katja laughed, but it was subdued. "You'll have to show me the sunset on the savanna." She looked Mayomi deep in her eyes. "Are you sure you want to do this?"

"They need me." They embraced quickly, then Mayomi started for the door. She paused for a moment and glanced back at Katja. "Put a guard on this door. A well-armed guard. You don't want any of what I'm smelling to come down here."

CHAPTER FORTY-SEVEN

ORA EARL

Konungr led a chant of a song, and the group repeated the ceremony with the Fire, each Delver stepping forward and saying his name and lineage to the dais, like he was introducing himself and his line to Kishar, then taking a drink in her honor.

Every once in a while, Ora thought he saw movement out of the corner of his eye, but when he turned to look, nothing was there. He shook his head. *This place must be getting to me.*

When the Delvers had finished, the group moved toward a door identical to the one they had used to enter this tomb. Konungr intoned the phrase of opening, and the scouts went ahead.

The group traversed several passages and mostly empty rooms.

A Delver scout came back to the group. "My lord Konungr, we've found some stairs that are now destroyed. I don't see a way up."

Konungr gestured for the scout to continue on, and the group advanced down the passage. Ora noticed a flickering in the light in the room they were walking toward.

They entered an enormous room, at least sixty feet in all three dimensions. All along the room's left wall was a massive network of webs scintillating with light. Across from the entrance to the room rose a sheer wall fifty feet high, and at the top was a door. Strewn along the floor of the room were the remnants of the staircase. The individual steps seemed to be intact, but whatever framework it once had lay in ruins.

Ora marveled at the lights that flashed along the webbing. "I've seen nothing like this."

"They are called sparkle spiders," Konungr said.

"Sparkle spiders?" Gverth laughed nervously and shifted to the right.

"Yes. Do you not have fireflies in the overworld?"

The non-Delvers in the party moved away from the webs.

Konungr laughed. "They're harmless unless you provoke them. One bite won't kill you, but twenty will make for a terrible day."

"You're sure they're not hostile?" Ora asked.

"They aren't. Why?" Konungr looked at him curiously.

"I have an idea." Ora surveyed the remnants of the staircase, then pointed at the wall of webbing. "What if I asked them to help us?"

"Just how are you going to do that?" Konungr seemed skeptical.

"I'm going to ask nicely." Ora smiled and stepped over to the giant web wall. He could hear Gverth choking behind him as he gingerly reached his hand into the web next to one spider that was busily working.

He sent Life Magic toward the spider. "Hello, little friend." The spider raised up, front legs out to ward off this great enemy.

"I'm not a spider, but I need your help."

The spider seemed to quiver for a moment, but then climbed onto Ora's hand and up his arm.

Gverth choked. "Ora…"

Ora smiled, then repeated the process until both of his arms were coated in spiders.

The wizard had backed against the far wall, with a horrified expression.

I probably shouldn't go shake his hand right now, thought Ora with a smile.

Instead, he eased over to where the base of the stairs had been. He channeled more Life Magic and fed it carefully into the little spiders.

"I need a way up to the door. Can you help me?"

He reached down gently so as not to disturb any of the spiders and picked up the first stair. Like the heavy boards in the earlier room, these were made of ironwood. He held the board steady, and the spiders poured off both arms and started spinning webbing. Some headed up the sheer wall and started casting the web down. Others wrapped the edges of the board in spider silk and started anchoring them to the webs being cast down.

When the spiders had cast enough webs. He let go of the first board then picked up a second and held it up a little higher.

He murmured to them, explaining what he wanted them to do. The spiders somehow knew what he wanted, whether guided by his will or his suggestions. They quickly wove the second step in, then the third, fourth, and so on. It took about twenty minutes, but when the spiders were finished, a scintillating ladder reached up to the top of the cliff wall.

"Thank you, friends." He pulsed some Life Magic out to all the spiders and then let it dissipate. Each of the little spiders seemed to quiver and then as a group headed back to their web wall.

Ora turned around and found the group staring at him in wonder.

"You are truly remarkable." Sera had a strange light in her eyes, which made Ora's ears hot.

Konungr whistled. "I have never seen anything so wondrous."

Ora smiled. "With the help of friends and a little magic, you can accomplish just about anything. Shall we go?"

The group gingerly made their way up. Even Gverth

CHAPTER FORTY-EIGHT

MAYOMI

ayomi raced up the stairs and moved quickly through rooms and passages following the scent of the group. She cocked an ear behind her when she heard a faint sound.

Spinning, she came face-to-face with a green and purple monster that looked as if a Troll had mated with a spider and had produced this horror.

It spat venom at her.

Mayomi pressed herself against the wall, avoiding the venom, then pushed off the wall when the creature approached.

It lunged for her with two of its legs, mandibles clacking together in front of a gaping maw of needle-like teeth. Stubby Troll arms with blood-caked hands flexed toward her. Mayomi drew her blade and slashed at the leg in one smooth motion, neatly severing it and evoking a scream from the Troll-spider. She spun around and raced down the corridor drawing her other blade, the creature followed her closely.

Mayomi's advantage was in speed and agility. She turned into the wall and ran up it, launching herself over the Troll-spider.

She twisted in the air, slicing a deep furrow across the creature's back. She rolled as she landed and came up with her blades at the ready.

The creature screamed in pain and took off into one of the rooms. Mayomi followed but only caught a glimpse of it as it disappeared into a hole in the ceiling.

"I wonder if the others ran into you?" Mayomi cleaned her weapons and moved on down the passage, sniffing for the scent of Ora and the others. The Troll-spider's blood distracted her, but when she passed the point of her fight, she caught the trail again.

Mayomi came upon the charred remains of the Delver in the cave. She took in the busted stalagmite and the burnt cave roaches and surmised what had happened. She avoided touching anything as she made her way through.

Some of the obstacles where the group had to use finesse, she used raw power. Mayomi easily jumped over the chasm and navigated the poles. She slowed down as she approached the sarcophagus room.

At the top of the ramp, she surveyed the dais with the sarcophagus.

She bowed toward it.

Off to her right, she heard a little girl humming to herself, which raised the hackles on the back of her neck. She stepped slowly past the sarcophagus and over to a curiously lit area where a small Wlewoi girl played in a plain, gray dress.

"Hello?" Mayomi called to her.

"Hello, I'm Key," the girl responded. "What's your name?" she asked without looking up, playing with some toy that Mayomi couldn't make out.

Mayomi sniffed the air but couldn't smell the girl. She caught the scent of prairie violets. It reminded her of home on the savanna. "My name is Mayomi. What are you doing here?"

The little girl turned to look at her with golden eyes. "I'm here because somebody woke me. I think it was your friends."

Mayomi tilted her head. "My friends woke you?"

The little girl nodded. "I think so."

"Why are you here?"

Key pointed at the sarcophagus. "Because I died."

Mayomi blinked. "You are Kishar, the daughter of the Giants."

The little girl watched Mayomi with her golden eyes. "I was. I don't know exactly what I am now. My friends call me Key." She stood and came over to stand in front of Mayomi. She tilted her head and twitched her feline ears.

"I smell my father on you."

That confused Mayomi. "I don't understand. I don't know who your father is."

"You have some of his power."

Mayomi's breath caught in her throat. With some trepidation, she asked, "Who's your father?"

Key looked amused. "Mushussu."

Mayomi's heart hammered in her chest. The Pentad. Key's father was part of the *Pentad*.

"What do you want?" Mayomi asked. "Why are you awake? How are you here if you died?"

"I'm not sure." She cocked her head and turned her feline ears toward Mayomi. "As to what I want, I want my parents to stop fighting."

That rocked Mayomi. Key's parents were Giants. She was trying to wrap her mind around the fact she was talking to the ghost of a Giant.

Key came over to stand in front of Mayomi. "Let me ask you this. What do you want?"

"I want to find my friends. I want to help them and keep them safe."

The girl cocked her head. "You're wrong. You want something else."

"No, I need to find them. Can you help me do that?"

Key looked at Mayomi for a long moment, then shook her head. "It's not my time yet. I need to marshal my power. I've been asleep for so long."

"If you're a Giant, why do you look like a Wlewoi?"

She morphed into an adult Wlewoi. "I wanted to put you at ease."

Mayomi shook her head. "Amazing. If now isn't your time, why ask me what I want?"

"I wanted to see what's in your heart. I wanted to see what my father's champion desired." Key's eyes glowed for a moment. "I can tell you something that might help."

Mayomi leaned in. "Yes?"

"Beware my brother, he is down below." She flickered out of existence, leaving only the lingering smell of prairie violets.

CHAPTER FORTY-NINE

ORA EARL

The passages and stairs led downward, reaching a section that had sagged. Water dripping from the ceiling had calcified into long, finger-like streaks and was feeding the pool that filled the passage.

The scouts stepped into the water and carefully tapped the floor to make sure there wasn't a sudden drop-off. The rest of the group stepped down and sloshed through the water.

Almost all of them had made it when a gray, shapeless mass dropped from the ceiling onto one of the Delvers. An acrid stench filled the room, and he started yelling in pain and fear.

"Acid, it's eating him! Quick, get it off him," yelled Ora.

They tried to scrape it with the edges of their blades, but it shifted and crawled around their attempts. The situation devolved to the Delvers beating their fellow with the flats of their weapons in an effort to subdue the strange creature.

Another Delver stepped close, and the gray creature lashed out with pseudopods, knocking him down into the water.

All the Delvers' yelling and the injured man's screams echoed up and down the corridor. Gverth shoved his way through the crowd. "Hold still if you can. Hold still, by the Giants." Gverth held a finger over the struggling Delver. *"Pir."*

He used it like a hot knife to cut the creature off of the Delver. It took several moments, but finally the creature sloughed off him, falling in the water, inert.

In a hurry, everybody sloshed forward up and out of the fetid pool further fouled by whatever the gray creature was.

"Bergmar, are you all right?" asked Konungr.

He groaned. "It ate... ate through my armor. I hurt all over. I don't know if that's from you or Dimas hitting me, you idiot."

One of the Delvers next to him said, "I'd want you to hit me if that was on me."

They examined Bergmar's hammer and armor. His armor was nearly useless, barely hanging from its straps, and his hammer had been eaten down to the wooden handle.

"Not much we can do for it, but at least you're alive." Sven helped Bergmar to his feet.

"And not much to do but continue on," said Konungr. He gestured for the scouts to continue down the passage.

The party passed several branches and forks, but Konungr guided them at each one. About an hour later, one of the scouts returned.

"We found a large room," he whispered. "You need to see it, and you need to be quiet."

Konungr nodded, and they followed.

The room had once boasted smooth, finished sides, but the ceiling bowed with large cracks that spider-webbed across the entirety of it. As they watched, a trickle of powder fell from one of the cracks and settled on the tables and chairs in the space.

Konungr said in a harsh whisper, "Everyone will move through the room one at a time. Go carefully and don't say anything. Sound could bring the ceiling down on us."

Ora went across first. Stepping gingerly, he looked up at the ceiling. Cracks ran across to the holes where the powdered stone had fallen from. He stepped around several pieces of furniture and made it to the other side. He waved for the next person which was Konungr himself.

He glided across the room like a dancer.

Next was Hohan. The big man stepped gingerly and tentatively, but he made it through without incident. Then the Delvers started to move through, one by one.

Bergmar glanced at the ceiling with narrowed eyes.

Sera leaned over and whispered to him. "You can do this."

He took three steps into the room, when a loud pop preceded another trickle of powder falling from the ceiling. Bergmar froze, staring up at the ceiling in horror. Several moments passed. Nothing happened. He took a deep breath and let it out slowly.

He took another step forward. The weakened straps on his armor picked that moment to let go. The breastplate separated from the backplate, and they crashed to the floor with a terrible clatter.

Bergmar only had time to look up before rocks crushed him.

A large cloud of dust coated the survivors with a fine powder and set everybody to coughing. Ora waved away the dust and examined the rocks, searching for a way through.

Once the dust settled enough, Ora crouched down. There was a slight space on the side that was mostly straight through. However, unlike the previous passage, only a mouse could make it through.

Ora cupped his hands and yelled into the gap. "Hello?" He enhanced his hearing, hoping the others were alive.

A faint reply came back from Sera, "We're here."

"Are you hurt?" Ora yelled.

"We're all right but Bergmar is gone."

"Can you get through?"

"No. We'll find a way around. Go on ahead and we'll catch up with you."

"Be careful."

"Aren't I always?"

Ora stood up and repeated what he learned to Konungr. "Do we try to find a way to them, or do we keep moving?" He tried to keep the worry from his voice.

Konungr looked at the pile and grimaced. "The Delvers still with them will help them get around this. We passed so many paths, there has to be another route. However, we don't know which way they went, so it would be futile for us to take a random passage and try to meet up with them." He put a sympathetic hand on Ora's shoulder. "Your friends are alive and capable. They will catch up with us."

The group continued down the passage past several corridors leading into darkness and more rooms. These were very similar to what they had found on the other side of the sarcophagus room, including sitting rooms, workshops, and some rooms whose purpose was unclear.

They reached another ornate door, just like the one they'd unlocked to get in the Lost Caves of Kishar. Fortunately, here the latch was on their side.

"Let's leave a lantern here," Ora suggested. "Hopefully, that'll help Sera and the others."

Konungr nodded.

He set his lantern in the middle of the doorway, and they headed down the stairs. At the bottom stood a plain stone door.

"I think this leads into the other half of Dragon's Reach," said Konungr. He put his hands on the wall and intoned the phrase in Delver that caused the seam to appear in the door. With a push, the door swung open, so well made that barely a whisper of stone on stone could be heard.

They stepped into the back of a large hall. It was easily as big as the Main Hall back on the other side of Dragon's Reach. It stretched a hundred paces before them and as far as they could make out to either side. Across from Ora was an antechamber. Beyond that antechamber, it opened up into a cavern.

In the antechamber there were figures. Some were moving around, others sat around a brazier. Ora enhanced his vision. He immediately recognized the enemy commander who'd stabbed Mayomi.

He raised his eyebrows in surprise as he also recognized the leader of the Blood from Draco. He didn't expect to see *that* Wlewoi here.

Ora spotted the Elvish woman Staveros had described, from tight-fitting, leather armor to the shockingly blonde hair.

There were no Wergoi, nor were there any other Human soldiers. But there was a clump of Humans dressed in the same red-black robes like the assassins that attacked him on the streets of Draco and the ones who had come after them in the Dragon's Cup.

Ora hissed, "Gorgon."

Hohan snapped his head up at that. His eyes narrowed and he flexed his hands on the haft of his war hammer.

Ora turned to Konungr and said softly, "We need to wait here for the others."

As the members of Gorgon moved, Ora glimpsed Ejvind in their midst. A thrill of excitement coursed through Ora.

He gave a sidelong glance at Konungr, and excitement quickly faded to fear of what the Delver would do when he spotted Ejvind.

He turned to Konungr and saw the Delver had a bronze, collapsible spyglass up to his eye, scanning the group on the other side of the hall. His heart sank as Konungr stiffened and his face flushed an immediate reddish-purple.

At the top of his lungs, Konungr shouted, "Ejvind!"

Then, as one, the Delvers shouted a low, deep battle cry that reverberated through the hall.

CHAPTER FIFTY

SANKARA MURCHALA

The war cry took everyone by surprise.

With the only connecting passageway collapsed, they had not expected anybody in this side of the Delver complex. Everyone's heads snapped around to find the source of the shouting. Across the large hallway they could see nine Delvers and two Humans. Ejvind staggered back, the fear stark on his face. The cat-man let out a growl.

"Where in the Shiva's name did *they* come from," snarled Sankara.

The only fighters here were the Humans who'd been doing Lavinia's bidding. They turned to look at the Delvers advancing across the hall. The red-robed Humans' lack of concern infuriated Sankara.

He shouted at them, "Form a line!"

They ignored him, looking instead to Lavinia.

I shouldn't have sent Rajan and the others back to camp. Sankara grimaced. It was supposed to be so simple. Just walk through the thuros. But now a group of Delvers charged at him, and his allies seemed to care little. He turned to Lavinia to see if she could get the men moving.

Lavinia and the cat-man bowed to Houshkulu as he came out from the room with the thuros. They made obeisance.

Houshkulu gazed past Lavinia to the advancing Delvers. He looked at Lavinia. "Deal with them while I open the portal."

She immediately snapped orders to the men Sankara had been trying to motivate, who obeyed her instantly. The cat-man went with her.

Sankara loosened his sword in his scabbard. "We will make short work of them."

Houshkulu gripped Sankara's arm before he could join them. "I need you to come with me."

"And leave them?"

"No. I need you to bring more troops. Lavinia and the Wlewoi are capable. Let my agents deal with them. If things go poorly today, I have another ally here in these lands. But you need to make it through the portal to talk with your uncle. Your men will surely die at the hands of the Eshitan soldiers if you can't bring support. And only you can convince your uncle to send more men."

Sankara narrowed his eyes. Reluctantly, he nodded. "I agree."

He watched the two lines approach each other. A part of him was envious of the fight about to happen, seeing the fighter he'd almost vanquished. He fingered his saber, then gritted his teeth. "Next time." He turned away and followed Houshkulu through the antechamber.

CHAPTER FIFTY-ONE

ORA EARL

Despite their rage, Konungr and the Delvers advanced in a disciplined line, gaining speed gradually until they trotted at the enemy. Hohan and Ora followed a few paces behind the line.

The Gorgon Human assassins ahead didn't line up, instead breaking into two squads, one with the blonde Elf and the other one with the Wlewoi leader of the Blood.

Ora craned his neck to see where Ejvind and the leader were. They were retreating with the robed figure.

That was when the Gorgon mage unleashed a torrent of magical death and destruction at Konungr and his squad.

Behind the line of Delvers, Ora gave a grim smile. "I guess they hadn't heard the Delvers are immune to most magic?"

Hohan smirked.

The mystical energies dissipated once they hit the Delvers.

Konungr's warriors didn't miss a step and just kept moving to the enemy.

Ora drew his swords. "Once the fighting starts, you and I will push around the right side, and we'll go after the leader and Ejvind, and whoever that is with them."

Hohan nodded.

The two lines smashed into each other. Hohan and Ora pushed around the right side. One of the Gorgon saw them moving and turned to engage, but the Delver at the end of the line cut him down.

And then they were past the major part of the battle.

Both Ora and Hohan ran to the antechamber and skidded to a stop at the threshold to the cave. The cave itself was huge, but that wasn't what stopped them. Heaps of treasure filled the room. Piles of armor and weapons. Vases filled to the brim with coins and jewels. Golden drums, platters, and every bit of art or ornamentation that Ora could think of. It had all been scattered about in a haphazard fashion.

In the center of the room, a large set of stairs ran up to a fifteen-foot tall archway with thick, elaborate columns on each side. Strange figures and symbols ran up the columns. They glowed, or at least Ora thought so.

The surface of the archway was a swirling mass of color, much like if someone had drawn a stick through an oily pond.

The dark figure in robes climbed the stairs.

The leader of the soldiers who'd opposed them in the Old Hall stood at the foot of the stairs, hand on the hilt of his sword. The man who had stabbed Mayomi.

Ora met his eyes for a moment and stepped forward.

The man shook his head, but then, with frustration on his face, ran up the steps.

At the top, the figure held up an object, and the surface of the archway suddenly blazed, the light filling the cavern. He stepped into the glowing swirl. The Human leader ran up the stairs and straight into the glowing swirl without even a slight hesitation.

The surface dulled and the colors just swirled. Both of them were gone.

Ora turned to Hohan. "What just happened?"

Hohan shook his head. "The gods only know."

The sound of battle raging behind them caused both men to turn.

At the far side of the hall, a door opened. Sera, Gverth, Staveros, and the other Delvers emerged from the Lost Caves of Kishar. They rushed toward the battle.

Ora took a step to join the battle.

A portcullis slammed down, cutting the cavern off from the antechamber. Somewhere up above and behind them, a deafening roar sounded.

Chapter Fifty-Two

GVERTH REDBURN

 verth identified the opposing mage off to his left and slid to that side of the formation. The Delvers and the Gorgon hacked and slashed at each other.

The mage saw him and sent three darts of bright light at Gverth.

Gverth held up his hand, and all three shattered in front of him, like snowballs, hitting a wall. He responded by sending a bolt of flame back.

The mage deflected it into the wall.

"So that's how it's going to be?" Gverth pulled up both of his sleeves and let loose another torrent of magic. A wild energy storm lashed between them as they each sought advantage.

CHAPTER FIFTY-THREE

STAVEROS

s Staveros approached the battle line, he spotted the blonde woman who'd betrayed him. He shifted in between the pair of Delvers who'd engaged her.

"My lady. How I've longed to see you again."

Lavinia blanched. She delivered a couple tentative blows with her serpentine dagger which he easily deflected with his Delver-forged blade.

All of his hatred and frustration poured into a cold, focused fury which he used as they exchanged strikes.

After her initial shock, a mask of arrogance settled onto her face. "Did prison make you soft?" she quipped as she slashed at Staveros. "Maybe it's your mongrel parentage. Which whorehouse were you raised in?"

Staveros quietly blocked her strikes, biding his time, looking for an opening.

With a fierce snarl, she dealt a series of vicious, but wild, blows.

Staveros calmly deflected or parried all of them.

"Giants take you," she said, her blows getting even wilder as her frustration increased.

A loud crash sounded behind her, and both Lavinia and Staveros paused for a moment to see the portcullis had closed.

"Nowhere to flee now, bitch," he hissed.

She took a glance behind her and paused.

"I won't die from scum like you." She slashed, then jumped forward when Staveros stepped back. Her foot slipped in a pool of blood.

Staveros stuck his blade in her heart.

She stood there, a look of surprise on her beautiful, Elven face.

Then she crumpled.

As the life faded from her eyes, he leaned down with a grin. "Don't worry, my lady. It was good for me too."

CHAPTER FIFTY-FOUR

SERA DEMOTT

Konungr's Delvers were pushing the line into the enemy forces. A flash of hatred coursed through Sera, as she spied the Blood who had threatened her back in Draco. He was anchoring the enemies' right side.

Sera wanted a piece of him and led her group to the left, chivvying them into order just behind Konungr's line to wait for an opening.

A Delver reeled from a blow, staggering back. An opening appeared giving Sera the opportunity she was looking for. "Charge!"

Her small group hit the line of Humans, pushing them hard, and she found herself facing the Wlewoi.

"Remember me from the Dragon's Cup, asshole?" She raised her blade, looking the Blood straight in the eyes. Spectral flame slid along her blade.

His ears flattened when he recognized her. He snarled and flexed his claws where they extended from the steel-backed gauntlets. "Come learn a lesson, *female.*"

He used his speed advantage to slash at her as she approached.

She punch-blocked with the cage on her hilt. "About time someone put you in your place, cat." She stepped forward and gave him a fiery slash.

He flicked her blade out of the way with the back of a gauntleted hand.

The Blood feinted to the right, drawing Sera's point after him. He swatted the blade further and stepped in on her, pounding her chest with a steel-gauntleted strike that knocked her to the ground.

CHAPTER FIFTY-FIVE

ORA EARL

From the other side of the portcullis, Ora watched in horror as the Wlewoi's strike landed and Sera went down. Helpless, he shouted her name and yanked on the bars with all his might.

* * *

As if the sky itself wept, the rain hadn't stopped for over a week.

King Ora stood with his queen as the bodies of Rella's retinue were brought into Draco Keep's courtyard in covered wagons. The wheels cut into the mud.

Rella was last. They'd shrouded her in purple and wrapped her in ornate ribbon.

Ora's retinue had erected a long pavilion for the occasion. The men in the procession laid out each of her slain entourage under it. They'd been wrapped in their cloak of service, a cloak that took years of training and undoubted loyalty to earn.

They put Rella at the head of the group.

His wife, Daphne, clung to his arm, openly sobbing.

Ora watched as the Reader and a priest of Enki spoke. He didn't hear what they said. There was just Rella's silent form.

CHAPTER FIFTY-SIX

MAYOMI

Mayomi stepped through the door, seeing the battle raging.

She ran toward the fray, noticing as a male Wlewoi reached over his shoulder and withdrew a long, steel falcata.

It was heavy with a broad middle section that tapered forward down the curved blade, ending in a fine point—a blade meant for chopping through armor and bone.

She started sprinting when she realized Sera lay at his feet, not moving, defenseless.

He bared his fangs and raised the falcata.

Mayomi jumped in between them, blade at the ready. "Get out of my way, cub," he sneered.

Mayomi pulled back the hood of her cloak, unfastened the clasp, and let the cloak drop behind her. She was wearing the harness of a full Esroi.

His eyes widened at the presence of, not just one of the true guard, but a Wlewoi female under arms.

She gave him a toothy grin. "Who's been a naughty kitty?" She bared her fangs at him and attacked, her blades a blur.

He tried to parry her blows, gasping, "Who are you?"

"Have you forgotten who hunts in the pack, *little one*?" She struck again.

His eyes dilated and ears lay flat on his head. "But—" Despite his strength, speed, and height advantage, her onslaught was unrelenting. He could not fend off everything.

First, there was one cut to his forearm, then to his side, then on the inside of his thigh and his right shoulder. She was picking him apart.

"You can't stop me," Mayomi taunted.

He screamed in frustration. He feigned a thrust to her face and pulled back sharply, turned, and ran around the edge of the fighting line toward the door to the caverns Mayomi had just come out of.

Mayomi checked Sera for a quick moment. She was breathing even if it was shallow. Mayomi met Ora's gaze through the portcullis where he was trapped. She glanced at the running Wlewoi, torn.

"Go after him, I'll take care of her," she heard Tess's voice float by.

She turned and went after the Blood. "Run, my little mouse. I do so enjoy the hunt."

Chapter Fifty-Seven

ORA EARL

O ra's heart sank when Mayomi disappeared through the door, leaving Sera laying on the floor. He looked frantically for a way to open the portcullis. At that moment, a blast of air hit Hohan and Ora, throwing both of them into the portcullis.

A loud crunch sounded behind them, and a deafening roar reverberated.

They turned to look. A dragon prowled toward them, barbed tail trashing behind it.

"Look, it's just a little one." Hohan's weak laugh turned into a groan. It was easily the largest dragon Ora had ever seen.

The dragon stood ten feet at the shoulder with four heavily muscled legs covered in red scale. A long, scaled neck ended in a snout. Its golden eyes blazed with anger, and it had its wings pulled back so it could move more easily. It dug its back claws into the pile of coins to get purchase, preparing for a lunge at the pair of them.

It snarled at Ora and Hohan, and then a squeak sounded to their left, drawing its attention off them.

"Move!" Ora said to Hohan and shoved him.

Ejvind cowered behind an ornate golden shield. When he saw the dragon coming for him, he threw the shield into the dragon's gaping maw. It bought Ejvind time while the dragon worked to get the offending object out of its mouth. Ejvind took off for the other side of the large room.

Ora and Hohan slid along the wall, away from the portcullis, searching for any sort of weapon or another way out.

The dragon brought up a claw and pulled the mangled shield free.

Ejvind moaned as he mounted the oversized stairs, stumbling on hands and knees. Ora heard him whining, "Oh please. I don't wanna die."

The dragon stalked towards the fallen Delver.

Fear must have motivated Ejvind as he made it to the swirling portal. He frantically pounded on its surface and screamed, "Houshkulu!"

With a lightning-fast snap the dragon bit Ejvind in two.

Hohan stared at the spectacle of the Delver getting slaughtered. "I don't want to do this," Hohan half-cried as he gripped his war hammer with white knuckles.

Ora grimaced at the gore, unable to tear his eyes away, as the dragon turned back to them munching on half of Ejvind. He tried to bolster his friend's courage. "You tell all kinds of stories about all the monsters you killed up north. Besides, it's just a wee little thing right?"

"I lied!" Hohan grimaced.

Ora turned to him. "You are a mighty warrior priest of Enki. We have slain trolls, Gnolls, and kegs of beer. There is nothing that can stop us." He grabbed Hohan's shoulder and pulled him, forcing him to look Ora in the eyes.

"Now, power up, ask your god to aid us, and let's kick its tail. Are you with me?" Hohan nodded, eyes still wild.

"I didn't hear you. Are you with me!" Ora shook Hohan's shoulder.

"Yes! I am with you!" Hohan looked better. He took a deep breath then gave a halfhearted smile.

"Good! You hit from the right. I'll come in from the left." The dragon spit out one of Ejvind's legs and turned its attention back to Ora and Hohan.

Ora pulled Shimmershield to give himself speed and strength and dashed around the left.

Hohan raised his hammer to the air and shouted, "Enki, give me strength." A blue nimbus surrounded Hohan for a moment. He darted to the beast's left.

Split as they were, the dragon's head wavered left and right trying to keep both men in sight. It snapped at the Northman.

As the dragon's jaw clashed inches from Hohan's face, Ora stabbed into the dragon's flank with all of his might. The scales turned the sharpened Delver-forged blade. It skittered along the hide until it caught in between a pair of scales and barely penetrated the dragon's hide.

The dragon yelped and jerked its head back towards Ora.

That gave Hohan an opportunity to strike the dragon's shoulder with his war hammer. The hammer blow rang, but didn't appear to do any damage to the dragon itself.

It did, however, turn the dragon back to Hohan. It ripped its claws at the priest.

Hohan jumped out of the way. "This isn't working!"

"I have an idea," Ora yelled. "It's not a good one though!"

"Do it anyway!" Hohan backpedaled, smashing at the dragon snout as it snapped at him.

"May all the gods bless me." Ora dropped his ancient, Delver-forged sword and pulled the Mavric iron blade from where he had strapped it to his pack. He quickly unwrapped it, letting the shimmering cloth fall to the ground. Since wielding the Dragon sword wouldn't allow him to use his magic normally, he chose to put all of his Shimmershield into the weapon as fast as he could.

The sword blazed, and the dragon shied away. He chased, forcing the dragon to sidestep.

I can only do this for a short while, so let's make it count.

"Hohan, go help Sera. The sword seems to work on the dragon. I'll keep it busy." Ora dodged a tail lash.

"But, Ora—" Hohan protested.

"Go! Please help Sera. You're the only one who can." Ora fed more energy into the sword. Something in the center of his chest felt as if it were tearing. At first, it was like a muscle strain, but the more energy fed into the sword, the worse it hurt.

Clang!

Hohan cursed, then snarled a prayer to Enki, followed by another *clang!*

As Ora moved, he saw Hohan bashing the portcullis with his hammer.

Then he realized the dragon was circling him, and if he didn't do something, the dragon would be at Hohan's back.

He jumped at the dragon. It flinched, and he got close enough that the next chopping blow reached the beast. Scales separated like so much butter, causing the dragon to roar in pain.

It reflexively snapped at Ora.

The pain in Ora's chest made it hard to breathe. Hohan's strikes had started slowing too.

Must go faster! He gasped for breath, then channeled more energy into the sword, feeling his soul rending in half.

As he fed his magic directly into the sword, he saw a wisp of blue arcing to his left, and it appeared to be flowing from the dragon to him. Ora had never seen anything like the swirling blue wind before, but the dragon's head followed the wisp exactly. He shifted out of the way just a moment before long fangs snapped the air next to where he had stood.

Ora ignored the pain in his chest and fed more of his core magic into the weapon. Another wisp appeared, flowing from the dragon to him, and again it showed him where the dragon was about to attack.

He dodged under the claws, turned around, and saw a third wisp, this one flowing from him to the dragon. Ora took a chance and swung his sword along that path. The dragon moved into the path of the blade, doubling the force of the blow. His blade struck the dragon's chest, sending blood spraying.

The dragon howled, and Ora staggered back from the pain that lanced through his chest. He hunched over from the agony, causing him to almost miss the blue wisp. The dragon's tail sent Ora slamming into the wall next to the portcullis, knocking the breath from him.

His chest blazed with pain as he struggled to get back on his feet. Ora touched his chest and felt blood. He looked down to see a hole in his armor.

One of the tail barbs must have gotten me.

The dragon turned and limped toward him, teeth bared. It raised up to strike.

"Ghendo donam!"

A tremendous boost of Life Magic flooded through him, energizing him, washing away the pain. The momentary confusion from hitting the wall and the wound the tail barb left on his chest all faded away, leaving the stabbing pain in his core. Hohan held the orb they'd found in Fagan Nuraghi. He had his back pressed to the portcullis, and all those who'd survived the battle in the other room had their hands on his shoulders, giving Hohan the gift to pass on to Ora.

"Now, by Enki, destroy that thing," growled Hohan.

Ora jumped up, feeding the sword, seeing another blue arc. He blocked a swipe of the dragon's claw with the blade of the sword, partially severing the claw from its arm.

The dragon roared in pain, then bit down at Ora.

Following the blue arc, Ora thrust the sword up. It sank into the dragon's jaw in a spray of blood and teeth.

The dragon howled again, this time rearing back.

Another blue flash went straight at its throat.

Ora swung the sword with all of his might, severing the base of the dragon's neck. A fountain of blood gushed out, coating Ora. It flopped forward to the ground, huffing through the hole. Ora struck again, this time with both hands, bringing his full weight down to sever the dragon's neck.

White-hot pain lanced through his chest. He fell to his knees, his eyes searching for Sera on the other side of the portcullis.

His arm fell forward, his hand opened, and the sword dropped to the ground, peeling the skin from his hand in the process.

His last sight before the world went dark was a green, spectral shape hovering over Sera.

CHAPTER FIFTY-EIGHT

ORA EARL

Ora slowly came to consciousness. He pried his eyes open and shifted his head. "Wha…" he croaked out. His throat was parched. A beautiful woman stood over him with long, blonde hair. "Rella?"

Smack! Sera slapped him so hard his eyes rolled back in his head, and he struggled to retain consciousness.

He felt a hand in the front of his shirt holding him up, shaking him. "I am not your Giant-taken daughter," she said in a tone that could freeze water.

She shoved him down. His eyes swam back into focus to see her stalking out of the room.

Across from him, Mayomi sat in a chair. She covered her mouth, shoulders shaking in mirth. "That looked like it hurt."

"Aren't you supposed to protect me?"

Mayomi had an enormous grin on her face and shook her head. "I can't protect you from yourself, Your Majesty."

Ora grunted. No sympathy from that quarter. He let sleep take him.

He woke up to find Konungr sitting there, two swords on his lap. Mayomi sat in a chair next to the bed.

"Konungr. What happened?"

"After you killed the dragon, we were able to get the portcullis up and everyone out before the other dragons came. Now, we're able to close the portcullis from the other side, cutting the dragons off. We can no longer access that side of Dragon's Reach, which is called Wyrmhome, nor can we use that path to Eshita, but our rear is secure."

Ora thought for a moment, nodding. "What about that thing."

"What thing?"

"The arch. The one that looks like a dirty pool? What was that?"

"That is a thuros."

"A what?" Ora asked.

"Thuros, that was a portal the Giants used to travel to other places, to thuroi."

Ora shifted in the bed. "The Giants? But there wasn't a Giant there. How did those people use the gate?"

Konungr shook his head. "Honestly, I don't know. We do know from legend the gates require some sort of key, but those keys were lost in time."

"Do you think that they'll be back?" Mayomi asked. "Do you think the people who went through the gate will come back through this thuros?"

"If they do, they'll have to get past the portcullis while dragons roam that side of Dragon's Reach. And we will always watch the door that leads into the Lost Caves of Kishar." He chuckled. "And perhaps we'll take some of our slaughtered animals to that hall. The dragons will learn there's food there."

Ora nodded. "An excellent idea. Use the dragons as your allies."

"Yes." Konungr placed one of the swords on the bed. "That's your sword, and as I said before, it's steel we Delvers are proud of."

"Thank you."

He held out the other one. "But you should have told me about this weapon. I could have told you about it." Konungr held the Dragon sword. Ora could tell from the hilt. They had found a scabbard that fit it.

Ora sat up but didn't take the sword from him "Oh?"

Konungr placed the blade on the bed next to Ora. "This blade was made during the War of the Giants. It has abilities, though no Delver ever recorded what they were. If we had a forge mage here, they might be able to tell you the specifics, but maybe not." He shrugged.

"I was able to put magic into the blade. And I saw things…"

"What kinds of things?"

"My memory of the fight is hazy."

Konungr shook his head. "You are a lucky man. These weapons were meant to be used by Giants. Mavric iron will kill Humans."

Ora smiled ruefully. "It almost killed me." He stared at the roughed up palm of his hand. It looked like he'd tried to fry it in a pan of grease.

Konungr and Mayomi stared at the blistered, torn flesh and said nothing for a long while.

The Delver turned to the Wlewoi. "I see you made it back safely. Did you catch your prey?"

Mayomi's ears twitched, and she shook her head. "No. He managed to elude me, but I have his scent, and if he comes back to Draco, I will find him."

Ora shifted in bed. "He didn't appear to be from any clan that I knew."

Mayomi nodded. "I'm familiar with all of the Wlewoi clans on Drakanon. He is not from Drakanon. He must be from—" she waved a hand "—that thuros. From someplace else."

The group contemplated that thought. That people from other places were invading their land.

"I may not be a king," said Ora, "but I know an invasion when I see one."

"As do I." Konungr grimaced. "What do you plan to do next?"

"Well, first thing I need to do—" Ora shifted in the bed and put his feet on the floor "—is make an apology."

"Indeed? Well, she is this way."

"Then let's go."

Mayomi helped Ora to the Main Hall. Konungr followed, carrying the swords.

On the way, many Delvers stopped and stared or whispered as he passed. Ora sighed. He threw a sidelong glance at Konungr.

"What's with all that, Konungr?"

Konungr smiled. "I don't know what you mean... Dragonsbane."

"What?"

They entered the Main Hall.

Cheers hammered at Ora, and only Mayomi's hand on his arm kept him standing up.

Ora stopped and stared. Where before, the hall had been practically deserted, now it was packed with Delvers, and all were cheering. He looked at Konungr.

Konungr guided him to the nearest table, stepped up on the bench, then onto the table. He held his hand down to Ora.

Ora shook his head, took the proffered hand, and Konungr pulled him onto the table. Konungr held up Ora's hand above their heads, and the crowd cheered louder. Ora smiled and waved. After a bit, the cheers died down.

"Show us the blade," someone shouted. Several in the audience shouted agreement.

Ora turned to Konungr and leaned in close. "I can't draw that blade right now. I still can't feel my Life Magic. Touching Mavric iron will prolong it further, and I need it to heal."

Konungr handed it to him. "So just hold it by the scabbard above your head. That's enough of a symbol for them."

Ora hesitated for a moment, then nodded, took the sword by the scabbard, and held it up.

The crowd cheered again.

"Dragonsbane," yelled one Delver.

Ora raised a hand to stop him, but another echoed it. Then another.

The cry echoed across the hall.

Finally, Konungr raised his arms for quiet, and the crowd subsided into silence.

Ora took a deep breath. "Thank you, everyone. The battle of Dragon's Reach and the taking of Wyrmhome was not done by me alone. Many of your brothers fought valiantly, and I would like to honor their sacrifice in your manner."

Konungr handed him his flask, and Ora held it high. "May the Giants bless your passing into the next life."

The hall thundered as the crowd repeated the phrase and drank.

Konungr put his flask away and addressed the crowd. "Ora and his friends will be here for a bit. He is still recovering, so be about your work. I'll make sure he gets healthy enough to drink with us all properly later."

The crowd laughed.

"Thanks a lot," said Ora.

"You're welcome." Konungr grinned, then got down from the table. Ora did not move, looking for a face in the crowd.

He grimaced, not finding it.

"She's not here," Mayomi said from behind him. "She is outside."

Ora found Sera in the top tower above the gate outside. She was there by herself, wrapped in a cloak against the wind. The setting sunlight illuminated her hair with reds, golds, and oranges.

She stiffened when he approached.

Ora stepped up to the wall and softly said, "Sera."

She turned to him, flint in her eyes. "What?"

"I'm really sorry for calling you Rella." She opened her mouth, but Ora held up his hands. She stared at his right hand and held what she was going to say.

"Rella was sixteen when she was killed. We had an argument the last time I saw her alive." He wiped his eyes. "My daughter's last words to me were in anger. The hardest day of my life was when they brought her body to me. That tore my heart in two."

"I'm not her."

He took her hand. She resisted at first, but finally acquiesced.

"I know I have issues, and I'm working to resolve them. I know you are your own woman, and a beautiful one at that."

She squeezed his hand. Then punched him on the bicep. "Then how could you be so stupid to almost kill yourself fighting that dragon?"

"When I saw you fall fighting that Blood, and I was helpless, I…" His voice caught in his throat, and he swallowed hard.

She shifted closer to him. "And what about me, huh? There you were, fighting a dragon, that cursed blade in your hand, and all I could do was lie on the ground and pray." She snorted. "I'm not Hohan. I can't remember the last time I prayed to *any* god, but I would have prayed to anyone if it could have helped."

"I did it for you. I fought the dragon so Hohan could get you the help that you needed."

She was quiet. Her eyes softened. "I'm not Rella. You don't always have to save me, you idiot."

He leaned forward and kissed her.

EPILOGUE

ORA EARL

ightning flashed, and the windows in the sturdy house rattled slightly with the accompanying thunder.

Ora stoked the fire in the front room while Sera slept soundly in the other room.

He felt unsettled. *What is it? I haven't had this much time to relax in centuries. Why—*

The front door flew open, pushed by the wind to slam into the wall. A large Draconian stepped into the house. His red scales caught the firelight and dripped both water and blood onto the limestone floor.

"Lightbringer," he gasped. "I am Vorcrath, and we need your help—" he held up a scroll "—the Pentad—"

His eyes rolled back in his head. The scroll tumbled to the floor, followed by Vorcrath slumping to the floor.

In the doorway behind Vorcrath stood a Human. He stepped inside, water sliding off his oiled leather cowl. He pulled back the cowl. His face was drawn, haggard, and eyes glowed with a sickly green light.

The Draconian's blood coated the long sword he held.

Ora gasped as he recognized him. "Kadryt? I thought you were dead?"

Ora thought for a split moment that Kadryt recognized him back, but the eye-glow intensified, and any recognition faded away. With a flick of his wrist, Kadryt removed the blood from his sword, a trick they had both learned in the Legion.

Without any acknowledgment, the man pulled the cowl back up and disappeared into the raging thunderstorm.

INTERLUDE

TE'ZLA HARDEN

e'zla sat at his desk reading. His apprentice, Anya, sat at the book stand reading the Chronicles, the secret records only permitted to the highest echelon of Readers.

The letter he had received was fascinating. He cleared his throat. "Anya, this letter from Gverth is unbelievable."

She put a card on the open tome to mark her place and turned to him and raised an eyebrow.

"He says here that they liberated the Delvers at Dragon's Reach." Te'zla continued reading for a bit. "Wergoi! He fought Wergoi." He looked at Anya. "Have the Chronicles that you're reading mentioned Wergoi?"

Anya shook her head. "No. I'm reading about the demons invading and the battle on the plains. Reader Aken has a strange writing style."

Te'zla nodded and looked back at the letter. "He described some of the Delver history. The Greater Dragons."

"Greater Dragons?" Anya asked. Te'zla glanced at her. She sat up attentively.

"Greater Dragons are the Giants that became Dragons and the children they sired."

Anya inhaled sharply, and her eyes grew wide. "Dragons are Giants?"

"Well, no. Not specifically. Not all dragons. Just the Greater Dragons."

Confusion spread across her face. "I don't understand."

Te'zla sighed. "The Drakanon Giants took dragon form and mated. Their children were both Giants and Dragons." She opened her mouth, but Te'zla held up a hand. "The dragons we hear about, killing cows or wrecking villages in the mountains. Those are lesser dragons. They are not Giants."

"How would we know the difference?"

Te'zla pointed at the book she was reading. "Have you read about the Pentad?"

Anya shook her head. "I haven't made it to that part."

"Well, read carefully. Because you and I are a part of it." Te'zla held her gaze for a moment, then went back to the letter.

Te'zla felt the call of the Aurora, the magical pulse that summoned the members of the Hand of Fate to the meeting place. He saw Anya stiffen, then turn to him with wide eyes.

"Is that…" she wondered.

Te'zla nodded. "That is the Aurora. We are summoned." He stood up. "Get your robe, and we will leave for the meeting." He moved to a wardrobe in the corner and opened it to retrieve his golden robe of office. In moments, Anya was back wearing her own robe.

Anya eyed him critically. "That robe looks awful on you."

Te'zla shrugged in the ill-fitting garment. It was overly large and slightly rumpled. "It fits their perception of me as a doddering old fool." He grinned. "To be honest, I enjoy playing the role."

Anya shook her head. "I can't believe they would think we would allow an idiot to run the Readers here."

The pair descended the back stairwell, several floors below ground level.

At the bottom, two Readers stood guard before the plain, double doors that were the only feature in the round room. Both men looked like they spent more time with weapons than with books.

Te'zla bowed. "Brothers, we need to enter the archives."

They both bowed their heads, and one put a key to the lock, then pushed the door open and stepped out of the way. Te'zla and Anya passed through the door, which was closed and locked behind them.

The room beyond revealed a well-appointed library. Rows of shelves lined every wall. Buckets of salt stood at various points around the library as squat guardians against moisture. Chairs and book stands occupied the middle of the room. The pair walked through the center before turning to the back corner and stepping behind the shelf there. Te'zla produced a small rod and pressed it into a depression in the stone. A door appeared and soundlessly swung back into a dimly lit passage. The passageway smelled of old rock.

Te'zla stepped through and picked up a lantern that contained a magical flame. Anya followed and pushed the door closed behind her. It sealed with a faint click.

The passage proceeded straight on for a long way.

"Why does it have to be so far?" Anya hiked up the hem of her robe and made her way after her Master.

Te'zla chuckled. "We couldn't very well go knocking at the door of Draco Keep every time we needed to use the thuros."

Anya sighed, but kept walking.

"Let's go over who is going to be at the meeting." Te'zla glanced at Anya.

She nodded. "The Lathranon Master is Ulient. He supports you. His Vice is Bakhar. She also supports you."

Te'zla smiled. "They are good people. I've known Ulient a long time."

"You said he was a friend of your Master's?"

His smile faded. "Yes. Ulient stood by me when Baagrem was killed." He shook himself as they continued down the passage. "What about Daemanon?"

"Their Master is Talliah. She does not support you."

Te'zla laughed. "She thinks I'm an idiot. Though let me tell you, when she was younger, she turned heads."

"Master!" Anya was shocked.

Te'zla cackled. "You're so easy. Anyway, who is Vice?"

Her expression soured. "Abissar. I really don't like him."

Te'zla looked at her. "Did he do something?"

Anya shook her head. "No, there is just something..." She took a deep breath. "The Noksonon master is Lengstrom. He supports you. The Vice is, um..."

"Elegathe," Te'zla prompted.

"Elegathe. Right. Did we meet her at the last conclave?"

Te'zla shook his head. "You know you met her. You just don't like her because she's pretty."

"Yeah, pretty ambitious." Her lips pressed into a thin line.

"You need to get over that. You have to work with her." Te'zla eyed her speculatively. "She's about the same age as you. So you're probably stuck with her for the next hundred years."

Anya grimaced. "Well, I would never kill you, Master."

Te'zla gave her a wide grin. "You definitely would, given the chance."

He cackled again at her shocked expression.

They came to a blank wall at the end of the corridor. There was a shelf with another lantern on it. Anya put her lantern up, and Te'zla once again pressed the rod to the wall, producing the door.

They stepped through into a rectangular, stone room. On one end stood a stone archway, the center of which was a mass of swirling colors. The other end held an enormous throne. No other exits from the room were apparent.

Te'zla turned to her. "Tell me about Pyranon."

Anya sighed. "Their Master is Jekka." She had an edge to her voice.

"Her too?"

"No," she said sullenly, then looked Te'zla in the eyes. "I'll work on it. She supports you. Her Vice is Traemic." The way she said his name made Te'zla watch her speculatively. "He's neutral."

"Okay. Let's go see who called the meeting." He put a hand on her arm. "I need you to watch them. Please don't let your bias loose over there." Anya nodded.

Te'zla grinned and held up the plunnos. "Want to open it?" He knew his impish ways irked her, but it was too much fun. "You need to know how to do it in case…"

Anya frowned and accepted the plunnos. She stepped up to the thuros and touched the coin to the surface. It reacted immediately, brightening and going translucent. She handed the plunnos back to him and waited for him to step through.

Even though he had been through the thuros over a hundred times, each time was like the first. It was both like jumping into an icy lake and settling into a warm, oil bath. He emerged dry on the other side, and Te'zla was once again unsure if he liked the experience.

The room they emerged into was built of the same stone as the one they left, only this one was pentagonal, with a space for each representative of their continents. A large, stone table stood in the center, with concentric rings carved into the surface.

Lathranon in their blue robes and Pyranon in their red were already at their spots around the large table.

Te'zla nodded each to Ulient and Jekka. "Did you call this?" Both shook their heads. Their Vice Masters each stood at their Master's elbow. In short order, the representatives from Daemanon emerged from their thuros, resplendent in their green robes.

Talliah wasted no time on pleasantries. "Why have we been summoned?"

"Why don't we wait until Lengstrom arrives?" Ulient replied. "It is he who declared this emergency."

Traemic of Pyranon added, "I'm sure he has good reason. I'm content to wait." Te'zla thought it interesting that he spoke for Pyranon. Suddenly, the thuros that led to Noksonon opened, and the pair of Readers emerged. To Te'zla's surprise, they had the hoods of their black robes up.

Not giving them a chance to step to the table, Jekka barked, "Lengstrom, why have you called us?"

Elegathe flipped back her hood. "Not Lengstrom, I summoned you."

"And who are you, a lowly apprentice, to summon us?" growled Talliah.

"Lengstrom, why did you allow your apprentice to break with protocol? She summoned us? Only the Master can activate the Aurora."

"Lengstrom is dead. I am the High Master of Noksonon now," said Elegathe. *Curious,* Te'zla thought. *Could she have killed him? Or, did the Giants get him like they got Baagrem?*

"What?" Abissar uttered. Surprise was plain on his face. Talliah put a restraining hand on him.

"It is as I feared." Ulient looked at Te'zla.

This was his moment, and Te'zla intended to make the most of it. "I told you! The Giants killed him."

"Calm yourself." Talliah glared at him. "It's far too soon to draw conclusions." As long as she had been on this Council, she still had her head in the sand.

Jekka gestured at the cloaked figure. "Then this is your new apprentice?" All eyes turned to the pair from Noksonon.

The other figure threw back his cowl, revealing a dead man. Darjhen smiled at the group, a smile that didn't reach his eyes. "In a manner of speaking." Te'zla forced his face to be passive. *That sly dog. This will really get their goat.*

"What is that doing here?" Talliah spat. "That was supposed to be dead. And if it's not dead, it should be executed immediately."

Jekka pulled her dagger. "I can make that happen."

"Wait. Let's hear what the oathbreaker says first." Ulient was the voice of reason. Te'zla narrowed his eyes. *Did he know?*

"No!" snapped Anya next to him, and Te'zla nearly jumped in surprise at the vehemence in her tone. "He has forfeited the right to live, much less speak." He glanced at her. Darjhen was gone from the Council long before Anya apprenticed to Te'zla. *Where is this passion coming from?*

Bakhar spoke up for the first time, "He is an oathbreaker, but Wyrd demands that we follow her, not our own passions."

Curiosity burned in Te'zla, and he nodded. "We must hear his warning."

Abissar leaned forward to Talliah. "Forgive me, Mistress. Perhaps we should hear him out and then kill him. Knowledge, after all, is the root of our power."

Talliah nodded once. She glanced around the group, and spat in a frosty voice, "Very well. If it is the will of the Hand of Fate, I shall listen to his lies." She looked meaningfully at Jekka. "I trust your blade is sharp."

"Hold." Traemic's simple word caused Jekka to snap her head around to him. Hand on the hilt of her dagger, she waited with an impatient look about her. Traemic turned to Darjhen. "Speak your truth and know it may not be Fate's."

"My truth?" Darjhen sneered. "Fate's truth. Soon enough, nothing we think or want will matter anymore. Not unless we do something right now." He threw a large, heavy metal disk across the table a short distance. It spun down to lie flat. It was four inches across and had five strange symbols etched on either side. Exultation coursed through Te'zla, and he struggled to appear calm while he was celebrating internally. *Finally, the proof I've been hoping for.*

Ulient leaned in and pointed at it. "This coin holds all of our symbols, not just our own." Several gasps flowed around the table as the others realized what it meant. It was all Te'zla could do to not crow in triumph.

"The Giants have returned." Darjhen folded his arms across his chest.

ABOUT THE AUTHOR

Mark Stallings is an Amazon Best Selling author living in Colorado Springs, Colorado since the early 80's. He is a member of Pikes Peak Writers, speaks at International conferences on Technology topics, is a writer of Wuxia, Fantasy, and Military Sci Fi.

Mark is a competitive shooter, avid martial artist, drinker of craft beer, and motorcycle enthusiast. He became an Amazon Bestselling author with his contribution to the Military Sci-Fi anthology in the 4Horsemen Universe *Set The Terms* released through Chris Kennedy Publishing Spring of 2020. Mark released the first book in the Silver Coin Saga – The Elements through Shadow Alley Press summer of 2020. He continues to sling the ink with further stories in the Silver Coin Saga, The Eldros Legacy, and the 4Horsemen Universes.

You can find Mark:
- on Facebook at facebook.com/markwstallings
- on the web at www.markstallings.com
- on Patreon at patreon.com/markstallings
- on Amazon at amazon.com/author/markstallings

AUTHOR'S NOTE

In early 2021, I was approached by Rob Howell and Quincy J. Allen to participate in a shared Fantasy world. We brought in two other people, Todd Fahnestock and Marie Whittaker. Over the next year and a half, the team worked, met weekly, and planned out the glorious saga that became the Eldros Legacy.

The excitement and energy of creating a world, races, places, and plots has been invigorating to say the least. We have brought in other authors to contribute short stories initially, and novels to enrichen our world.

This specific story concept came about in early 2018 when I was having breakfast with David Farland. I have always been a fan of *The Belgariad* by David Eddings and had recently finished the audio books of the initial finve books. David Farland asked what I wanted to work on as far as story concepts and I posed the question: What if a Wizard-King who lived forever, watched his family die, got bored?

I hope you enjoyed the answer.

If You Liked...

If you enjoyed this novel and the world it's set in, then the creators of the Eldros Legacy would like to encourage you to don thy traveling pack and journey deeper into the mysteries of the world Eldros and all the myriad adventures set therein.

The mortal world of Eldros is coming apart. The Giants, who once ruled its five continents with draconian malice have set their mighty designs on a return to power. Mortals across the globe must be victorious against insurmountable odds or die.

Come join us as the Eldros Legacy unfolds in a growing library of novels and short stories.

You can find all the novels at:

www.EldrosLegacy.com/books

Our website is, of course:

EldrosLegacy.com

The Books by Series

Legacy of Shadows
by Todd Fahnestock

Khyven the Unkillable

Lorelle of the Dark

Rhenn the Traveler

Legacy of Deceit
by Quincy J. Allen

Seeds of Dominion

Demons of Veynkal

Legacy of Dragons
by Mark Stallings

The Forgotten King

Knights of Drakanon (Forthcoming)

Sword of Binding (Forthcoming)

Return of the Lightbringer (Forthcoming)

Legacy of Queens
by Marie Whittaker

Embers & Ash

Cinder & Stone (Forthcoming)

The Dog Soldier's War
by Jamie Ibson

A Murder of Wolves

Valleys of Death (Forthcoming)

Other Eldros Legacy Novels

Deadly Fortune by Aaron Rosenberg

The Pain Bearer by Kendra Merritt

Short Stories

Here There Be Giants by The Founders (FREE!)

The Darkest Door by Todd Fahnestock

Fistful of Silver by Quincy J. Allen

Electrum by Marie Whittaker

Dawn of the Lightbringer by Mark Stallings

What the Eye Sees by Quincy J. Allen

Trust Not the Trickster by Jamie Ibson

A Rhakha for the Tokonn by Quincy J. Allen

CPSIA information can be obtained
at www.ICGtesting.com
Printed in the USA
JSHW022114260323
39499JS00001B/23